Ian Hickman (actually his two middle names) is one of the pennames used by the author, David Ian Hickman May, a professional electronics engineer with more than 50 years' experience. With a BSc Hons, C.Eng., MIEE, MIEEE, he is a chartered engineer and a sometime member of various national and international standards committees concerned with equipment and system level applications of electronics and communications. He is the author of over two dozen books (12 titles, counting second and later editions) and over 300 magazine articles concerned with electronics.

My Friend Farringdon is Ian Hickman's first venture into fiction, a 'novel' experience for him – at 86 years of age. His book *My Friend Farringdon* was instigated by a dream, completely forgotten, of which only the phrase 'spanking cat' remained. This prompted the present work which seemed to write itself, as ideas for the story flowed in abundance. The tale is told by Yellow Laughing S. Catt, and covers his life and that of his friend Farringdon Spanking Catt.

To my wife, Dot, for patience while books are in progress.

Ian Hickman

THE SAPES

AUSTIN MACAULEY PUBLISHERS™

LONDON * CAMBRIDGE * NEW YORK * SHARJAH

A CIP catalogue record for this title is available from the British Library.

ISBN 9781398451995 (Paperback)
ISBN 9781398452008 (ePub e-book)

www.austinmacauley.com

First Published 2024
Austin Macauley Publishers Ltd®
1 Canada Square
Canary Wharf
London
E14 5AA

Table of Contents

Chapter 1: Chance Encounters   9

Chapter 2: At the Conference   17

Chapter 3: At the Office   26

Chapter 4: To Tokyo, the 6th WPC 2266AD   44

Chapter 5: The Baritone in the Bath 2268AD   56

Chapter 6: Simian Amazonians Versicolor 2280AD   70

Chapter 7: The Seventh WPC 2283AD   76

Chapter 8: Snuggling Up and Old Acquaintances   89

Chapter 9: Demijohns 2291AD   104

Chapter 10: Music, Art and Nightcaps   116

Chapter 11: Red Roses and Poison Ivy   127

Chapter 12: Green Baize and Straight Lines AD2300   134

Chapter 13: Soldiers and Shop Assistants 2301AD   142

Chapter 14: Clandestine Courtship 2309AD   149

Chapter 15: Double Celebration 2310AD   156

Chapter 16: Psophometers 2311AD   162

Chapter 17: Encounter on the Bridge 2314AD   172

Chapter 18: Zimba 2316AD   181

Chapter 19: A Wedding and a Funeral 2316AD   186

Chapter 20: Overdue Cleaning and Nuns' Sighs 2317AD   193

Chapter 21: The Battle of Mbalala-Ville   196

Chapter 22: Epilogue 2323AD   **200**

Chapter 23: Postscript 2323AD   **204**

Chapter 1
Chance Encounters

As he took the only spare seat, at the front of the carriage next to a stout swarthy man, he soon got the impression that the man was watching him, out of the corner of his eye. But Julian's eyes were now peering out of the window of the uncomfortably full carriage. Before his unseeing eyes – his thoughts were far away – the countryside processed by monotonously, already this spring more brown than green, with the sky above a painfully bright deep blue. He had seen that sky a year ago – how could it be such a deep blue and yet so bright? It had stopped him suddenly in his tracks in wonder; a man coming along behind had swerved to avoid a collision and had hissed *'COÑO'* as he passed. Julian's Spanish was more than adequate to recognise a grossly indecent swearword when he heard it, though he couldn't imagine how when or where such improper words had found a place in his Spanish vocabulary.

Julian, a figure of medium height, slim build and blue-green eyes, found his thoughts gnawing obsessively at something that happened almost a year ago – but now a sort of recurrent visual disturbance was beginning to demand his attention. Coming slowly out of his reverie, he noticed that every two seconds or so a concrete post sailed past the window, and that running between the tops of the posts was a wire or cable of some sort. As each passed, the wire drooped gently down, a metre or so at most, gracefully climbing up again to the top of the next post, down and up, down and up. It struck a chord somewhere deep in his subconscious; he knew he had seen something like it before, and now his brain – never idle – was worrying, without outcome, at this new puzzle.

He wondered whether it was a blessing or a curse to have such an inexorably active brain – *probably a bit of both*, he thought. But now, the posts had disappeared and the train of monorail carriages in which he was travelling from the airport, slung beneath its overhead rail, was rounding a bend, accompanied by an ear-splitting screech of metal on metal. He hoped the system was safe, monorails were old technology and this one was the last one still in use anywhere in the world. Thankfully, the bend passed and, on the straight the carriages started to slow down as they approached the Estacion, in the suburbs of Buenos Aires. As he descended the passenger who had been sitting next to him said, "Buenas dias, Señor Broffi."

Utterly taken aback, Julian just managed to mutter, '*Buenos dias*' back, with a puzzled smile before the stranger disappeared. Although the pronunciation of his surname Brophy amused him somewhat, here was another puzzle – who was this man and how did he know Julian?

This was Julian's second visit to Argentina. Now he was walking along a side street, making his way from the station towards his hotel. Taxis were few and expensive, he knew, and anyway on such a lovely day he preferred to walk. At one metre eighty tall, young and slim, though well built, he was, to any observant passer-by, clearly a man of rather old-fashioned tastes – his neat suit and tie said as much; suits had long been abandoned by most, in favour of a much more casual style of dress. But that said, perhaps he was ahead of fashion which went around and round in cycles, as it always had in the past, or so his mother said. She played piano and sang, encouraging in him a deep love of music. Almost always there was a theme running round in his head like an earworm, typically one of the extended melodies typical of Berlioz, Tchaikovsky or Bruckner. But at the moment his mind was occupied by a crude refrain he must have picked up as a child from a playmate.

Hundred and one, never been – Oh shut up! he said to himself and diverted his mind by dwelling on the striking minor thirds solo trumpet opening of the fifth symphony of his favourite composer – *Tatatadaaa tatatadaaa tatata^{daaa} tatata^{daaa} tatata^{daaa}* followed by a rising minor arpeggio finishing on the octave, shortly followed by a crash as the whole orchestra burst into action and then by a ghostly dead march, said to have been inspired by the funeral of a fireman in New York.

He was clearly a man with something on his mind. His fair wavy hair and oval face with its rosy complexion proclaimed him a foreigner, as he strolled distractedly along, not hurrying, a raincoat – superfluous on this warm spring day – draped over his arm. He was preoccupied with a vision that had dogged his thoughts during the railcar journey from the airport to the Estacion, during the whole of the flight from Heathrow also, and indeed on and off for close on a year. Passing a shop window, he noticed his reflection showed a tousled mass of hair, a strong wind had been sweeping the high open platform of the monorail station at the airport and he had meant to tidy it but had forgotten. He ran his fingers through his hair, which obediently settled itself down almost as neatly as had he used a comb in his bedroom at home. Wavy, to the envy of his mother Kitty, it conveniently fell of its own accord into this one natural style – fortunately, he had never wanted to change it.

He was heading now for the Centro, a few hundred metres beyond which lay a small family run hotel, a little run-down but friendly, hiding its charms in a back street. He had stayed there the previous year, covering the Fifth World Population Conference for his paper the Telegraph and vividly remembered the engaging if eccentric elderly couple that ran the place, the rotund wrinkled Antonio Gaudi with his crooked discoloured teeth, and his equally ample wife Maria, clearly once a beauty and still agreeable to behold, with her thick wavy black hair, despite a heavily lined face.

Another reporter, more senior than he, should have covered that Conference, but he was involved in another important ongoing story, and besides, Julian's Spanish was fluent. His degree was in French with German but fascinated with words since a child, he was a voracious reader and reading contemporary novels in Spanish and Italian had left him quite competent in those languages also.

So now, a year later, here he was back again in Buenos Aires, this time to cover a story of massive corruption in the government of the day. He had a clear picture in his mind of where he was going, but soon had to admit to himself that he was lost. He asked the way of a passer-by and set off in the indicated direction. But he could only remember 'first left, second right' and then something about a big theatre, so after that he asked again. This time he was instructed to proceed in the direction from which he had just come, followed by another maze of directions; his life had always been hampered by a poor memory – except, strangely, when it came to learning languages – nowadays, in his spare time he was learning Mandarin. However, nearby was a stationer's, where he purchased a city street plan, as it happened, the same as the one from last year which he had forgotten to bring with him. He entered.

"Si Señor?"

"I'd like a town plan or street map please."

"Certainly, I have two sorts, but I'd recommend this one." *Obviously the more expensive one*, Julian thought, *but no matter, it would be on his expenses claim.*

"Gracias. Er…could you point out, please, whereabouts on the map I am?" The shopkeeper, without a word, marked the place with a blob of red ballpoint pen. "I have to get to the Avenida Santa Fé, opposite the turning for Calle San Juan." Without another word, the shopkeeper added another blob and Julian left.

With map's aid, he soon arrived at the Avenida Santa Fé, where, the previous year, it had happened.

*****

Then, he had been going to cross the road, coming from the Centro on his way home from the Fifth WPC, deep in contemplation of the disturbing papers he had heard presented. The population of the world was then just forty-nine percent of that at the turn of the millennium and falling steadily. Indeed, the presenter of one paper speculated that, extrapolating from the mean rate of population decline over the past hundred years, the human race might be virtually extinct within a century and a half. Another presenter, reminding delegates about the 49% figure mentioned by the prime minister in his opening address, made two positive points; firstly, that over the last decade, there had been a small but measurable reduction in the rate of decline of the world's population – it was still falling but not quite as fast as previously. Secondly, he pointed out to delegates that it was the decline in the world's population which had led to the welcome easing of conflicts, especially in Africa and the Middle East, observed during the previous hundred and more years.

"Since most conflicts are basically about ownership of land, particularly the more productive agricultural land, the greatly reduced population density in most areas of the world has had a marked beneficial effect," he mused. However, this was the only consoling fact to emerge from a conference notable for gloomy reports and even gloomier predictions. His musings continued. "Mind you, while population decline has had a markedly beneficial effect as far as conflicts are concerned, it presents severe manpower problems." These were exacerbated by the pressing shortage of all sources of energy, particularly oil, necessitating a great resurgence of manual labour in the field of agriculture, if mass starvation were to be avoided.

Engrossed in these sombre reflections, he had been about to step off the kerb when an unseen hand had pinioned his arm in a vice-like grip, and he froze. A fraction of a second later a large electrically powered bus whooshed past with no noise but the swish of its tyres. Had the driver seen him at the last minute and swerved? Or would he have been hit and injured, or worse? He did not know and did not care to speculate.

The hand slowly released its grip and, turning, he saw that he had been saved by a young woman, little more than a girl really. Embarrassed at his stupidity, he apologised profusely in Spanish, and thanked her for probably saving his life.

"Oh, that's alright – but do be more careful next time." A little shocked and breathless herself, her captivating smile expressed a range of emotions, most of which he could not fathom, but uppermost – he realised – was concern.

"How did you know I was English?"

"Your Spanish is good, very good but accents are difficult to capture. That's what my professor always said."

It was true, her English was excellent – even the accent, probably better than my Spanish he thought ruefully – but there was a charming colouration to some of the vowel sounds and the occasional slight misplacement of the stress that subtly but unmistakably hinted at Spanish.

They had crossed the road without further incident – as in most cities there was very little traffic and virtually no private cars; it made one careless – and he found this enchanting creature going in the same direction as himself. Clearly interested in people and in the world around her, she soon discovered that he had been at the Fifth World Population Conference and was questioning him avidly on the subject when suddenly she said, "Oh, this is my turning. You will be more careful about the traffic, won't you? Goodbye." And, lightly squeezing his arm – the one she had so recently fiercely gripped – she disappeared down a narrow alleyway. He was still wondering if it was a through way or a private entrance when she turned a corner and disappeared from view. At the time, he had really noticed nothing about her except that beautiful face expressing concern for him, the long dark hair and the collar of her blue-grey coat.

*****

Now, a year later, as he made his way with the aid of his newly purchased street map, along the Avenida 9 de Julio towards the Centro and his hotel, his thoughts turned yet again to this girl he had not seen for a year, and almost certainly never would again. The peculiar thing was that, vividly as he could remember her face with its long black eyelashes, finely chiselled nose and pink lips, and above all that smile – exasperatingly he had been unable to forget it for a whole year – he was no longer sure of anything else about her at all. What had she been wearing, dress, skirt or trousers? Was she tall or short, fat or thin? Exactly what colour was her hair? Even the colour of her eyes eluded him, leaving him with just the memory of that enigmatic smile and the silvery sound of her voice.

He was still engrossed in trying to conjure up a fuller picture of her as he reached his hotel, where Maria gave him a motherly hug and a moist kiss, as though he were her long lost son, and Antonio said cheerfully, "Ah, Señor Brophy, your bags is just delivered a few minutes soon and in now the room." He chatted volubly to Julian, about the latter's visit the previous year, about the weather, about politics and a thousand other topics. Like hoteliers around the world, Antonio spoke hotelier's English but his was of the less refined kind. Completely fluent, his speech was rapid and with such a thick accent that at times it was difficult to understand. *One might almost be excused for not realising that it was English at all*, Julian thought. It was so ungrammatical as frequently to be comical, either unwittingly or when he realised his mistake and corrected himself, hugely to his own amusement. Nevertheless, he would make a useful sounding board for the views of an average Argentinean on the corruption and on the related trials which it was rumoured were pending. Having signed in and collected his key card, at last Julian could make his way towards the narrow staircase – there was no lift – glad to get away from the torrent of words.

But Antonio followed and there on the first floor just outside Julian's room, away from Maria, whispered, "I hope Señor will find the room comfortable, and if the night will be lonely, Morella would be happy to keep you company."

Julian remembered the comfortably upholstered part-time chambermaid with her plain but pleasant face and thick black hair (more abundant even than Maria's, which was thinning) – her English was more atrocious even than Antonio's. Antonio had hinted at the same arrangement last year and after a moment's hesitation he had courteously declined; after all he dreamed of a soulmate who would love him as much as he loved her, not of a strange woman in a strange bed. Antonio doubtless remembered the slight hesitation and had asked again this year – perhaps he was a shrewder judge of character than Julian realised. Hardly realising what he was doing, Julian nodded, and the deal was struck without a word said. Almost immediately he regretted the arrangement, but to back out now, he realised, would look silly: Certainly, it would be a new experience for him, a virgin.

Still, they tell me that it's a hundred times more enjoyable than the mean miserable disappointing little relief you get from masturbation, he thought to himself.

He entered his room, which was small and slightly shabby but spotlessly clean, with its outlook – or lack of it – onto the lower floors at the back of a towering hotel block with its large windows, in a parallel street. In the room, his bags awaited him, and he showered, did some unpacking and prepared to go down to dinner, all the while unable to forget his troublesome vision of last year for more than a few minutes together.

He dined in the hotel; he knew from his last visit that Maria was a fantastic cook and did wonderful things with pastry – as both her and Antonio's figure attested. After, he took a stroll around deserted back streets in the cool of the evening, realising that at the back of his mind, almost subconsciously and quite unreasonably, was the vague hope that he might meet the vision again. Returning, he enjoyed a nightcap with Antonio and then headed off to his room. Morella appeared as if by magic and whispered, "Bed you first."

Once he was in bed she slowly and coyly undressed in full view and then slipped in beside him after shaking out a freshly ironed and folded gents' handkerchief by one corner and leaving it on the bedside table. She murmured, "Darling." And he felt the web of skin between her right thumb and palm contacting the rear of the glans and her fingers and thumb slowly and gently closing around the shaft with its great erection. After a few seconds, without warning, she squeezed it briefly but firmly and it jumped to attention, thicker and longer than he would ever have thought possible. After what seemed an age but was actually only three seconds, it relaxed, leaving him aglow all over. A replay followed a few seconds later, but this time it took fully five seconds to relax, during which time he was concerned that priapism might set in, with its possible permanent damage to the organ. He needn't have worried but lay there in ecstasy wondering what would happen next. Again, a momentary firm squeeze and after four seconds feeling that it would burst it started pulsing wildly, uncontrollably, recklessly, deliriously – Morella was there with the handkerchief at the ready and not a single drop fell either onto his body or the bedclothes.

Suddenly he felt as exhausted as if he had just finished a day's hard labour; trenching a virgin plot of London clay, three spits deep. Would he ever be able to get to sleep after such a mind-blowing experience? Eventually as he was dosing off he heard Morella whisper, "Morning we do proper." And he slept soundly. He awoke to find the room in complete darkness with Morella lying beside him, her slow deep stentorious breathing verging on snoring. He wondered if he would get any more sleep that night; but in fact, the next thing he knew the room was brilliantly lit by the light of the sun reflected off the windows of the hotel opposite. Wasting no time, Morella made sure he was fully erect and rolled on top of him, deftly guiding it inside her. Without warning, with a great heave she rolled them both over, still coupled – he found himself on top of her, her legs wide apart, their pubic bones grinding together, her hands fiercely cramponned onto his buttocks, the fingernails digging into his flesh.

Chapter 2
At the Conference

Thirty-five minutes later Julian was up, showered, dried and talcum powdered, shaved, teeth cleaned, dressed, hair combed, tie adjusted, shod and ready to make his way down to desayuno – breakfast – taking his briefcase with him to avoid the need to go upstairs for it after breakfast, before leaving for the Conference Centre. His dalliance with Morella meant he was running late – there had not been time for his morning prayers. He usually said them, at night also although he did not really know why. He consoled himself with 'Pascal's wager', the philosopher, scientist and theologian said that though people laughed at him for praying, if it turned out that there were an afterlife the laugh would be on them, whereas if there weren't, there would be no one to laugh at anyone.

On the first morning of his visit last year, Maria had prepared half a grapefruit the night before, cutting the flesh free from the core and the pith, leaving it overnight covered with a thick layer of sugar. She had seen his frown of disapproval as he scraped the sugar off and thereafter prepared his grapefruit, sugar free, moments before he came down. As he made his way down the last few steps and crossed the hall to the breakfast room he noticed a faint smile on Maria's lips. Did she know of his escapade with Morella? He certainly hoped not but could not be certain.

He sat down and savoured the fresh tang, using a grapefruit spoon with its serrated tip, looking forward to the main course to follow. A choice of cereals was available, but he waited for Maria to serve up her generous interpretation of an English breakfast. After coffee, glancing at his watch, he set off for the Conference Centre. That night, as he undressed for bed, he noticed something odd about his socks – literally. Each had a ring about a centimetre wide near the top, made up of narrow rings of black, grey, white and blue, this motif being repeated at three-centimetre intervals down to just above the heel. Between these the background was a mid-grey, as was the foot. However, on one, this background was a slightly deeper grey than on the other. He realised that at home in London, in his tiny flat, there must be another pair of unmatched socks.

I hope that was what Maria was grinning at this morning, not my night with Morella, he thought. The days passed, Julian worked hard each day at his investigations, assisted by various contacts he had been given. These he had acquired in a vaguely mysterious way. The day before his departure for Argentina he had been climbing the stairwell to his small apartment in a large block near Charing Cross, when a tall lean figure, whom he thought he recognised – or should have done – was descending. The lean man had silently slipped a folded piece of A5 paper into Julian's top breast pocket as he passed and from the next landing down had grunted 'good luck' in sepulchral tones. The contacts, just names addresses and telephone numbers, had evidently been photocopied from two pages of a small notebook which had been opened out flat. There was no other information, except for 'B. Aires' at the top of the left-hand page, in handwriting as small and neat as were all the entries.

Julian filed his copy each evening straight after dinner, describing how minister after minister had assured the conference attendees that there was no corruption in his department. At a break in the proceedings for morning coffee, the man from the train came and sat at the same small round table as Julian, saying, "Buenas dias Señor Broffi, we meet again!"

"Buenas dias. But I'm afraid I don't know your name."

"Felipe MacGomez of the Brazilian Times, at your service."

Seeing Julian's raised eyebrows at *MacGomez*, Felipe went on to explain. "When my Scottish forebears came to Argentina in the early twentieth century to settle, at the port of entry they had to have details; name, current nationality, age, names of parents and grandparents, marital status, dependents if any, etc. recorded by an immigration clerk onto a form in quadruplicate, one copy of which was handed to them after they had signed all four copies, as, in effect, their identity card. The clerk got the Mac bit but was completely confused over the rest and had simply opted to add the common name Gomez."

"That's what the form says, so that's who we are."

"How did you come to know my name?"

"Like you, I attended the Fifth World Population Conference and having a photographic memory for names and faces I was particularly interested in delegates from other continents, particularly Europe. It's all in here, you and several others." He took out a little black notebook and tapped the cover with his fingernail. To his surprise Julian took out an almost identical black notebook and was busy entering his name.

"Email, home and office phone numbers please, oh – and if you don't mind, home address as well." Felipe obliged and Julian provided his, to fill out Felipe's own record about him.

"I see, like me, you don't use an electronic notebook."

"I have it back at the hotel and after dinner I will update it with today's entries. Of course, it's also backed up on a couple of different bulk storage devices as well."

"Just like me; double belt and triple braces, eh?"

They met again at lunch, which was a buffet affair. Julian satisfied himself with just one sandwich, knowing the scale of the provisions that Maria would serve up that evening.

"Can I get you a drink?"

Julian hesitated. "Just a small cerveza, please, actually I'm T." It was Felipe's turn to raise the eyebrows.

"I'm semi TT, you know." What he didn't say was that he was very wary about how much alcohol he consumed, bearing in mind that drink had mastered his mother and eventually brought about her death.

They returned to the main hall for the afternoon session. In the comfort break mid-way through the afternoon, Felipe pointed out to Julian a carafe covered with an upturned glass, next to more upturned glasses, on a small green baize covered table in the foyer.

"Gin, for those who can't manage more than hour or two without a drink," said Felipe, apparently quite seriously. For a brief moment, Julian wondered if that could be true, then broke into a grin along with Felipe. Julian did not see Felipe again that day, or indeed for the rest of the Conference.

And then came the difficult part. His work engrossed him during the day, but that still left him with a few hours to fill, somehow, before retiring. During the five days he was there, in his evening wanderings he explored much of the city on foot, wandering the streets until late at night; he knew that going to bed earlier would lead to a wasteland of sleeplessness. One night, returning late and sharing a nightcap with Antonio, he said, "I've been exploring all sorts of parts of your lovely city. Parts of it are very run down, specially round what looked like an old town hall."

"**Never** go into that district again, and certainly not after dark," said Antonio with all the emphasis at his command. Julian had, in fact, had a nasty feeling that he was being followed, but fortunately his steps had led him into a well-lit main street and away from danger.

In his nocturnal wanderings, he even discovered one or two vaguely familiar-looking alleyways turning off this street or that. But he could not decide which had been the one down which the young lady, with her impeccable English, had disappeared. Gradually, over the course of the week, any hope of seeing her again faded and at last he prepared to leave for the return journey to the U.K. Antonio said, "Here is your receipt for the stay." Handing him the receipt. It was very grandiose, more than the top quarter of the A4 page was taken up with the name of the hotel in letters 4cm high and a picture of the frontage taken with a very wide angle lens making it look twice as imposing as in real life. Without taking any great notice of it, Julian handed over his credit card. The card machine spewed out a ticket with the details, which Antonio stapled to the top left hand corner of the receipt: Julian folded it in two and two again and slipped it into his wallet. After bidding Antonio and Maria farewell, he found himself retracing his steps to the Estacion where he boarded a railcar for the airport. He had left the usual luggage tickets attached to his bags and handed in the counterfoils at the airline's office on the way past – Antonio would have them ready for collection by the baggage service and he would not see them again until they arrived back at his flat.

As he entered the nearly deserted airport building – there were only two scheduled international flights that day – his heart missed a beat. There ahead of him, going in almost the same direction so that he only got a three-quarter rear view of her head, was a smart young lady in a blue-grey coat. Her long black hair hung down over the collar, and he involuntarily quickened his pace. When she was still about twenty metres from him, she paused and started to turn round. For an agonising moment that seemed like ages, he was sure it would be she. But the woman's gaze passed over him with no sign of interest or recognition and he saw that she was much older than the young lady on his mind. Suddenly, seeing the person she was expecting to meet, she hurried away. Julian felt a sinking feeling in the pit of his stomach, as his unexpectedly aroused hope had crumbled into dust.

The return journey passed with the usual tedium of any long flight, punctuated by a visit to the restaurant. With time on his hands, he studied the receipt from Antonio and Maria's little hotel; he felt sure it was much more than he had paid the previous year. He saw that it included a not inconsiderable charge for 'personal services'.

That's really very reasonable, he thought but it occurred to him that he could hardly expect his employer to pay for his escapade with Morella. Thinking back over their night together he thought, *Come to think of it, at the time there was no mention of a condom, it just never occurred to me. I wonder if, at some time in the future, a young Argentinian will learn that his or her daddy was an English gentleman. Surely not – doubtless Morella had precautions permanently in place, but if that were the case, most likely some other man would have been the Father – certainly, judging from her experienced approach, I'm far from being her only customer.*

The plane was a sleek newish jet, quite unlike the wide-bodied type which in an earlier age would have carried 500 or more passengers, crammed in like sardines in a can. The Brentwood 907 however had spacious accommodation for just 90 passengers and their luggage, together with a restaurant and capacious holds for commercial air cargo and mail etc., in addition to baggage.

Brentwood was an international financial consortium, which had purchased the famous North American plane maker after it virtually went bust, following years of losses. With the decline in world population and the severe restrictions on air travel, all the North American plane makers had amalgamated, but even then the corporation could not be supported by the dwindling requirements of a dwindling number of airlines. The share price had dropped to a few cents and Brentwood had picked up what was still the largest plane maker in the world, though much smaller than in its glory days, at a bargain price.

After a less than satisfactory meal in the restaurant, Julian returned to his seat, relaxed, and wondered if he would drop off to sleep. But his ever-active mind had other ideas and started one of its favourite games, playing with words. At one of the press conferences, he had met a reporter from another paper, and they had fallen to comparing notes over dinner one evening. Julian learnt that he came from Halifax, and now, relaxing in his window seat, Julian's brain began to play with the word. It was so malleable, could become Hafilax or Falihax, Haxifal etc. – and he searched for other words which could metamorphose as well, if not better. He failed to find one – though later in the flight Kilimanjaro came to mind, offering hundreds of possibilities. One could swap the vowels around, as well as the consonants – and he fell to wondering if there were other people whose brains played such bizarre games, largely beyond their control. He assumed there must be; no way could he believe that he was unique, though just how common it was, he had no idea.

Suppose it were just one in a thousand, then with current population of the UK, there must be tens of thousands of people like me, he thought. So, he resorted to a pocket-sized paperback with its collection of cryptic crossword puzzles, reprinted from the paper. But after a while, it ceased to hold his attention and he fell into a sombre mood, reflecting that his visit to Buenos Aires had been successful, yes, as far as his job was concerned, but had left him with an empty feeling. Only now did he realise that from well before setting out, as soon as he had received the assignment, he had been subconsciously expecting, quite irrationally, that he would meet her again.

At last, the plane touched down at Heathrow and Julian, with all the other passengers, was soon through all the familiar airport formalities. He caught a tube train, one of the new super quiet ones as people still called them, although they were in fact over fifty years old, and was soon arriving at Leicester Square. Turning up his collar against the unusually chill autumn breeze, he set off towards Trafalgar Square on the way to his flat, his mood becoming greyer with every step, matching the deepening gloom of the evening. As he turned into Duncannon Street, head down against a suddenly bitter blast of the east wind, a hand gripped him fiercely by the arm and a voice said in Spanish, "Do be careful of the traffic!" She laughed. There was not a vehicle in sight, indeed the street was now a pedestrian precinct, having narrowly escaped plans a century or so earlier to bulldoze it out of existence as part of an over-ambitious but ultimately unsuccessful development plan.

Julian was struck dumb in a whirlwind of conflicting thoughts and emotions; he had had the greatest difficulty all year in trying to recall exactly the sound of that voice, yet now he heard it again, it was as familiar as if he had heard it daily, ever since their first meeting. At last, he recovered his composure sufficiently to reply, awkwardly, in view of the strength of his feelings for this young lady, whom he barely knew. But there was that same heart-warming look of concern on her face – was it for him, personally, or was it just her natural expression? "Please, come in, out of the cold." A he guided her into a narrow coffee bar a metre or two up the street.

They sat down on one of the long bench seats down each side of the warm interior with its steamed-up windows, a small table for two in front of them, took off their coats, and he ordered two cappuccinos. His heart pounding, his mind in turmoil, he blurted out, "I never expected to…what are you doing here? Oh, my name is Julian, Julian Brophy." He learnt that hers was Inez da Silva, that she had been in London on business for a week, for the import export firm for which she worked in Buenos Aires and that she was just twenty one years of age. Inez was articulate, poised, talkative herself and, Julian found, so easy to talk to. Consequently, in the ensuing minutes, she found out much more about him than he had about her.

"Tell me about your parents."

"That's Bill and Kitty, I was brought up by them in their charming cottage in the country, with a garden next to woods where there are wood pigeons. From dawn to dusk, the woods, the garden – even the house resounded to the mournful sounds of the pigeons." Feeling a little self-conscious, he mimicked the sound…

ooo OO OO oo oo

And then continued, "Actually they are in fact my adoptive parents. I did well at school – in the sixth form I studied Latin, Ancient Greek, History and Economics, and at uni I tackled both classics and modern languages."

"That was ambitious – must have been hard."

"Later, at twenty two I joined the Telegraph as a cub reporter."

Slightly long-sighted from birth, he still needed spectacles, but for reading only – she noticed the rimless demi-lunettes as he had conned the menu and read the notice on the back of the menu card, which proudly proclaimed that the establishment had been founded in 2200A.D. by the grandfather of the present proprietor. What Julian didn't say was that he had come to live with his adoptive parents when he was five, after his parents separated, he was careful not to reveal the exact circumstances of that painful stage in his life.

Yet he had felt no hint that she was prying, just that she was, for no reason that he could imagine, genuinely interested in him. Or was it simply that she was a naturally warm-hearted person, who would have greeted just as charmingly any other person she had unexpectedly met for a second time, by a strange coincidence? He could not make up his mind which, leaning to one view one minute, the other the next. Julian ascertained that she had already eaten that evening, and he said he had too though in fact he had had nothing but that disappointing meal on the plane in mid Atlantic.

So, they talked on – and after a while he felt sufficiently confident to steer the conversation around to learn a little more about her.

"My parents live near a small town fifty kilometres from Buenos Aires, they come from a rural background where all their relatives and neighbours are small farmers, catholic and very traditional in their outlook, but I only attend mass on occasional visits back home."

Having no sons – Inez was an only child – her parents' hope was that she would marry a local lad, a second son of one of the neighbours, say, and that the couple would in due course take over the running of the farm. But she had never had a boyfriend and now lived in Buenos Aires, where she had a small flat, a few hundred metres from where they had first met.

The door opened and a customer was about to enter as another was leaving. In a protracted exchange of courtesies as to who should go first, a bitter wind swept in, and with an involuntary shiver Inez moved further away from the door, closer to Julian who surprised himself by slipping an arm around her waist. She gave no hint as to whether she was surprised, pleased or otherwise. They talked of his plans for the future, though when he enquired as to hers, she was a little evasive – but she did draw his hand up ten centimetres so that it rested on the side of her breast, his little finger tucked underneath. She turned her face up and towards him and smiled a smile which he could not decipher; he was as though turned to stone, too entranced to move. After a moment or two, the smile became a little wistful and she nestled her head on his shoulder. He knew he should have taken the opportunity and kissed her, even here, in this public place; he had missed the chance, had muffed it – had she been disappointed? Even as he was reproaching himself, her hand on his leg, just above the knee, gave a little squeeze, and he knew she understood, had forgiven him. He was overwhelmed by such a delicate, understanding nature; he could not conceive of such a person ever being angry, sarcastic, confrontational or bitter.

And still they talked on – he was devastated to learn that she was returning to Argentina the following morning – and on, until the coffee bar closed. He was not expected in the office the following day and having learnt that she was to catch a plane at Heathrow in the morning at ten o'clock, he arrived there himself at half past eight and waited expectantly. With so few flights, there was only the one terminal in operation, and only one check-in desks in use. At a couple of minutes past nine, Inez appeared and, on seeing him, broke into a warm, surprised, but perhaps just slightly knowing smile; he suspected she had more than half expected to find him there. After she had checked in and secured a seat by a window, they sat and talked, facing each other across a small table for two in the coffee area. This morning he was determined that if an opportunity to kiss her arose, he would take it. If he leant forward, it would be easy, but only if she leant forward too. Somehow it didn't happen, she made no move – he wondered afterwards, was she waiting for him to make the first move? So, they talked on, until it was time for her to go through to the departure lounge. He accompanied her to passport control where they had at last definitely to part, and he looked so plainly disappointed that she kissed him lightly on the cheek before turning to go. At the last minute, he desperately thrust his card into her hand and begged her to let him know she had arrived safely. He watched her, the long glossy black hair hanging down her back dancing as she walked. She turned a corner out of sight: He felt keenly disappointed that she had not glanced back even once. He was about to turn away, feeling empty, when she momentarily reappeared and waved. Then – perhaps as an afterthought – she blew him a kiss and was gone, this time for good.

Chapter 3
At the Office

Julian returned home and spent much of the day sorting out old papers, backing up files on the computer and on the local and main company archive storage devices, deleting various other files, doing some washing and tidying up the flat. The following day he was due in at the editorial offices. These had moved around from place to place over the centuries but were now situated back in recently rebuilt accommodation in a Fleet Street that had been flattened and redeveloped, back in fact to where they had been situated a century or more earlier, and conveniently only a few hundred yards from the block where he lived. When he arrived, he was in for a shock: The receptionist beckoned him over and directed him up to the office of the Deputy Foreign News Editor. He knocked and was invited in by the latter's secretary, a slim petite blonde, a good head shorter than him. On hearing his business, she looked slightly embarrassed, knocked at the inner office and showed him in.

"Ah, hello there, Julian. While you were away, we've had a bit of a reshuffle," said the DFNE pompously, a large paunchy balding thick-necked red-faced man in late middle age, leaning back comfortably in his large leather swivel chair, twiddling a fat ball pen in his hand, as though it were the cigar he was only allowed to smoke at home.

"I hope you'll be pleased. From now on, you'll be sharing an office with young Raynor – Hal – he's the same age as you, I believe. Could be a bit embarrassing, finding your desk and all your stuff's been shifted while you're away – not my idea though, the boss'." Julian wasn't quite sure who was supposed to be a bit embarrassed; it clearly wasn't the DFNE.

"By the way, we quite liked your stuff from Buenos Aires. There's something else interesting coming up, not sure whether you'll get it, or Hal. He's the more senior of course, started here straight from school – sensible chap, while you were…er," he paused while he consulted a personnel folder, "studying modern languages and other things." He pronounced 'other things' with some apparent distaste, as though he could not understand why anyone in their right mind should want to study classics, let alone anyone intent on becoming a newspaper reporter.

In truth, that had not been Julian's intention originally; he had always studied his chosen subjects simply because he liked them, not with any particular career in view. It helped not only that he liked them but that they were also the ones he happened to be best at. In any subject in which he was interested, he had a prodigious memory for facts; while for mundane things like birthdays, appointments, anniversaries et cetera, he was hopeless, relying totally on his diary, if he remembered to consult it, and if he had remembered to enter the items in it in the first place. Only near the end of his university career did he start to consider, belatedly as he realised, how he was going to earn a living for the rest of his life. It was purely following a chance remark from a fellow graduate, who had pointed out a job requiring fluency in several languages, advertised in that paper, that he had applied for a job with the Telegraph, and had been accepted.

The DFNE closed the personnel file, pushed it away and pressed a button on his desk. His secretary appeared so promptly that Julian wondered if she had been listening at the door. He got up and followed, as she led him along a corridor, tip-tap-tipping briskly along in bright red glossy high-heeled court shoes, a perfect colour-match to her just-below-the-knee pencil skirt, her breasts in a brief lacy bra with elastic straps bobbing gently up and down in her silky white semi-transparent blouse. Julian noticed the slim shapely legs, in their glossy stockings, and those shoes with their eight centimetre high heels, and wondered how on earth she coped in them, all day long.

She probably spends most of her hours at work sitting down, he thought. She chatted gaily as she led the way, turning her face with its warm attractive and completely unselfconscious smile towards him, with each new bit of gossip she retailed. She was enchanting and he wondered whether he had not better forget Inez altogether and turn his attention to – he realised he did not even know her name – but had noticed there were no rings on her third finger, left hand. She barely came up to his shoulder, and he was resisting a forceful impulse to put a strong protective arm around her waist, when just at that moment she turned right up some steps, and the moment was gone.

They continued along another corridor and on the way, beaming at Julian. "You'll like Hal I'm sure, everyone does. He's quite reserved really, never gets in a flap. Oh, and he's just a bit devious, I've heard some people say. Looks a bit raffish – but don't be taken in by it; he's always very friendly and helpful," she said, in her high soprano tones.

"What he'll think, getting a new office mate on the Day of Doom, I can't imagine." Finally, they arrived at an office in a different part of the building from Julian's previous one, which he had shared with three others. They went in and the tall lean dapper man who had passed him on the stairs eight days previously got up.

Ignoring Julian completely, he said, with a face at the same time completely serious but totally expressionless, "My dear Sandra, you look ravishing today." Then, wagging a didactic finger, added solemnly, "Not that I'm suggesting for a moment that you don't look ravishing other days."

She laughed lightly, turned to Julian smiling and said, "You see what I mean?" Before going on to introduce Mr Julian Brophy to Mr Hal Raynor.

Julian was impressed with how it was done, with consummate artistry. The flattery was delivered apparently in all seriousness, as though he really meant every word, yet somehow in such a way that there was no danger of the recipient thinking he was in earnest, was seeking to start a romantic attachment.

If only I had such an easy natural way with women, I might have had girlfriends, might even have been married by now, thought Julian. Only when Sandra had left did his new office mate turn to Julian, who noticed that he then had his full attention.

"Welcome to our new home, such as it is," he said, in his gravelly voice, waving a beautifully manicured hand around the office. He said that they had met twice before. This was true, but Julian had only the haziest recollection of the first occasion, probably because it was on his first day with the paper and he had met, in passing, easily a couple of dozen people that day and the next.

"What did Sandra mean, saying you might not be pleased, getting a new office mate on the Day of Doom?"

"Is that what she said, the superstitious little sparrow?"

"It didn't mean anything to me."

"Well, well; I'm not surprised. It's a superstitious belief that something bad is going to happen on the twenty-third of the month. Some old crones forecast it in the middle ages, it was found on a folded up scrap of parchment, badly stained, walled up in the ruins of an old priory, you know – something after the style of Mother Shipton or Nostradamus."

"I've never heard of it. Anyway, twenty-third of which month?"

"Ah well, that's the art of prophecy, keep it a bit vague, then you can never be proved wrong. It's been in all the tabloid rags – both of them, that is. Someone's just unearthed that old parchment, it's been dated to around fifteen hundred A.D. Didn't warrant a mention in our paper of course. Got a mention on television I believe – one of the commercial channels."

"I can see why thirteen was always considered unlucky, one in thirteen apostles was a bad 'un, but why twenty-three?"

"Good point. P'raps it's something to do with prime numbers. Three, thirteen and twenty-three are all prime. So are forty-three and fifty-three, seventy-three and eighty-three, a hundred and three and a hundred and thirteen. Then no more till you get to a hundred and sixty three and a hundred and seventy three."

"Gosh! Do you know all the primes off by heart?" Hal laughed.

"Nope, fat chance, anyway there's an infinite number of 'em. Only up to four hundred and one."

Julian was to discover in the following months that Hal was a fount of knowledge on all sorts of arcane subjects, sometimes flaunting it as a party piece, but in a totally undemonstrative way, as though it were the sort of thing that anyone would know, sometimes revealing it only reluctantly, as though it were too important to be noised abroad.

The office he now shared with Hal was but little if any smaller than the one he had previously shared with three others, and moreover this one had an outside window, overlooking the street. His fellow reporter was, he decided, a curious character with a somewhat raffish manner and ambience, just as Sandra had said. This went well with his appearance; he was a few centimetres taller than Julian and slightly cadaverous, both of figure and of countenance, with jet-black hair swept back and plastered down. Julian was to learn later that Hal more commonly dressed in black, which, with his aquiline nose, hawkish features and the glitter of his piercing blue eyes, emphasised his cadaverous looks. Today however he sported an open neck check pattern shirt, revealing a Paisley pattern cravat and an old Harris Tweed jacket with leather patches on the elbows, such as Julian had only ever seen in old black and white movies from two centuries earlier.

Only really noticing this jacket at that point, suddenly a picture flashed into Julian's brain. As a child he had seen on television an old black and white film about a family in the Second World War. A couple with their two children were travelling in the dimly lit corridor of a crowded steamtrain, swaying as it sped through the dark moonless night. The father in a jacket with leather patches on the elbows, with his wife and teenage daughter were standing, but the boy, about nine or ten, was sitting on a large up-ended suitcase, next to a sailor. Each time the lad started to nod off, his head fell forward, and he woke up. The sailor cupped the lad's chin in his hand and in no time at all he was asleep. The hours passed and dimly the dawn appeared; the lad awoke, and a procession of poles was passing outside the window. At the time, Julian had identified with the boy in the train, and much of the film had stuck in his memory. All this flashed into Julian's mind, and now he knew what buried memory had stirred in him, in the railcar on the way to the Estacion. Kitty had told him that they were called 'Telegraph Poles'. So, there was a moment's distraction before he replied to Hal's next question, as to how he would like to be known. "Mr Brophy if you prefer, or perhaps something a little less formal." Hal took the view that all familiar names should be monosyllables, like his own. But after trying 'Joo' and 'Yoo' he settled on 'Yan'. Julian concurred and was offered a cup of coffee, from a pot that Hal kept on the go all day. Julian gratefully accepted it. It turned out that neither took sugar, and only a little milk, which Hal dispensed from a small vacuum flask which he brought in daily from home. 'Home' turned out to be a flat in the same building as Julian's, two floors higher, explaining their brief encounter on the stairs.

Julian found, to his relief, that his desk and other items had been moved carefully; nothing was missing except a couple of ballpoint pens, which were standard office stores issue anyway. Not that they ever saw much use at that time: Schoolchildren learnt keyboard skills at the same time as 'joined-up writing'. They were all expected to become proficient at the former, while some never entirely mastered the latter. Settling into the seat behind his desk, he said, "Thanks for that list of contacts in Buenos Aires. Some of them were really helpful. Where'd you get 'em all?" Without a word, Hal rummaged in his desk and held up a small black notebook, tapped it significantly with the long, neatly manicured nail of his right forefinger, nodded slightly to it and carefully stowed it away again, locking the drawer. Over lunch in the canteen, Julian made discreet enquiries of Dick, one of the reporters with whom he had previously shared an office, about Hal's notebook.

"He's the same age as you," Dick said. "We all regard Hal as an old hand, he has a reputation for sniffing out scandal; of the commercial, political and financial sort, rather than the sexual."

Hal had built up an extensive range of contacts throughout the world, details of whom he kept in his famous but jealously guarded little black notebook. For no very good reason anyone could fathom, he affected to scorn the pocket electronic notebooks most others used.

"Although I suppose at least there's no danger of the battery running out just when you want to use it," his former roommate had said. His contacts would often pass on to him snippets or leads, in return for the same sort of assistance from Hal in their own enquiries.

The picture of Sandra slowly faded, unnoticed, from his mind and throughout the day he kept wondering if Inez had arrived home safely. He told himself that of course she must have done, but there was no call to his mobile, which he kept permanently on nor was there an email to his work address, nor yet to his home one either, when he arrived back that evening. This left him feeling deflated, and even just slightly peeved. He had hoped – expected even, remembering her blown kiss – that he would indeed hear from her again, but now he began to doubt it. The following day he settled down to work at his desk, having absentmindedly returned Hal's gruff but a friendly 'morning, Yan', and tried to forget Inez by immersing himself in his work.

"By the way, Hal, I must put in my expenses for the Argentina trip. You don't happen to have a blank claim form, by any chance?"

"'Enquire within upon anything' is my motto, like the once famous Pear's Encyclopaedia," said Hal as he fumbled in his desk drawer and produced a blank form, like a rabbit from a hat. Julian filled in the details and attached the various receipts. He had cut off the bottom of the receipt from Antonio's hotel bill, with its mention of 'personal services', just slightly askew and had touched the middle third of the bottom edge with a finger dripped in red wine.

Halfway through the afternoon, he realised that he was sitting there gazing, unseeing, into the far distance. It had not gone unnoticed. Without a word, Hal got up and poured a cup of coffee, brought it over and placed it in front of him. Laying a sympathetic hand on Julian's shoulder, he opened his mouth to say something but closed it again, having thought better of it and returned to his desk, sat down and pretended to be busier than he really was.

There was no message that day, or at home that evening. The following day he felt not so much disappointed – he had told himself firmly the previous evening as he went to bed that he had best forget Inez entirely – as tired, indeed exhausted. He had not slept well; telling himself to forget was one thing, carrying it out was another thing entirely. He had always had a fear of insomnia, knowing how it had troubled his mother; he had often wondered if it had contributed to her uneven temper, and even ultimately to her drinking. Near the end of what seemed to him another interminable afternoon, Hal broke into his thoughts, out of the blue, with 'still waiting to hear?' Julian started; *what did Hal know, what could he know?* Julian assumed he meant 'waiting to hear from someone', although the question had actually been more vague than that.

"Yes, but I don't suppose I will, now." He had been surprised by the query and had replied without thinking.

"From someone?"

"Yes."

"In Argentina?" Hal did not need a reply; Julian's look confirmed it more than words could have done.

'Another cup' was Hal's banal riposte; Julian was to learn that more coffee was his invariable prescription for any contingency, from a minor irritation to a dire calamity. Later that afternoon, Julian had taken the expenses paper work along to the cash office. Jane, the clerk, raised her eyebrows at the sight of the mutilated hotel bill. Julian hastily explained. "Er, I accidentally spilled a glass of red wine over it and the bottom part dried all wrinkled and crinkled." Jane nodded, and the claim was duly settled in due course.

He arrived home that evening and prepared himself a meal. Like the vast majority of people, he fed on ready prepared meals, the freezer and microwave oven being his quick and simple servants, reliable and uncomplaining. He felt slightly guilty at this laziness; Kitty had prided herself on always preparing dishes using all fresh ingredients, and had insisted on teaching him simple cookery, against the day when he would leave home. But all ready-made meals were subject to Ministry of H.& R approval, both as to the quality of their contents, and the balance of the various ingredients, unlike in former ages when the sort sold by supermarkets at the cheaper end of the market were of very dubious quality, containing excessive quantities of fat, salt and sugar. He finished his meal, accompanied by a glass of Kentish dry white wine

He washed up the pots and pans, cutlery and crockery and put them away; for one, it took almost no time at all, and he could do without the expense of a dishwasher.

"Disposable plates and cutlery would have saved me a little time." He reflected. He knew that, though now banned, they had enjoyed a brief popularity, not just for picnics but even for everyday use, a century earlier. But apart from the expense, after use either they contributed to atmospheric CO_2 if burnt or to the demands for landfill if stored for the fortnightly refuse collection. In the latter case, for most of the year they still needed rinsing anyway, if they were not to become a smelly and unhygienic attraction for flies and were still regarded as unrecyclable.

So, one might as well have proper things – cheaper in the long run, he ruminated.

The domestic chores out of the way, Julian turned on the computer to see if there were any emails. Since Inez returned to South America he had hurried home each day and checked, but with steadily fading expectations, so that today it had not even occurred to him to do so before getting himself a meal. There, to his surprise, was a long videomail, in which Inez explained, with an apologetic look on her face, why she had been incommunicado. It appeared that as her plane landed, she had received a text message from a neighbour of her parents: Her father had suffered a stroke and her mother was in a crippling state of anxiety, unable to attend to anything. Inez had hurried to her parents' home and taken charge of the day-to-day running of the household, while her cousins had rallied round and lent a hand running the farm.

"Only now have I been able to get to a neighbours, where there's a computer and a connection, my parent s have never given houseroom to such things."

Over the following months, their acquaintanceship had blossomed, albeit at a distance, mainly by videomail, and at weekends by videophone. While commodities generally, food, transport and heating in particular, were very expensive, modern technology had made communications of all sorts almost ridiculously cheap. So, their weekend videophone sessions had been long and intimate, but regrettably no substitute for the physical presence of each other.

Thus, it was a complete surprise when there was a knock on his door, one evening in the spring of the following year, and on opening it, he found Inez standing there. Instinctively, he put his arms around her and kissed her. He had not thought of the consequences beforehand and was immediately worried that he might have been too forward; after all, they had only met in the flesh three times before, the first time literally for no more than a few minutes. Shy, and so not naturally a success with the ladies – he envied those men like Hal who had 'the knack' – he had had no girlfriend before. Perhaps because of this, he had been totally unprepared for the strength of the feelings which surrounded his acquaintanceship with Inez. But his fears were unfounded; she was completely relaxed in his arms, and returned his kiss, lingeringly.

"Come in." She did so, and he took her coat and brought her a cup of coffee. She apologised that she had given him no warning of her visit, had been worried that he might be out, or might have moved from the address on his card. But although she had not liked to mention it in case it did not materialise. "I applied some months ago for a transfer to my firm's London office. Only at the last minute an offer came through, and judging that Mum could now cope, with the help of relatives and neighbours, I accepted it."

She had mischievously thought that it might make a nice surprise if she kept it a secret for another day, until she actually arrived. In fact, she had arrived late the previous afternoon, booked into a hotel for the night and then scoured the accommodation section of the local paper. Her first call had been to a frail elderly landlady in Bayswater, who was more than pleased to have a lady lodger in place of the troublesome man who had left a few days earlier, much to the dear old lady's relief.

"I spent my first day at the offices of the London branch of the firm, returned after work to the hotel to collect my bags and took them round to my new digs." She had then came straight on to Charing Cross.

"So here I am. Are you glad to see me?" Of course, no answer was necessary, nor expected.

Julian plied her with questions, about the journey, about her new job, about a thousand things, as the evening wore on and darkness fell. All the while, at the back of his mind (which, like any good computer, was used to multiple tasking), he was thinking about her imminent departure for some anonymous bedsit in Bayswater. When he had taken over the lease of his tiny flat, with its one good-sized bedroom, it had been unfurnished. He had filled it with furniture bought locally, much of it second-hand, but the previous occupier had left a perfectly serviceable double bed behind, which he had never replaced. He found it difficult, but attractive, to imagine her staying the night in his bed – perhaps while he offered to sleep on the settee but realised that however much he might like the idea, it was not in his nature to propose it.

It was true that there had been a remarkable, if largely unexplained, change in the mores of society over the last hundred years and more, from the casual sexuality of preceding centuries. This was possibly due to the proliferation of a number of new sexually transmitted diseases which had appeared – apparently from nowhere – virulent and in some cases untreatable, many with alarming consequences in the short term and even more dire in the long. But the current attitude to extramarital relations was not what held him back from suggesting it. It was rather a vague and ill-formed yet powerful feeling that it would be inappropriate, that she did not belong to him – yet. He fervently hoped that in due course, sooner rather than later if possible, she would do; not because he wanted her to, but rather because she wanted it. He thought to himself, wryly, that it must be something to do with that old-fashioned and much-maligned word 'respect'. In the end, he suggested that he should see her safely back to the little house in the quiet Bayswater backstreet which she had described to him, and she did not demur. Moreover, she seemed pleased when he mooted that they meet again the day after next: Eventually after some discussion as to exactly where and when, it was agreed they would meet at 1900 hours the very next day in the coffee bar in Duncannon Street.

In the coffee bar the following evening, they arranged that she would come round to Julian's flat the following Sunday morning, and later, as they prepared to leave, she produced a small packet, saying, "I've brought this for you, all the way from Argentina." When he got back home late that evening, after seeing Inez back to her bedsit, he unwrapped it. It looked like a glass jar, although in fact it was plastic, and on the label were the words '*Dulce de Leche 500gm*' plus a list of ingredients and a host of other matter. The contents were listed as caramelised milk with sugar and a little preservative. He put it on one side, not sure what to do with it.

Sunday morning dawned bright and fair, and Julian hastily tidied up the flat. He had scarcely finished when, a minute before ten, there was a knock on the door and Inez arrived, with a small shopping bag. After they had kissed, Inez said, "Have used the dulce de leche?"

"No."

"Good. Can I have it, then?" as she pulled a packet of digestive biscuits, a small packet of icing sugar and a box of half a dozen eggs out of her shopping bag, in the little kitchen.

She peered into the cupboard where he kept his pots and pans, and fished out a frying pan and a few saucepans, together with a dusty square metal baking dish, all of which Kitty had insisted he take with him when he left home. It had seen no use since then and Inez washed it out thoroughly and dried it. With the ingredients she had brought with her, and some butter from Julian's fridge, she set to work. Julian watched, intrigued, as she prepared a delicious desert of dulce de leche over a crushed biscuit base, topped with whipped sugared egg white, and popped it into the oven, which she had turned on beforehand.

They relaxed in the lounge and just talked – there was still so much to learn about each other. Just after noon, Julian busied himself in the kitchen and prepared them a simple meal of vegetables, duchesse potatoes and chicken pieces from the freezer which she had asked Julian to transfer from there to the fridge the previous evening. For desert, they enjoyed some of the mouth-watering sweet Inez had cooked; she had rescued it from the oven as the meringue topping was just beginning to show colour and had put it on one side to cool.

"I've put the rest in the fridge; you can finish it tomorrow," she said.

Inez was with Julian again all day the following Sunday and the one after that, after which it became a regular fixture, as did meeting most evenings – at first in the coffee bar and then in Julian's flat. One evening Inez said, whether mischievously, seriously or for what other motive he had no idea, "Do you love me?" He studied her face; there was the suspicion of an enigmatic smile which he could not interpret.

"Of course, don't you know that?" And added, blushing, "From the first time I ever met you, when I nearly got run over."

"I don't know that I believe in love at first sight."

"But you love me now, I hope?"

"Silly," she said and threw a cushion at him. "'Course I do."

"But if you didn't at first, when did you decide you did?" Her expression changed abruptly to a deeply thoughtful one. After a pause, she said, "I've always been a very private person: I always hated it when anyone touched me, especially a man. When I was a teenager, Uncle Miguel would lay his hand on my shoulder – he and Aunt Anna never had any children – and I used to shrink away, I hated it. And when I started work, in the crowded Metro often a man would stand with

his body pressing up against mine, much closer that was really necessary –
horrible. But with you it was different." He remembered putting his arm round
her waist in the coffee bar in Duncannon Street, the first time they ever went
there, and how she had moved his hand up to rest against her breast.

"From the first, I didn't mind you touching me – in fact, I rather looked
forward to it. I don't know why, that's just how it was." He knew he would
remember that conversation for the rest of his life. It was a warm Saturday in
autumn of the year 2255AD as Hal and Julian arrived at the nuptial suite in the
new Guildhall. Julian's parents Bill and Kitty were there already, as was the little
landlady and a few other friends and colleagues, and Kitty straightened Julian's
tie.

"That'll be someone else's job after today," growled a taciturn Hal who was
flattered but not entirely sure he was pleased to have been prevailed upon to be
best man as they awaited Inez. She arrived accompanied by two friends she had
made at work, both dressed in pink, she in white. Her mother could not attend,
being no longer steady on her feet and daunted by the thought of the journey, but
repeatedly urged her father to. But her father, despite having long recovered
almost completely from the stroke, would not, not approving of Inez marrying a
non-Christian and not even in a church. This had hurt Inez more than she would
have thought, which surprised her, but it certainly did not deter her. If her father
was stubborn, she was equally, if not more so.

Over the last year or so she had come to know Julian well, better than he
realised, and could see in him a transparently honest man, if a little over-reserved,
with infinite patience and application when he set his mind to a task and a definite
streak of obstinacy to match her own, but a truly gentle nature. At no time had
he actually proposed to her; somehow they had just found themselves making
plans for the future, plans which always seemed to involve them both. A
mutually agreeable date had been set, Hal did not readily get involved in other
people's affairs but had agreed – after a little persuasion from Inez – to be best
man, and she had asked Bill to give her away.

Bill had been more than ready to comply; he and Kitty had taken a great
liking to Inez.

"She's like the daughter we always wanted, but never had," Bill had said to
Kitty, after the second time they had met her. Steady sturdy undemonstrative old
Bill, with his big frame, heavy features that always looked unshaven, thinning
grey hair – once sandy – ready grin and a bit of a paunch, was in particular

delighted with his prospective daughter-in-law, and it showed in his obvious affection for her. Inez was surprised, and not a little relieved, at the warmth of her reception by her parents-in-law to be.

I've always imagined English people as being polite but distant and reserved, she thought. Perhaps his warm feelings for her were a partial consolation, for he was not without his disappointments. Sharp-spoken Kitty, one metre sixty seven tall with sharp features, a turned-up nose and a tendency to nag, apparently welcomed Inez warmly also. For her part, Inez had never expected such affection from her in-laws, but noticed, with relief that it seemed to be tempered by respect for Julian's and her privacy; with gratitude she felt sure there was no danger that Kitty might like to hang on to her son, or interfere in their new life together, and she hoped the same applied to Bill.

Julian was not quite sure that Kitty's apparent warmth towards Inez was one hundred percent genuine, but if that was the case, fortunately it did not show, at least to Inez. Indeed, Julian was the one person in the world who might have noticed, having grown up under Kitty's kindly guiding hand, gentle but, when necessary, very firm. With her stocky figure, high cheekbones and grey hair tending to white – he never remembered it having been any other colour – she had always been an excellent loving mother, but he had always been vaguely aware that perhaps she was so, because that was her place, her duty. She was in fact a much better mother than his own had ever been, but when his own mother had shown him affection, which happened more and more rarely as he grew up, it was of a complete and unreserved nature that Kitty's had never quite evinced.

The honeymoon was modest indeed; they explored the twin cities – of London and Westminster – on foot, discovering vestiges of the Roman wall around the original Londinium, the remains of mediaeval prisons and bishops' houses, explored the many parks, gardens, wharves and jetties, and found a thousand interesting sites and views. There were so many attractions that were free, such as the museums – Inez was particularly fascinated by the eccentric Sir John Sloane Museum at Lincoln's Inn Fields – whilst the dozens of marble memorial plaques in the tiny Postman Park moved her deeply.

"Look at these, they record the heroic self-sacrifice of ordinary citizens, builders' labourers, housewives, children even, in the period 1890–1910, who saved the lives of others at the cost of their own," said Inez, in wonder.

They would look back on this phase of their lives as one of the happiest, if one of great self-imposed financial stringency if they were ever to own their own home. Inez had moved in with Julian, into what was now their marital home and he remembered how, on the night of her first visit, he had tried to imagine her in the bedroom – perhaps with him: Now it was the norm, for real, and he was supremely happy. And yet…

Late that autumn they spent a few days visiting his parents, in their lovely old cottage a few miles from Tonbridge. The cottage had belonged to a reclusive great aunt of Kitty's, who had died at the age of one hundred and seven, and they had gained permission to move in after the old lady died. Bill had had to pull a few strings in 'The Department': Few indeed were the folk who were permitted to live outside a town. Inez had several long talks with Kitty, about people, while the two men talked about things, reflecting – Kitty said – the differing primary interests of men and women.

Inez learned that soon after she and Bill were married, Kitty had borne a son who suffered from spina bifida. To her great regret, she never saw the baby, and Bill only once, after repeated requests to see their child. In a little less than two days, the baby died, causing serious trouble. It appeared that the elderly matron in charge of the ward had arranged that the baby was kept warm and comfortable but fed only on a bottle of warm water; naturally after exhausting its original stock of energy, it ceased to live. The government policy was that in the face of continued population decline, every child should be raised and helped to become a useful citizen, however disadvantaged. Opponents of this policy maintained that the special care often required was an overall disadvantage to society, while supporters pointed to disabled people who had none-the-less turned out to be gifted, such as Hermanus Contractus, a cripple who in 11th century became an expert on music, astronomical instruments, clocks and in many other fields.

The matron had been charged with a grave offence and the case was reported and commented upon nationally. Bill and Kitty never succeeded in having another child, although the doctors assured them that Bill's sperm count was normal for the population at that time and that there was no assignable reason why Kitty should not be fertile.

When it became clear that another child was unlikely, they had adopted Bill's nephew Julian. Julian's parents, Colin and Hannah, had divorced when he was three, his stoutish impatient red-faced fiery-tempered father remarrying and emigrating; he had never been heard from again. Subsequently, as Hannah had become ever more depressed, her drinking had become more and more serious and when Julian was five, the little lad had come to live with his uncle and aunt, being formally adopted four years later, on the first of several occasions when Hannah was committed to an institution for the treatment of alcoholics. Inez wondered if these traumatic experiences explained Julian's reserved nature and felt a sudden flush of tenderness for him. Now, years later, the thought of a future grandchild partially consoled Kitty for her own childlessness.

Remembering Julian's reticence about his parents, at the coffee bar in Duncannon Street, Inez never revealed to him that she had learnt of what must have been a harrowing time for a five-year-old. Julian, meanwhile, telling Bill of his first encounter with Inez in Buenos Aires, made a startling discovery. When Bill heard that Julian had been at the Fifth World Population Conference two years before, Bill raised his eyebrows and said quietly, "I was there."

"I never saw you."

"I didn't see you either."

"But I know I scanned the delegate list, I'd have noticed if you were on it."

"The boss of the Department's name was. But he was taken ill and at the last moment, I was sent instead. The Department, you know, had been created some sixty years previously, when the population had long been decreasing and the press barons were pressing the government of the day to do something about it. The previous Health and Welfare Department had been split in two, the Health part doubled in size, renamed Health and Reproduction, and the Minister responsible for it raised to a senior cabinet post, second only to the Chancellor of the Exchequer."

Subsequent governments had continued to throw money at the problem, in the wake of numerous reports and special inquiries, but the population of the country continued to decline, as it was doing throughout the world. Bill had joined the department at the age of thirty-one, bringing with him into this Civil Service job years of experience in the rough and tumble of the commercial and financial worlds. He had progressed well, and eventually became Deputy Head at the age of fifty, two years after Julian left home to go to University.

Their visit passed all too quickly, and they returned to London, Julian bringing with him on loan a spare copy of the Report of the Proceedings of the Fifth World Population Conference belonging to the Department. Much as Inez had enjoyed the visit, they were both glad to be back in their own home again. That evening when they got back, Inez said, "Oh, do make me a cup of coffee please." Julian busied himself with the task in the little kitchen while Inez sank into an armchair in the living room and watched idly. He brought the two cups of coffee, set them down on the coffee table and Inez said, "Thank you, darling" and gave him a kiss. Again, at the back of his mind was this little niggle of a worry, which he could not pin down. Somehow, life with Inez seemed too simple, too easy.

That night as he lay in bed, having woken at two in the morning and unable for the moment to get to sleep again, the answer struck him, so obvious that he could not understand why he hadn't realised it earlier. During their recent stay with his parents, Bill helped Kitty around the house as a matter of course, just as Julian did Inez. But he recognised the very precise way in which Bill did each little job, and the memories flooded back to him. He too, when he lived with his parents, had had to do each little thing in precisely the prescribed way, or he would be instantly corrected by Kitty, who knew exactly how everything **should** be done, even if it was something she can't do or won't do or couldn't do or wouldn't do. One had to do the job precisely that way, or one was making a complete and utter mess of it, no deviation whatever – however small – was ever admissible. Strangely, he had missed this – that, he realised, was why life with Inez had seemed somehow just too simple.

Over the next month or two, Inez noticed her husband's mood becoming perceptibly more sombre. She was concerned, even though he was no less attentive and loving, both by day and by night. One evening, after dinner, she tackled him.

"What is it?" He knew exactly what she meant; they had developed a sort of sixth sense about each other's moods and feelings.

"I've been reading that report from the Fifth World Population Conference. It really does seem that the human race is doomed. In some ways, considering what a mess we've made of the planet, perhaps it's a good thing," he added bitterly. She came and sat next to him on the settee and leant her head on his shoulder.

"Can't they do anything about it? Doesn't anyone know what's causing it?" On the news they had just heard the latest projection for the crunch date for humanity. It was only a few generations away – if they had children and then grandchildren, what was the outlook for them?

"Most think it's the effect of pollution."

"What, like pesticides, ground fill and that sort of thing?"

"Maybe. There are lots of known bio-accumulative substances, and hormone-disrupting ones as well, out there in the environment. It could be just one of them, or the effect of a combination of two or more. A scenario that just never occurred to Malthus: It turns his weltanschauung upside-down completely."

"You'd think someone could do something. It makes me feel so helpless, trapped." He patted her arm.

"Lots of people are working on it, around the world. Perhaps something'll come of it. Perhaps I'll help to do something about it, one day." This strange comment stuck in Inez's mind: She could not see what it could mean but refrained from asking at the time. So, it was a bombshell for Inez when one afternoon, after returning from Fleet Street, he said, "Well, I've done it!"

"Done what?"

"I've stopped working for the newspaper and got a job in the Department."

Inez knew all about the department from talking to Bill who was by now high up in the organisation, though naturally Julian started at the bottom.

Inez returned to the subject of the world's falling birth rate the following December, when she announced to Julian that she was certain she was pregnant. Despite her problems with morning sickness, Inez managed to keep working up to three weeks before her confinement. That had brought their savings up to the point where, in April 2257, they could move out of the tiny flat, purchasing the freehold of an apartment just the other side of the Thames, with the aid of a mortgage – the falling population meant that accommodation was steadily becoming less expensive, in real terms, than in former centuries. The move involved some domestic disruption that she felt she could well do without, in her condition, but the new flat had been available at an attractive price, provided they moved without delay. After her troublesome pregnancy and a difficult delivery in St George's Hospital, Inez had produced a healthy son. Julian had been with her all day throughout her labour, holding her hand, except for the actual delivery, which had been difficult. He was mortified to hear Inez's cries of pain throughout; he wondered why evolution had subjected female members of the human race to such terrible toil in parturition while females of many other species managed so much better, often without any outside assistance whatever. Late that evening, as she held her son in her arms, they were both delighted with his chubby, wrinkled pink features, although Julian was pained to see how absolutely exhausted Inez was.

Back home, Inez breast-fed her child; James William they had named him, but from the first always called him Jim. Julian suggested they should include his wife's maiden name on the birth certificate also, and so he became J. W. de S. Brophy. As soon as they could, Bill and Kitty had come up to see their grandson: videomails and even the videophone were no substitute for the real thing.

Their new home was on the first floor, and on the ground floor was a crèche-cum-nursery. So it was that when Jim was six months old, Inez was able to return to work on Tuesdays and Thursdays and then later on Mondays, Wednesdays and Fridays. Kitty said to Bill, "It's a scandalous arrangement, leaving the child in the hands of strangers half the time."

But Bill pointed out that they had been very glad of Kitty's earnings early in their marriage. She had been well enough to return to work full time just a few weeks following the loss of their son, indeed she had been glad to do so, to keep herself from brooding on what might have been.

"But even so, it's far too early to leave the poor mite in someone else's care, even for one day a week, let alone three."

"It's a decision we unfortunately never had to make," Bill reminded her.

Chapter 4
To Tokyo, the 6th WPC 2266AD

It was some years after Julian had joined the Department; he progressed extraordinarily well, partly on merit and partly as a result of chance opportunities as, for one reason or another, more senior people had left, had had to retire, or had died. With the extreme shortage of experts of all sorts, staff were from time to time tempted to move on to better paid posts – legislation to impede this, at least in the case of government employees, had often been mooted, but never actually enacted. At about this time, the Department arranged for Julian to attend a medical school part time, not with a view to qualifying as a doctor, but to have someone in the Department with medical knowledge in general, with emphasis on anatomy. But if things were going well with his career, things were going badly for the career of mankind: The news about population trends was as gloomy as ever, if not more so. Certainly, the faint hope raised by the observed slight decrease in the rate of world population decline, reported at the Fifth WPC, had evaporated: The trend in following years showing a return to the previous rate of decline.

Nevertheless, it was the year that saw Julian, Inez and Jim move from their tiny first floor flat just south of the Thames, to a two hundred and forty year old semidetached property in Tunbridge Wells, which had been – until recently – well maintained and, over the years, modernised. The reasons for the move were many and complex, but among the major considerations were a wish that nine-year-old Jim, with his freckles, chestnut hair and passion for rugger, should grow up in a less densely urban environment, together with concerns for the health of Bill and Kitty, now sixty-seven and sixty-five respectively, with Kitty particularly becoming rather frail. Bill had in fact just retired, early and unwillingly, on the advice of his doctor who was concerned at his high blood pressure and one or two other potentially worrying symptoms.

With the pressing shortage of labour of all kinds, people were encouraged to work until they were seventy, or even older, wherever possible.

Inez was looking forward to the move, though she voiced a little concern when she learnt that Julian had arranged for the removal van to take all their possessions to the new house on the twenty-third of the month.

"What's the problem?"

"It's supposed to be an unlucky day, isn't it?" she replied. It just had not occurred to Julian, he had forgotten all about the Day of Doom Prophecy, not having heard it mentioned since that day in Hal's office ten or more years ago.

"Oh well, I don't suppose there'll be a problem, anyway, everything's insured. Really, you're as superstitious as Sandra was."

Inez pounced on this comment. "Who is Sandra? Was she a girlfriend or more? Are you still in touch with her?" Julian insisted the answers were no and no, though he could not forget his impulse to slip his arm round her waist as she had led him to his new office with Hal.

With Julian's recent promotion, they could now afford a move, although they would still be left with a big mortgage, even though the 'new' house was a bargain. The last owner was a widow who had done nothing to the property for some five years, so some expensive works were needed, the costs of which were added to the mortgage. For the first few months after they moved in, both Julian and Inez spent all their spare time cleaning and redecorating; even Jim proudly helped get the place tidy and shipshape, to the best of his ability.

With his sturdy frame and huge hands, which seemed incongruously out of scale with the rest of his body, he could lift and carry surprisingly large heavy objects, but Inez always had her heart in her mouth whenever he carried anything breakable: A lively, cheerful, happy-go-lucky lad, he was definitely a little on the clumsy side. So, she was horrified when she saw him carrying a stack of books with a vase perched precariously on top, out of the front room which they were clearing ready for redecoration. She was about to shout, 'be careful!' But bit her lip instead – realising it might do more harm than good. Sure enough, in the hall the vase toppled off, and she shut her eyes and ears against the imminent crash. But there was none: Jim had instinctively thrust his foot forward, breaking the vase's fall, and it survived, to roll harmlessly along, coming to rest against the kitchen door.

Money was tight, and for the bedrooms they found some very cheap red self-colour carpeting which would do at least for a few years, until they could afford something better. So thin was it that Julian called it 'woolly lino', using a term that had been handed down in his family through the ages. Out of curiosity – it was not a word she had ever heard – Inez looked it up on the internet and found that lino (an abbreviation for 'linoleum', also known as 'oil-cloth') consisted of 'a heavy canvas backing thickly coated with a preparation of linseed oil and powdered cork etc., used especially as a floor covering'.

One Saturday evening they were relaxing after having been busy all day long. They had had a cold meal to save time and effort and Julian had washed up. Now, as they enjoyed a cup of coffee, Inez said acidly, "I never thought when I was a carefree professional young woman in Buenos Aires I'd finish up one day as a household drudge." Watching him closely. Julian looked at her anxiously; he had become attuned to listening out for, and dreading, that tone of voice which he had come to recognise as a danger signal, betokening a rupture of peaceful relations. But he saw no trace of anger or displeasure on her expressionless face.

At first, he did not understand, then, when she could no longer contain a hint of a smile, he boomed, "You did that purposely, didn't you?" She nodded and broke into an even broader smile. He had no comparable way of winding her up in return; he was not given to using that tone of voice. Instead, he made as if to smack her bottom, she resisted, they struggled, and finished up in each other's arms, with a brief but tender kiss. Julian was greatly relieved; such spontaneous innocently childish moments of intimacy had been a part of their daily lives from the day they married, but had been conspicuously absent for some time, he did not quite know why. Had Inez come to the same realisation, and engineered the result that evening, he wondered? It somehow brought them closer together again – he realised how much he missed such apparently trifling but important moments.

As before, Julian worked mainly from home, with only a fairly rare journey up to town, to an occasional particularly important meeting in the Department. For less important meetings, there was the 'v-phone', a more complex version of the videophone which had formed a part of his workstation in London. The v-phone was controlled by a little box on his desk, which was rather like a combined mouse and miniature joystick, with a row of four buttons. When used, a screen would automatically unroll from a long narrow box on the ceiling of the bedroom – the smallest of the three – that served as his office, stretching down in front of the bookshelves which lined the opposite wall from where he sat at his desk, shelves already half filled with the books he had brought with him. In use, a life-size 3D image on the screen would show the caller or called person. There was also 'conference mode', in which as many as six persons could be displayed, their images being adjusted size-wise by the software and displayed as appearing on the other side of an electronically generated virtual conference table. For even larger conferences, up to twenty 'pages' of conferees could be handled, the relevant page – showing six including the one who was speaking – being automatically selected for display. The joystick on the desk controller enabled the viewer to select and zoom in on any part of the display, while a cancel button returned the screen instantly to the default display format. By a piece of technology that Julian did not understand, a video camera viewed him, apparently from a point in the middle of the screen, transmitting the image that others saw of him.

Meanwhile, Inez announced she intended to leave the import/export office of the London branch of the Argentinian company, where she had worked.

"The two friends from there who had been my bridesmaids had both left and the work I once found so interesting I now find, frankly, boring."

In Tunbridge Wells, she soon found a job as a secretary with a legal practice. The work she found difficult to start with, as she had to become familiar with all sorts of legal terms, many of which formed no part of the vocabulary even of an English person of above average education – she certainly had no idea of the Spanish equivalent of any of them. But the work was well paid and more than interesting; she found it fascinating to learn of the twists and complications of what might, on the face of it, seem simple cut-and-dried cases. In one case, an application for a divorce was lodged by a woman, one of whose complaints being her husband's attempts to persuade her to fellate him. She had roundly declared, "I would never countenance any such thing, any more than I would submit to cunnilingus – both unutterably disgusting perversions."

One day she had to prepare papers for a case dealing with an appeal against an 'R.O.', a Relocation Order. With the greatly reduced size of the country's population, many city centre properties had stood empty for years and in other areas inhabitants had been sprinkled sparsely. But it was now government policy that the populace should live in conurbations of not less than a specified size, depending upon the area of the country in question, in order to minimise the distance travelled by public service vehicles of all sorts – recycling collection vehicles, ambulances, police cars et cetera. There were exceptions, of course, many farmers for example, but the case in question concerned a couple where the husband no longer worked on the land. She asked the partner working on the case whether they really would be forced to move, if so how, and what would result if they refused. 'Trouble!' Was his laconic reply – he had the reputation of a string of successful cases behind him as well as of being a man of few words – but he would give no more details at that time.

That evening, she related the story to Julian, and asked how it was that Bill and Kitty were still allowed to live in their isolated cottage nearly three kilometres from Tonbridge. Julian had never thought about it, though he was aware of the policy; he confessed himself as puzzled by it as Inez.

One morning as he was busy with his work, the desktop box buzzed, and he pressed the 'accept call' button.

"Are you there, Julian," said a disembodied voice from the other side of the room, as the screen started to unroll.

"Yes, is that you, William," he replied, recognising the voice. As the screen finished unfurling, it flickered into life, and there was a life-size William Hacker with a query as to how the report was progressing. Julian dealt with that point and one or two other trifling queries from the Head of Department, who then closed down the link, and the screen retracted. Julian's office was on the first floor, and Inez, who as it happened was coming out of their adjacent bedroom, had heard the initial buzz. Curious, and not having seen the v-phone in action before, she had hovered outside on the landing till the call was over.

"What was all that about, darling?"

"Just a routine call. Actually, I think it was all just an excuse to see whether I was at my desk or not." Even now, the time was only five minutes past nine: It was known that William was a stickler for timekeeping himself, and Julian had heard of his habit of seeing whether others were too, although this was the first time he had been on the receiving end.

Later, in the winter of that year, Julian had to make one of his rare excursions to the offices of the Department in London. The occasion was a meeting with others from the continent, also working on the possible employment of simian labour; an international videoconference was considered inadvisable, due to the sensitivity of the subject. As Julian and William Hacker (known to the younger employees in the Department, from the gold-blocked initial and surname on his briefcase, as 'whacker') were having an after-hours pint just before Julian caught his train back, he learnt the reason why Kitty and Bill had never been the subject of an R.O. Bill had been passed over for Head of Department on grounds of age when he was fifty nine, the post going to Mr William Hacker.

"I've often wondered how my parents were able to remain in their secluded little cottage – it was surely a case for an R.O. if ever there was one," said Julian.

"That was my doing. When I joined the department as head, I wrote a report critical of another department, but based upon my basic misunderstanding and misinterpretation of the facts. Bill had happened upon a copy before the report was distributed, and had alerted me to its inaccuracies, and the substantial discomfiture that the Department would have experienced if it were distributed."

William had never said anything to Julian's adoptive father about this realisation, but when Bill came to retire, he had pulled a few strings with a friend in the Heritage Department, who had had the cottage declared an example of vernacular architecture of sufficient interest that it should remain inhabited: Continued occupation would ensure the maintenance and preservation of the fabric. Thus, he had made sure that there was no question of the Brophys' having to move out of their delightful home when Bill retired. Julian, who was still not very senior in the department, was quite impressed by William's candour in unbuttoning himself in this way, and his respect for the Departmental Head increased considerably.

It was in the autumn of 2269 that William next asked Julian to come to town and see him. Julian arrived one Monday morning at Waterloo station in good time and made his way towards the Department, cutting through some back streets. On the corner of one, he noticed that an ancient and dilapidated block of public conveniences was in the process of being demolished, only the back wall was still left standing: It carried – exposed for the first time to the daylight – a white vitreous enamelled notice, now chipped and besmirched, with the legend in bold black letters 'GENTLEMEN, PLEASE ADJUST YOUR DRESS BEFORE LEAVING'. Julian glanced down at his trousers, then smiled at the involuntary action.

He crossed the river, arrived at the Department and was shown into William's office, to be told by his boss that he had intended to lead the British delegation to the Sixth World Population Conference himself, but that he had to go into hospital for an operation that would keep him out of action for a few weeks. The Deputy Head of the Department would therefore have to take charge in his absence, so he could not go either. Of the remaining personnel in the department, several were candidates for the job, but he judged Julian's qualifications to make him the most suitable, by a small margin, even though he was somewhat less experienced and senior than one of the other possibilities. There were some other matters that they discussed, some important, others less so and Julian wondered, at the end of the day, why William had considered it necessary for him to come to town, when secure mode on the v-phone would surely have been adequate. Julian did not relish the thought of a week away from Inez and Jim, and knew that Inez would be even more reluctant, but accepted with apparent alacrity as to do otherwise would hardly promote his quest for the increased salary his further advancement in the Department would bring.

Inez, devoted to her husband, was nevertheless visibly disappointed at the prospect of Julian's approaching week's absence, although she tried, unsuccessfully, to disguise the fact. It reminded her all too vividly of Julian's foreign assignments as a newspaper reporter. Since her marriage she had experienced a strange gradual change in her personality: Gone was the brio with which she used to handle life, she could scarcely imagine or remember the insouciant composure with which she had travelled between her employer's offices in Buenos Aires and London. Although she still took an active and lively interest in the arts, the important things in her life were now her home, her husband and her son. Indeed, she would have liked to have another child, but despite expensive fertility treatment – another drain on their resources – there was no sign in that direction. Reluctantly, then, she fully supported his going to the Sixth WPC – like him, hoping for his future further advancement in the Department.

The Sunday before he was due to leave, she helped him pack his suitcase, alternating between an all too obviously forced cheerfully busy mood and a subdued, almost sullen one. Julian recognised the symptoms all too well: He adopted a tenor midway between these two extremes; no point in his appearing moody as well – that would simply add to the general atmosphere of gloom and doom, while undue cheerfulness would suggest he was unconscious of, or worse still impervious to, her distress. Despite his best efforts, the day did not end well, with Inez falling silent, and pointedly sleeping that night with her back to him.

It was a cold wet Monday morning in late October as Julian left the house.

"Have you got everything you need?"

'Yes' was his gruff reply, barely concealing his anxiety to be gone. *Their relationship had been as frosty that morning as the night before, and the briefer the parting, the less would be the mutual distress,* he thought. So, he was touched that, despite her obvious pain and annoyance at the prospect his absence for almost a week, at the last moment she kissed him hurriedly on the cheek before shutting the front door with a bang.

Bowing his head against the driving rain and clutching his bulging suitcase in one hand, his briefcase in the other, he made his way the few dozen metres to the end of the pedestrian cul-de-sac where they lived, to where an official car was waiting to take him to the airport. The driver, a big bony glum-faced fellow, got out and, taking his bags, put them in the back of the large electrically propelled estate style vehicle. He knew that, in a sense, he was lucky to be chosen for such a sought-after 'jolly', travelling by car and plane: With the state the world was in few people were able to travel anywhere. Only the prime minister and the most senior of cabinet ministers were allowed private cars in Great Britain and throughout the Euro Plus Union, as in most other countries of the world. All business, very nearly, was carried on by communications, including the v-phone.

"Carting bodies around just makes too much pollution," William had said, on informing him that nevertheless, he, Julian, was to be the leading British delegate to the Sixth World Population Conference in Tokyo.

He checked in at the only remaining operational terminal at Heathrow, disposing of his case but hanging onto his briefcase; there were only one or two other passengers in sight. One turned out to be a certain Ken Robinson, his fellow delegate, from the Population Statistics Department of Whitehall, a tall gawky sour-looking loose-limbed individual with a sallow face and drooping jowls, but obviously once handsome enough. They mutually re-introduced themselves – they had only met once before, and that years ago – and wandered along to the deserted café bar where they ordered themselves coffees.

"As a kid I remember my grandfather telling me when he was young, his grandfather told him that this place used to be teeming with travellers, and lots of airlines ran services to all sorts of destinations, all the time," said Ken with a sigh, between sips. "Still, at least the coffee's not too bad."

That's rather a generous description thought Julian; the coffee was strong, certainly, but had that peculiar bitter taste of coffee that has been 'stretched' with too much chicory and kept hot for hours.

"What are you people in Health and Reproduction doing nowadays?" asked Ken, in a voice which suggested that, whatever it was, it was pretty ineffective, as he stroked his chin – he was one of those unfortunate individuals who never looked really clean shaven, no matter how recently he had shaved. Julian considered his answer carefully; the antagonism between the Departments was palpably deep as both knew, and he knew that Ken was of a disagreeable, carping disposition. So, he was determined not to say anything that could be twisted to show Ken's Department in a better light than his own. Ken's was the older Department, having been created almost a century previously, when the then government bowed to pressure in the popular press to do something about the falling population. In the popular economic wisdom of preceding centuries, a small rate of population increase had been seen as essential to the maintenance of the great political shibboleth, 'sustainable economic growth', but even that long ago, the impossibility of perpetual growth (obvious to anyone whose knowledge of maths included the exponential function) was acknowledged, even by politicians. The establishment of the department had had precisely the result hoped for and expected by the government; now that they were 'keeping an eye on things' on behalf of the population, interest in the topic waned, and newspaper proprietors judged it to be no longer newsworthy, just passé.

Julian's department had been created years later, when the population was still showing signs of decreasing steadily, and the press barons were on the rampage again. Julian pondered his reply to Ken's loaded question but could not think of a suitable riposte. Later, an absolutely crushing reply occurred to him – why was it always like that, too late, he thought? Instead, he lamely referred Ken to the latest Health and Reproduction Department's report, which was due out shortly. They finished their coffee and at the same instant there was a loudspeaker announcement, requesting passengers Brophy and Robinson and several others to report to Gate 7. With so few passengers, each was known and checked on constantly while on Airport premises.

The necessary passport facilities having been completed they passed through to the checks at the gate and then straight onto the plane, a Brentwood 907, like the one in which he had twice travelled to Argentina, in previous years.

A few hours into the flight, as much to get away from Ken as anything, Julian got up from his comfortable seat and wandered around the passenger compartment.

"I say, have you seen this?" asked a portly man, whom he thought he vaguely recognised, in a seat next to the aisle, a few rows back. He moved into the window seat, and Julian sat down beside him, taking the proffered copy of The Times. 'Security Alert at Japanese Conference Centre' read one of the headlines.

"Aren't you with the Department of Health and Reproduction?"

"Yes, how did you know?"

"I thought I recognised you," said the man, who introduced himself as Professor Henry Wilkinson of Oxford University, and proffered his card. He was one of those comfortable rotund settled-looking middle-aged individuals who gave the impression that they had always looked the way they did now. Scarcely beyond middle age, Henry looked as though he might have been born looking just like that, with his heavy frame, smooth rosy features, black-rimmed powerful glasses and thinning black hair.

"You were at the seminar on Population Dynamics at Baliol last year, weren't you?" said Henry, in his high tenor voice that seemed wildly out of character with his general build and appearance.

The professor's memory is a great deal better than mine, thought Julian, as he grunted his assent while reading the newspaper story, and then commented that it looked as if he was in for an exciting time.

"You too, I guess?" said Julian, and the Professor affirmed that he was indeed on his way to the same Conference as Julian.

"You were the mainspring behind the statistics in that report and its rather gloomy predictions, weren't you?" Professor Wilkinson nodded, and Julian added, "*He* won't be pleased to see you, he's from the Population Statistics Department." Nodding in the direction of the row he had come from, where Ken was doing the Telegraph crossword puzzle. "He'll think you were treading on his territory."

"I don't see why, if anything, it might be construed as impinging more on your field," said the Prof.

Julian replied that, "The outlook for mankind was so problematic, that the more brains focussed on the problem, the better."

"Is there still no conclusive evidence on exactly which pollutant's mainly responsible for the global downturn in fecundity?" It was, of course, a leading question; Julian did not really expect to learn anything he did not already know.

"Lots of theories, but nothing substantive." And the Professor went on to recount numerous facts concerning the problem, which Julian already knew about, bar one which was new to him, and of which he made a mental note.

After a long boring flight during which Julian only managed to snatch an hour or two of sleep, they landed at Tokyo's main airport where it was now early in the day after they had left London. They retrieved their bags and negotiated the 'passport desk', a quaintly if anachronistically named formality – passports had been replaced a century earlier by credit-card sized International Identity Cards holding a vast amount of individual-specific information. Each had to swipe his card and face the inspection camera while holding his right hand flat against a scanning screen. This resulted in some delay as Ken had cut his forefinger the previous day and it now sported an adhesive dressing. Eventually a security officer was located and convinced that all was in order. Customs checks followed, occasioning no great further delay and they went outside to where an official car was to await them. There they saw a man in a smart chauffeur's uniform (which contrasted markedly with the casual dress of the driver who had ferried Julian to Heathrow – *a comment on the two countries' different attitudes to work, perhaps,* thought Julian) who bowed stiffly and asked if they were the gentlemen for the Sixth World Population Conference, to be held at the Taguchi Conference Centre. They applied in the affirmative and looked around for a car, but they saw none, and the driver did not move. After a hiatus that seemed like half an hour but was in reality was probably less than thirty seconds, Henry said, slightly impatiently, "Well, we're ready." The driver, who had been looking at the door of the terminal, turned to them and apologised, explaining that he was expecting four gentlemen.

"Oh, who's the other?" asked Ken. The driver consulted a piece of paper on his clipboard, and said it was a delegate from the USA.

Julian and Ken looked at each other in concern. There were so few flights nowadays that today there was only one trans-Pacific landing expected. It was from San Francisco, and though due to have landed an hour before their flight, was listed on the board as delayed by seven hours.

"Oh, well can't you?" said Henry, but at that moment a short stout red-faced man with a briefcase, hair which was ginger where it was not turning grey, and a rolling gait emerged from the terminal. He came straight up to the uniformed driver and spoke.

"I'm due to be picked up by an official car somewhere here, do you know anything about it?"

"Doctor Goldsmith?" asked the driver.

"Sure, that's me."

The driver led them to a car parked some little distance away, an identical model to that which had ferried Julian to Heathrow. Julian was glad of the little wheels on his suitcase, while Ken struggled with his, which had none; their respective Departments had found the Civil Service's travel office on strike, so no arrangements had been made for their luggage. Henry and Dr Sam Goldsmith were the lucky ones; theirs would be delivered straight to their hotel rooms.

Now that Julian saw him afoot, he realised that Henry was really quite short, only a centimetre or so taller than Sam. They piled into the car and as it left the airport complex Dr Goldsmith said:

"Well, I guess we'd better introduce ourselves: I'm Sam Goldsmith, from Harvard Medical School."

Julian, Ken and Henry introduced themselves likewise, and Sam said, "Gee, doesn't the driver talk just perfect English! I wonder how many other Japanese speak English." With his inscrutable face unmoved, the driver volunteered the information that English was taught in all schools, starting after the first year and continuing up to school-leaving age.

"Many, especially those living and working in the countryside, never use it and soon forget it. In the big towns and cities, it's different," he said, and they noticed that all the street names were in English, with the Japanese names underneath, in smaller Japanese script. He whisked them away through streets crowded with pedestrians, but devoid of traffic, towards the Holden Hotel. They wondered what perils lay ahead, in view of the security scare.

Chapter 5
The Baritone in the Bath 2268AD

At the hotel, they checked in and went up to their rooms, having agreed to meet up for dinner after a shower and unpacking.

"Where have sprung from, seeing the flight from the USA was delayed?" Henry enquired in the bar before dining.

"I was on the same flight as you!" said Sam. Henry vaguely recalled the recumbent figure in one of the back seats, reclining blissfully unconscious with a handkerchief over his face.

"I had a word with a relative in the administration and got permission to come via England; it gave me a chance to look up Great aunt Bertha who lives at Potters Bar, and to go up to Saffron Walden to see where my folks came from originally."

Dinner was a leisurely affair and the conversation ranged far and wide, on into the night. The population crisis was of course discussed, as were a host of other topics, including languages. Henry noted that English was spoken by about 85% of the world's population, at least to a basic usable level. And nearly all countries had English language newspapers. However, the language of the home was everywhere the native language of the country, except perhaps in the homes of cosmopolitan professionals. This was confirmed by fellow delegates Henri Duparc, a tall thin dapper moustachioed slightly balding Frenchman in an immaculately cut suit of palest grey – despite his great height there was no hint of a stoop, and Hans Eisenkreuz, a stolid thick-necked tousle-headed German in a chunky dark brown sweater which matched his hair, who had joined them for dinner after introducing themselves in the bar. They said that with English being the universal lingua franca, very few ever bothered to learn a second foreign language. Ken said, "Julian here's an exception – he's fluent in French, German,

Dutch, Spanish and Italian, besides Modern Greek of course, and can get by in most of the Slav languages."

From anyone else, it would have sounded like a compliment, but somehow Ken managed to use a tone of voice that suggested he thought such an accomplishment somewhat unnatural, outré, positively excessive.

"Gee," said Sam, "what set you off down that line?"

"I don't know, but Kitty – that's my mother – she was an English teacher, with an interest in languages generally, besides reading a lot of French."

"I am glad to hear that. French is a more logical language, it would have made a much better lingua franca than English," said Henri.

"Maybe," said Henry, "but it still strikes many people as odd that a man may be referred to as 'elle'."

"No, don't believe it," said Sam, who had just a little French.

Henri countered with, "Mais oui." And Henry, who was also a keen student of French literature explained:

"For example, 'Le Tsar s'ennui. Sa Majesté ne sais que faire. Elle veut aller chasser'. See? That's what happens if you make your possessive pronouns agree with the thing possessed, rather than the possessor. Elle refers to Sa Majesté and Sa Majesté refers to the Tsar. It's just that in French 'majesty' is feminine. I guess the same sort of thing applies in German." Hans nodded in agreement.

"Yes, majestät in German also is feminine." Julian thought there goes an academic for you, explaining everything three ways over, as though talking to a backward child.

Ken said, mischievously, "Is it the case that Frenchmen never wash their hair?"

There was a silence and then Henri said, "Yes."

"Surely not," said Sam and Julian thought he'd better explain.

"To a Frenchman, washing ones hair conjures up a picture of an Englishman washing each individual hair one by one. A Frenchman simply washes the head, whether he's bald or not. Alors, on lave la tête," Sam said to no one in particular.

"What's your hotel room like?" The question was picked up by Henry.

"My hotel's alright generally but the bedroom walls must be mighty thin. In the room next to mine, there's a baritone with a powerful voice, who insists on singing in the bath every morning – always the same thing, something about a loch, a kilt, porridge and I know not what else," Sam said.

"Sounds intriguing, listen out and let us know next time what it's all about," Henry said.

"Sure, if I remember to."

A newcomer joined their little group and introduced himself as John Keith Nostyn. It turned out that Henry knew him already and explained that everyone called him Jake, adding, "Whenever he books into a hotel, he always includes the K, otherwise he gets an incredulous look from the receptionist and the query 'Like the famous lady novelist?'"

The conversation moved on, returning inexorably to the population problem and the Conference, which opened the following day. Finally, they all said Goodnight and retired.

At breakfast, the next morning the hotel was fuller than it had been for many months, the waiter commented. With few exceptions, the guests were all delegates to the Sixth World Population Conference, and Sam, recognising a fellow American, introduced him to the previous night's little dinner group.

"This is Nick Wagner, from UCLA," he said, pronouncing the name like 'wagoner' without the 'o', and they all shook hands with a tall slim fresh-faced athletic-looking man with blue eyes, a crew cut, open features and large ears, whose age they would have found it difficult to guess.

"We've never had a chance to shake hands before, but we've often had dealings with each other over the v-phone," Nick explained. So much so, they were like old friends, although this was their first meeting.

At 09.15 hours, all the delegates assembled in the hotel foyer ready to make their way to the Conference Centre. As it was within the prescribed maximum no-transport distance from the hotel, they all prepared set off on foot, accompanied by a courier. All except Dr Anton Plessner from Poland, who was wheelchair bound.

"What's going to happen about him?" asked Ken.

"I heard the courier talk to the receptionist and heard that some transport for him will be arranged," said Hans.

"Well, if they're sending a car for him, why can't some of the rest of us go in it too?" However, as there was no sign of a vehicle, they all set off together, following the courier. As they neared the Conference Centre, a rickshaw passed them, and Dr Plessner waved.

"There's your answer!" said Jake.

They all filed into the Conference Centre, through security, and then reception, where they picked up their name badges, which also gave their titles and qualifications, the firm, university or government department etc. for which they worked and the country from which they came. They also each picked up a huge folder of notes about the organisation of the conference, the Conference Centre itself, timetables for the main conference and a score of subcommittee and working party meetings, abstracts of some of the papers to be presented, list of delegates, etc. etc.

After some confusion and milling about, finally all the delegates were seated in the huge main auditorium of the Centre, and an official introduced the first speaker, the Prime Minister of Japan. His speech was lengthy, and strong on rhetoric, but at the end left little if any impression on the minds of the delegates.

"A typical politician's effort," commented Ken dryly, and they all felt the same. When it eventually drew to a close, the meeting broke up for coffee.

"Gosh, I'm desperately needing it after that speech," Sam confided in Nick. They chatted on as they sipped their coffee and Sam said, "I'm feeling definitely a bit old today."

"I've just reached the 'big four oh'," said Nick.

"Gee, sex at forty ain't a patch on sex at twenty-five," Sam just murmured.

"Mm." Nodded sympathetically, smiled and wondered.

Should I tell Nick that sex at sixty isn't a patch on sex at forty? But what's the point? He will find out for himself soon enough.

Sam remembered fondly his ecstatic joy at making love with his wife when they were first married, especially piercing the hymen on the first night of their honeymoon.

"Ah, but that was forty years ago, about the time Nick was born, actually. I'm glad we waited till we were wed before we slept together – I get the impression we were fairly unusual in that respect," he soliloquised.

At the morning coffee break, Julian was surprised to find that a selection of biscuits was provided – he had never seen this before. Like almost everybody else, he chose a chocolate digestive biscuit but afterwards found himself carefully brushing off crumbs from his suit jacket. A lady delegate whom he vaguely thought he recognised and guessed to be about thirty years and 36C, wearing a very fine knitted fabric jumper which showed off her figure to perfection, said, "Tut tut," and finished brushing off the crumbs for him, adding, "hold the biscuit chocolate side downwards and as you bite, breath in deeply through your mouth at the same time; any crumbs will be swept up into your mouth."

I must remember that, thought Julian.

After coffee came a worthy paper from an Austrian academic, which ran over the history of population decline over the century. It contained little new but was useful as a background to the following proceedings, explaining that the falling birth rate in the developed nations which appeared first in the twentieth century was followed by a similar trend in the rest of the world commencing in the late twenty first, with the terrible sudden collapse at the end of that century caused by AIDS, Asian Bird Flu and Bubonic Plague. Only the last minute success in developing vaccines had saved humanity from an even greater disaster. It was copiously illustrated with tables and other data from a laptop computer operated by the speaker, after a hiatus of five minutes or so, during which a number of technicians struggled to persuade the laptop to talk to the projector instead of the latter showing the dreaded 'no video' error message. The speaker showed a graph which illustrated the steady decline in population which had set in again following the dramatic collapse; apart from some very minor wiggles the continued downward trend was all too evident.

This paper was followed by a buffet lunch, which was not to Ken's liking, though everyone else seemed contented enough. During the lunch break, the afternoon tea break and before returning to the hotel in the evening, Julian engaged as many delegates as possible, from various different countries, in conversation about conditions in their respective countries, and their views on the questions of the day. He was making full use his reporter's skills to gather as much information as possible, about items not on the official agenda, and found out some strange and disturbing facts.

The first paper after lunch, given by a Dr Kwang Lee from Korea, dealt with population decline and its economic consequences, and described a computer model the presenter had developed, which could be run to predict population trends. He enumerated a number of parameters, upon the exact values of which depended the future course of mankind. He then outlined some interesting forecasts of possible future scenarios – one being the continued decline leading ultimately to the extinction of mankind, or else possibly a reversal of the trend leading eventually to overpopulation pressures even worse than those which had been experienced in the twentieth century, or, perhaps the least likely – but most desirable – of the three, a population stabilised at a manageable level, by common consent of both governments and their peoples. The latter two scenarios presupposed, of course, a solution to the infertility problem.

The speaker then agreed to a request from the chairman of the session that he should take questions from the floor. Sam's hand shot up as he rose smartly to his feet, and an attendant brought a radio microphone. He mischievously asked, "Which of the three scenarios does the speaker considered the most likely?"

With a disarming smile, the speaker said, "If the honourable delegate will quote me figures for the seventeen parameters I outlined earlier, I could then run the model and answer the honourable delegate's question."

A tea break followed, and Julian helped himself to a chocolate biscuit. Despite his best efforts, he still got crumbs on his suit. After the previous lengthy but interesting exposition, there followed a paper which Julian thought by far the most important so far; a joint paper by delegates from seven different countries, including a section by Nick, describing work carried out to date to try and pin down the factors which were contributing to continued erosion of the world's population. Much of this work was the subject of more detailed discussion in some of the sub-committees and working groups, as was pointed out by the chairman of the session, Dr Plessner, when at length he regretfully said he could not accept any further questions from the floor concerning the paper, due to the late hour. Julian looked at his watch and found to his surprise that it was 18.35 hours, long after the scheduled close of the day's proceedings.

That evening the previous night's little dinner group reconvened, joined by Nick, Jake and Dr Plessner, but the conversation was more muted than then, being concerned almost exclusively with the present plight of humanity. Dr Plessner said, "Tomorrow's papers should be at least as interesting as today's have been, probably even more so in some respects." An opinion supported by Henri Duparc, from the Curie Institute, who was to chair the next day's sessions.

Sam said, "Come on now Henry, you promised to tell about your bathroom baritone's aria!"

"I would never have been able to remember it, so I've jotted it down." As he pulled out an A5 sheet of paper from the notepad provided in each hotel bedroom, cleared his throat and striking a pose, said, "By Loch Aber and Loch Tummel, by Loch Erne and Rannoch Moor, ye can roam and roam and roam for bloomin' miles, wi' yer porridge in yer sporran and yer haggis up yer kilt, ye'll never feel the tangle o' the isles."

Ken, who had a remarkable memory, repeated it word perfect, adding, "There, now look what you've done – it'll stick in my memory 'till my dying day."

There was another knot of people around a table on the other side of the dining room, and a further, smaller group at another table, all delegates to the Conference. Apart from that, there were only two other tables occupied, both by elderly Japanese couples. Julian looked around the once smart dining room with its faded hangings, now distinctly shabby. The room, like the rest of the hotel, was badly in need of a facelift, and Sam commented that there must be scores if not hundreds of delegates staying in other hotels.

"I was supposed to be in the Bristol, the one next to the Conference Centre, but by the time my government had decided to fund my attendance, it was fully booked," said Dr Plessner.

"So here you are in the one furthest away!" Quipped Nick.

Hans chipped in. "No, one of my colleagues is in the Kyoto-Brooklyn; it is so far out that those delegates must come by transport."

"Just my luck, in between, so we don't get a car," said Ken.

"They do not also – they must come by Metro."

The following day brought more papers, some interesting as Henri had predicted, some less so. During one of the latter, out of his professional interest in languages, Julian put on his headset, there was one by every seat, and switched around the different channels. He knew that traditionally, international conference centres, such as that of the International Telecommunications Union in Geneva, had always provided simultaneous translations, by highly paid interpreters, available in the official languages of the organisation and others. In the case of the ITU, the official working languages were, for historical reasons, English, French and Spanish, and the proceedings were conducted in English, with French, Spanish, Arabic and Russian available on the headphones. But here, he found all the channels carried the same version, which he recognised as Japanese, though he could not follow it. Just an example of the hegemony of English.

If you don't speak English, tough, he thought.

One of the more interesting papers painted a more optimistic picture than the others. The presenter reminded delegates of the statement by the prime minister in his opening address that the world population now stood at just 43% of the figure at the start of the third millennium. But he pointed out that over the last few years, there had been a small but measurable reduction in the rate of decline of the world's population – it was still falling but not quite as fast as previously. Julian recalled that there had been a similar glimmer of hope reported fifteen years ago at the 5th WPC, but it had faded in the years following. He had a feeling the same might happen again.

The last paper of the day dealt with the energy crisis and provided a gloomy perspective, in contrast to the previous one. The speaker reminded his audience that since the near complete depletion of the world's natural resources of oil in the previous century, international co-operation in energy conservation had become a necessity, however unpalatable to some of the larger nations. He expounded the implications at length, although most were well known to many of the delegates, including Julian. Other possible implications he hypothesised were sinister in the extreme, should they ever come to pass.

The following day they passed into the auditorium, and it brought more papers, one of which dealt with the severe problems caused by the world shortage of skilled scientists, engineers and medical professionals. The proportion of the world's population endowed with the inherent intellectual apparatus to cope with these subjects had not changed over the centuries, while the demand for such people to maintain and advance civilisation, in a world increasingly dependent upon technology, was insatiable. Indeed, advances in technology had largely come to a standstill, since most of the available technical talent was stretched just to maintain the world's various infrastructures, such as communications, medicine, agriculture, chemical engineering and pharmaceuticals, electrical power generation and supply, water, etc. The economics of the labour market had seen major advances in the relative remuneration of scientists, engineers and others in the last fifty years, but this had not greatly increased the flow of new science, engineering and medical specialists. Science and engineering in particular, the paper stressed, were heavily mathematics based, and the proportion of individuals with mathematical aptitude, among the declining population, was constant; ergo, the shortage was only likely to get worse.

"The bit about increasing engineering salaries should please my grandson Al – he's in his last year at college, doing control electronics. Still, pity they can't do something for us poor old academics," said Sam.

The fourth day passed with more papers, and a few of the earlier reports, from two of the working parties and one of the sub-committees; the rest were to follow in the Proceedings of the Conference. Julian was beginning to get a little jaded by the less interesting aspects of the proceedings and looked forward to the fifth and final day on the morrow. It duly arrived and consisted mainly of 'wash-up' sessions, considering the early reports, detailing the future work of the various sub-committees and their working parties, and finishing with an extended interactive session between the floor and a panel consisting of the chairmen of the various sessions. Henri summed things up neatly by saying, "The principle cause of population erosion is a worldwide decrease in sperm count in men of all ages from puberty upwards, probably due to an environmental factor or factors unknown, and a suspected decrease in female fertility, also currently unaccounted for."

Back at the hotel over dinner that evening Hans, who was a chemical engineer, said in his thick German accent, "The problem is that ever since the late eighteenth century man has been releasing large quantities of many chemicals into the environment. Many of these naturally do not occur, and will indefinitely, almost, persist. Man finds a small but finite correlation between any of them to male and female infertility both. But the compound correlation of several pollutants with infertility, in practice is not calculable." He paused for several gulps of Japanese lager from a huge glass – most of the others had opted for the indigenous wine – but no one spoke as he clearly hadn't finished. "Even the combined effect of two specific pollutants is difficult to handle, but signs of progress in that area are promising. If the REACH directive had been introduced worldwide a century earlier, or even fifty years earlier, things might have been…"

He paused, seeing one or two blank faces around the table. Henri filled in with, "Registration Evaluation and Approval – er, no – Authorisation of Chemicals."

"Yes, it was due to be adopted in the European Union by 2005, but in fact until many years later was it not in force, and very much later before similar controls became worldwide." Henri took up the story.

"There were more than thirty thousand chemicals to be examined, and in the meantime, they could continue to be produced and used. Of course, chemical concerns introduced minor variations on existing products before the directive came into force. These would also all have to be tested before they could in turn be approved or banned, so they could go on selling one or other of them for years. Once the directive came into force, development of safer products ceased.

Because these would all have required expensive safety testing, to be paid for by the manufacturer, naturally."

Julian thought to himself that with the vast number of chemicals, not existing in the environment before the activities of man, it would be a long time before anything came of Hans's research. They all retired early, in a sombre mood, to pack their bags for an early departure the next day. After packing, Julian took a hot shower and turned in, but sleep eluded him for several hours. He kept turning over in his mind the huge range of problems facing mankind, many of which of course he had been well aware of previously, but the Conference had illuminated other facets of which he had been less conscious. He turned over yet again and, thinking what a good job it was, he had decided against a cold shower, eventually drifted off into a sleep troubled by dreams of bizarre catastrophes raining down upon the unfortunate human race.

He woke later than he meant to and hurriedly shaved and packed his last minute overnight things. He arrived down to breakfast still in time and took a seat at a table with Sam and Dr Plessner who were at the toast and marmalade and second cup of coffee stage. As he arrived they were talking animatedly, and there was an unusually excited buzz of conversation at all the tables. Julian looked at Dr Plessner and raised his eyebrows. The good doctor handed him an English language newspaper and indicated an item at the top of the second page. This was a report of an in-depth investigation by one of the paper's reporters, concerning developments in China. The results of the introduction of a strict population control regime, in the twentieth century, had not been seen until much later, and these results were certainly not foreseen. Like other countries which had embraced the communist experiment, an emphasis on meeting over-ambitious industrial production targets at all costs had left the country badly polluted with all sorts of chemical by-products, wastes and residues. This, combined with an ageing population brought about by the population control measures, had resulted in a spectacular population crash in the twenty-second century, on top of the AIDS, Asian Bird Flu and Bubonic Plague problems. As a result, China was desperately short of agricultural labour. Immigrants and convicted criminals were all employed in the paddy fields and the reporter had obtained leaked information which made it clear that plans were further advanced in China than in any other country, for the wholesale employment of simian agricultural labourers, in particular simian simian amazoniensis versicolor. It was rumoured that a number of such gibbon-like animals, captured from their native habitat in the Amazon jungle, had been obtained from an unidentified source or sources in Latin America.

"Well, it appears pilot trials have already been completed," said Julian as handed the paper back, thoughtfully. He made a mental note to pass this information on to the Department – it would not of course appear in the official Proceedings.

Breakfast finished, they returned to their rooms for any last minute packing and then assembled in the foyer where they all took their leave of the various new acquaintances each had made. They disposed of their baggage and were ferried to the airport, negotiated security and customs, and settled down in the departure lounge for the call to go to whichever gate their flight was leaving from. Julian's was from Gate 3, and he was glad that he did not have long to wait. One or two others had several hours, and Nick had said his flight was so late in the day, he would not be accompanying them to the airport but intended to set off to see a little of Tokyo. Julian's flight took off on time and took a great circle root direct to Britain, passing over the spectacular Stanovov mountains, the Jamal peninsular, a point some hundreds of miles north of Moscow, and on over Finland and Sweden before crossing the North Sea to Heathrow. En route Julian fell to wondering what sort of a welcome he could expect from Inez on his return. He was disturbed at the memory of their frosty parting and wondered whether he should apologise for accepting the assignment when he got back. But surely that wouldn't do; hadn't they both agreed that he should go, in the interests of his career and their future income prospects? In the end, he decided that he would have to play it by ear – a daunting prospect, as he never seemed to get it right in such circumstances, his efforts to be diplomatic usually finished up making matters worse.

It was early evening British time when he finally arrived back at his home in Tunbridge Wells, after a flight of some 9600km, taking a few minutes less than ten hours. He found, to his great relief, that he needn't have worried. Inez, obviously delighted to have him back, greeted him with a tender kiss and a cup of strong coffee from a freshly made pot, with milk but no sugar, just as he liked it. But he realised that her joy and relief at his return was, nevertheless, vaguely tinged with the slightest hint of resentment still. That this could be the case, while she had specifically supported his going in the first place, was one of those inconsistencies which the feminine mind could accommodate in a way he could not understand, but which he knew he had to accept if life with her was to be at all practicable.

While he unpacked, she quizzed him about the trip, enquiring anxiously first of all about the security scare at the Conference Centre that she had heard about. Julian realised that he had forgotten all about it, and so assumed it must all have been sorted out before the delegates arrived. He was not expected in the office until a meeting on the fifth of the following month, so the following morning he allowed himself an hour's lie-in, while Inez continued to ask questions about his trip. But suddenly she broke off, insisting that they get up at once. She said it was just that she needed to make sure that Jim was up and getting ready for school, and it was true that he sometimes needed chivvying along. But later Julian realised that actually she was concerned lest there be another early morning call from William, to see if he had his nose to the grindstone. It was just like her, to think methodically of all these things related to his job, while at the same time being resentful about them; all sorts of mental dichotomy were, he had come to the conclusion, a characteristic feature of the female psyche.

Back in his home office, Julian started straight away preparing his official report on the conference. It recounted all the main information presented and the conclusions drawn, in due order, including the fact that news on the world population level was every bit as bad as had been feared, at 43% of its value at the start of the millennium. The hopeful point about an apparent slight reduction in the rate of population decline, mentioned at the Fifth WPC, had turned out to be illusory, though in the last year or two the decline had moderated again. The finished report went first to William and after that to the Minister and thence to Cabinet, followed by copies of the official Conference Proceedings when at length they arrived. Julian also produced an unofficial report, containing all the background information that he had gleaned from his contacts with other delegates, the circulation of which was strictly limited to the Department, William insisted.

"On no account is anyone outside the Department to see it and especially not the Department of Population Statistics," Warned William, the very future existence of which Department was in some doubt since the retirement of Ken Robinson's boss. Julian's unofficial report recounted in detail various disagreements between the participating nations, disagreements that were glossed over or simply omitted entirely from the Proceedings of the 6th WPC, when copies finally arrived. But the really startling news, which Julian retailed also to Inez in strict confidence, concerned the development of the trade in simians. These Amazonian creatures had long been domesticated by the aboriginal inhabitants of the Amazon rain forest and trained for jobs such as picking fruit from trees. If one fell to its death, it was much less of a loss than a child. They were now being bred on what might be described as an industrial scale, and the Conference had sought, unsuccessfully as it later turned out, to bring the trade under tight international control, with strict conditions on the rearing of and trade in the animals. These conditions were to be worked out by a series of subcommittees, charged with reporting back to the Seventh World Population Conference. Animal Protection Societies from many countries around the world had lobbied hard to have the trade banned outright, but to no avail; it was too late to shut the stable door or get the genie back in the bottle. Julian's unofficial report recorded apparently well-founded rumours that many highly placed people, including several heads of state, had a financial interest in the lucrative business of the breeding and trade in 'simian auxiliary population elements', known as Sapes for short or 'servant apes' by the popular press. These had earlier been known as 'simian simian amazoniensis versicolor', referring to the contrast of their white paws and face to the rest of their fur. But that was old terminology, it was now agreed that they were a species within the genus Hylobates, itself a member of the family hylobatidae.

That evening Inez prepared a special dinner. She had once served up a meal with a gammon steak each, but being small eaters, they had found this too much, so Inez had bought a large gammon steak and served up half each accompanied with a fried egg, half a tinned pear, some baby sweetcorn each and additionally, for Julian, some crinkle cut chips; Inez, he knew, professed not to like potatoes in any form. That night, they made love, then at three o'clock in the morning, Inez woke Julian saying, "I think I'm going to be sick." Remembering Inez morning sickness while carrying Jim, Julian had a plastic washing up bowl from the kitchen in front of Inez just in time. As she threw up, Julian placed a cool hand upon her forehead, which she always found comforting.

Later that day when they were both up, Inez said, "Don't want any breakfast, thank you."

"Perhaps you picked up a tummy bug."

"Maybe, but I can't imagine where."

"But it can't have been the meal – you're perfectly okay with all those things."

Julian was aware of Inez's allergies and what to avoid. She was fine with soft fruit, citrus fruits and pears, but avoided the plum family and particularly apple like the plague. Later that morning, he fished the empty pear tin out of the recycle bin and read the contents. He handed it to Inez and spoke. "There's your answer."

It read **Contents: 'Pear halves in apple juice, acidity regulator citric acid, 140 mgs'.**

"Well really" – Inez exploded – "if I buy pears, pears are what I expect to get, not some mongrel mixture of pears and something else. I've a good mind to complain to the supermarket."

"It's not their fault – it's a case of caveat emptor, let the buyer beware. We should have read the label."

"You mean I should," said Inez bitterly.

Chapter 6
Simian Amazonians Versicolor 2280AD

It was thirteen years since the last WPC and the memory of Julian's absence had slowly faded from Inez's mind. During that time Julian had been up to the Department in London for meetings on several occasions but had only once ever been away from home overnight. Up to five years ago, apart from the mortgage, they had been paying for horrendously expensive fertility treatment. It had been free up until Inez was thirty-five and they had elected to pay for continued treatment thereafter in the hope of another child, although the odds of success diminished with age. But in 2277 when Inez was forty-three and Jim was already nineteen they had finally given up and accepted the inevitable.

Now, Jim was a grown man of twenty-four, weighing in at 78 kilos, five and a half centimetres taller than his father and still living at home. Long gone were the freckles, but the passion for rugger remained and he played regularly, presenting his mother with a pile of dirty kit twice a week. After school, he had taken a degree in economics and disappointed his parents, and himself even more, by only gaining a 'Commended', the equivalent in earlier ages of a Lower Second. However, having obtained employment with Baker and Daley, a firm of economic analysts, he had studied as an extramural student for, and just obtained, an excellent higher degree in Economics and Politics, thus rehabilitating himself in his parents' eyes and indeed in his own esteem.

"As you're clearly capable, if you'd worked harder earlier, you could've have taken this higher degree as a full-time student and qualified that much earlier," Julian commented dryly.

Jim countered with, "By learning on the job with my employers, my studies had held much more meaning for me and consequently I found the work both easier and more interesting than that of my first degree." Inez was of course pleased at her son's success, but a little puzzled – and even disquieted – that he seemed to have no interest in girls. This was not natural, she thought; after all, at his age she had already been married for two years. She wondered whether to mention her disquiet to Julian, but decided to keep her fears to herself, for the moment.

In any case, a week after the welcome news of Jim's academic success, less welcome news arrived in the shape of a phone call from Bill. Inez had just finished lunch and Julian was still eating, so she took the call. "Hello." There was a long pause, so long that Julian stopped eating and watched her, in concern. He was about to ask what was the matter, but she impatiently signalled him to be quiet. Finally, she handed the phone to Julian with the words.

"It's Kitty," Bill said.

"Kitty fell over a quarter of an hour ago. It's not the first time and initially I thought she was just winded. But she's having great difficulty breathing and can't speak."

Julian was instantly concerned. Bill continued, "I've called an ambulance –
"

But broke off in mid-sentence. Julian guessed that it had just arrived. Bill phoned again later that afternoon, from the hospital in Tunbridge Wells, to say that Kitty was in intensive care but that the outlook did not seem good. Fifteen minutes later when Julian and Inez arrived, it was to find a nurse trying to console Bill with a cup of tea. With an indescribable look, he rose as they entered the room, muttering, "She's dead." And slumped back into the chair, burying his ashen grey face in his hands, his whole body crumpled, shaking in despair. On hearing of Kitty's death, Julian was at a loss as to what to say or do, but without a moment's hesitation Inez was kneeling beside Bill, with her arm around him as his whole burly frame was shaken with sobs.

*****

One autumn morning, two years and a day after Kitty was cremated, Bill was feeling confused, dazed and not a little annoyed with himself. He had been upstairs to get a clean handkerchief and tripped at the top of the stairs coming down. He had tumbled down to the bottom and was lying there in considerable pain. He had forgotten to put on the emergency beacon Julian and Inez insisted he must wear, and as he tumbled down, the cordless phone he always carried with him had slipped out of his pocket and disappeared. He managed to reach up to a low shelf and lift down the old-fashioned corded telephone handset by the front door, wondering if it still worked. Yes, there was a dial tone, and shakily he dialled Julian's number. A woman's voice that he didn't recognise answered.

"Is Julian there?"

"I think you must have a wrong number – sorry." And the phone went dead.

Bill reached up and felt for the little booklet where he kept all the personal numbers he was likely to need. Checking, he found he had indeed remembered it correctly. "Must have misdialled," he groaned. He redialled and was relieved to hear Julian's voice answer.

He explained what had happened and heard Julian say, "Don't worry, Dad, just stay where you are and try and relax; I'm coming straight over."

"But really, I'm –" But Julian had rung off.

He rang the county transport officer who could authorise either of the only two car hire firms in the county, to accept a travel request, but he was not available neither on the office number, his home number nor yet his mobile number, while a journey on the infrequent buses would have involved a change and a long walk. Rather than waste further time, Julian got out his bike and set off for the country cottage where his father, now aged eighty-four, still lived following the death of Kitty. He arrived breathless and vowing to take more exercise in future, having covered the thirty-four kilometres from his home in somewhat over an hour. He let himself in with the spare key that Kitty had always insisted he should keep 'just in case'.

Julian felt around the parts that hurt and having satisfied himself that there were no broken bones, helped his father to the lounge, settled him down on the sofa and prepared a light meal for them both.

"It's ridiculous, I've lived here more than half a century and never had anything like this."

"But you're not as young as you were."

"It was like a dream, or more like a nightmare. I suddenly realised I was going – I should have grabbed the banister but there wasn't time, it all happened so quickly."

Julian phoned Inez and said he would stay there overnight but expected to be back the following day. After that, his father watched the news and then said he had better go to bed, insisting that Julian help him upstairs.

"I've brought you up a cup of coffee, Dad," said Julian, entering Bill's bedroom just after 07.30 am the following morning. Bill stirred, rubbed his eyes and grunted; his alarm clock had failed to wake him, and there was Jen lying on the bed at the foot end. After Kitty's death, Bill had visited the local animal shelter and adopted a five-year old black and white border-collie-cross bitch, who was now his constant companion. Jen was normally shut out of the bedroom overnight, but Julian had left the door ajar, and the dog had taken the opportunity to be near its master, but not so near as to be noticed and risk being turned out again. Julian sat on the end of the bed and enquired how the patient was. Much improved, was the answer, but Bill seemed worried as much as anything by the fact that he would not be able to take Jen for her morning walk – despite his age they normally walked into Tonbridge and back, always once and occasionally twice a day, whether there was any shopping to do or not.

Julian cycled to Tonbridge and back with Jen running alongside and then prepared some breakfast for the three of them. When he had arrived back, he found Bill had got up and come downstairs, uneventfully this time, and seemed much more like his usual cheerful self although he was moving stiffly and with some difficulty. After breakfast, Julian handed him a copy of the Telegraph, which he had bought in Tonbridge. Soon Bill was totally engrossed in the paper and lost to the world. He had great powers of concentration and when busy reading – or just with his own thoughts – the outside world and other people might just as well not exist. It was a trait which had constantly exasperated Kitty, who seemed to think that her husband's brain should be just like an airport's PPI radar – sitting there with nothing to do all day but watch out for any approaching plane – or for anything that she said – his full attention should be instantly available to her at all times. Julian knew that he was the same, evidently a trait that ran in the Brophy line. So, he waited patiently until Bill had finished, and then asked what he had found that was so interesting. His father handed it to him without comment, simply pointing to an extended article on an inner page. This described how in Peru and some other South American states, simian labour was being exploited on an increasing scale.

From small beginnings with initially private entrepreneurs, later big business had moved in, establishing breeding colonies of Sapes. The article recounted much that was already known to Julian, had indeed appeared in the unofficial report that he had prepared.

"Have you ever actually seen one?" asked Bill.

"Not in the flesh, no. But I once saw an information film at the Department. It'd been prepared by the WSPCA as part of their drive to have simian labour banned worldwide. Of course, it rather sentimentalised the creatures, but gave quite a good idea of what they looked like and so on."

"And?"

"Well, they're just a largish tailless monkey, like a gibbon only bigger. Standing about forty-five centimetres shorter than you at a guess, short fur light brown – except white on faces and backs of hands – quite cute looking really. Faces can look quite expressive, almost human. But watch out for the toothy grin – it's a threat, not a smile. It said they can give a very nasty bite if they get really upset. Normally walk upright, with no more than a hint of a stoop, but fantastically agile in trees. Can't think of anything else to say about them, really, except that *simian simian amazoniensis versicolor* is outdated terminology. It's now agreed that they are a species within the genus Hylobates, itself a member of the family Hylobatidae."

Bill commented on how Kitty, with her enthusiastic support for the World Society for the Prevention of Cruelty to Animals, would have hated to read that newspaper story. The article, however, quoted the suppliers of these animals as insisting that their intelligence equated roughly to that of humans with mild learning disability (in earlier less civilised centuries dubbed 'morons'), with an IQ in the high seventies.

"It's well known that beings with a very modest level of intelligence can positively enjoy showing how they can cope with simple repetitive tasks, provided that they receive timely approbation and encouragement, like food, for their efforts," said Julian. The article was news to Bill and left him in a thoughtful mood. Julian heard Bill recount again the business of the 'ayudante simiesco manual' that he had heard about thirty years previously, at the Fifth World Population Conference in Buenos Aires.

At lunch time, Bill insisted on getting the meal ready, and in the afternoon after they had done the washing up – which prompted a quip about how handy a domestic simian would be – Bill maintained that he was quite recovered enough to manage on his own. So, not without some misgivings, Julian left the cottage where he had grown up, and rode home. Inez inquired anxiously after her father-in-law, of whom she was very fond.

"He really shouldn't be living there, all alone in that cottage at eighty-four. Anyway, it's far too big for his needs," she said.

"I know, but he won't hear of leaving, too many memories of happier times there, I suppose." Bill seemed, if not positively happy now, at least perfectly content living in the cottage with just Jen for company, and pottering in the garden, trying unsuccessfully to keep it as neat and tidy as it had been when Kitty was alive.

It was only a few weeks after this, in early autumn, that William called Julian, to tell him that he was to lead the British delegation to the Seventh World Population Conference. Why William himself was not going he did not say. *I wonder why; after all,* – thought Julian – *he's barely fifty.* There was some rumour of an attachment to a secretary who worked in the Minister's office, but Julian did not credit this story. So, the mystery if there was one, remained.

Inez was as visibly dismayed at the prospect of Julian's approaching absence at the Seventh WPC as she had been fifteen years earlier, on learning that he was to attend the Sixth, although she tried to hide the fact. Again, she fully supported his going, for the sake of their finances. Now Julian would be going to see what had happened in the intervening years since the last WPC. He had heard some rumours, from contacts he was still in touch with, from his days with The Telegraph. Some of these seemed far-fetched, if not incredible – he would soon find out.

Chapter 7
The Seventh WPC 2283AD

The Seventh World Population Conference was to be held in Antwerp and would be attended by a larger number of nations than any of the previous WPCs. They were held under the auspices of the United Nations, an organisation which had very nearly collapsed into disintegration on a number of occasions, but always, rather to its own surprise, risen like the phoenix from the ashes. The larger tally of countries was partly because several, with mixed ethnic groups, had split into two entirely separate states, usually accompanied by severe internal disruption and inter-ethnic violence in the process. Some countries sent only a single delegate, or even just an observer, but Julian found that the information for delegates that William handed to him, a week before he was due to leave, listed five delegates from Britain. Julian thought he ought to recognise some of the names, perhaps he had heard his father mention them in the past. The largest delegation by far was twenty, from the USA.

The day before his departure arrived, and Inez was visibly subdued, but very solicitous in making sure he had everything he could possibly need. On seeing that the pullover he was about to pack had a frayed cuff, and his others were even worse, she insisted on his packing one of hers. When he protested, she said, "Nonsense, there's no difference in men and women styles in simple vee-neck pullovers."

When he came to put it on later though, he noticed that she was correct except that the sleeves were slightly too short. Jim, now 26 and progressing well at Baker and Daley, had grown into a hulking great fly half, and at one metre eighty-six, was seven and a half centimetres taller than his father, and positively dwarfed his petite mother. He put his arm protectively around her and gave her a hug.

When the morning came and Julian was about to leave, he shook Jim's hand, and winced at his son's iron grip, then took Inez in his arms, in an embrace which lasted fully half a minute. Then he left the house hurriedly without looking back, as he had fifteen years previously. As for that earlier journey, and indeed his father's fifteen years before that, an official car was waiting, though the driver was a much more affable one than previously. Julian had heard all about his father's journey, and wondered, though the driver was obviously different, if it was the same car.

[[The design of cars was quite different from that of two centuries earlier, when built-in obsolescence, designed to maximise carmakers' profits, was the order of the day. Nowadays, cars were expected to last almost indefinitely, instead of dying of rotting bodywork in ten or twelve years at most. Proper underbody protection, the increased use of aluminium and plastics and a straight-through chassis meant that a replacement motor or batteries could be fitted, when and if necessary, to bodywork that was virtually everlasting.]]

Unlike his journey to Japan, Julian travelled to the conference by road and sea. The driver seemed quite chatty and asked where Julian was going when they got to the ferry at Sheerness.

"To Flushing, and then on to Antwerp, for the 7th World Population Conference."

"What, as a delegate, or a reporter?" Adding facetiously, "Or just for fun?"

"Don't suppose there'll be much of that for anyone. As a delegate, as a matter of fact. Went to the sixth one in sixty-nine, too."

"Did it do any good?"

"Not much I suppose; since then, the population of the world's dropped again, from forty three percent to thirty seven of what it was at the turn of the millennium."

"Holy cow; when's the crunch date?"

"Extrapolating from current trends, the last man snuffs it in about twenty two seventy three."

"The last woman, more like. My old woman says she's gonna outlive me if it's the last thing she does. Says…women are ten times more likely to outlive their husband than the other way round."

"I wouldn't put it quite that high, but she's not far wrong."

Julian would be travelling alone, or so, he thought. But on the ferry, up on deck where he had gone for fresh air – he was not a good traveller – he got talking to three men who turned out to be other British delegates. Scythrop Read was an academic from Oxford, Dick Bailey was from the Benson Pharmaceuticals research department and Rodney Follet, a psychologist.

"I hope you don't think it impertinent, but Scythrop's an unusual name surely," said Julian.

"Everyone says that, I have my mother to blame for it. She was mad on the novels of Thomas Love Peacock – apparently that's the first name of one of the characters in the one called 'Nightmare Abbey' – or is it 'Headlong Hall', I forget which. In fact, I've never read it or any of them. Ought to get around to it when I have some spare time."

By this time, they were all in the bar and another came up and introduced himself as Sandy McIntosh of Edinburgh University. He was looking sadly woebegone, Rodney asked him what was wrong.

"I've just heard that my local football club have lost another game, the third in a row. We're likely to be relegated, I should think."

"Oh Fortuna," said Julian.

"Sicut luna," added Dick, picking up the quotation.

"Semper variabilis," said Scythrop.

"What's all that then – sounds like Double Dutch to me?" Sandy's face indicated bewilderment.

"Not Dutch."

"Or Greek?"

"It's Latin. It means, 'oh fortune, like the moon, ever variable'. Perhaps your club will have a run of wins next," said Scythrop.

Scythrop's features were regular in the extreme: His nose was neither too large nor too small and situated exactly in the right place relative to his other features, which were similarly unremarkable, set in a face that was neither pale nor sunburnt, under short neatly brushed black hair. His whole face seemed the epitome of the appearance of an unremarkable urbane thirty-year-old, though he was in fact in his mid-forties. Yet such regular features somehow did not add up to a strikingly handsome male face, far from it; together with his average height and average build, they merely contributed to an eminently forgettable appearance. Dick was a complete contrast. His nose looked slightly too small for his face and was tilted slightly to one side, the effect of a fracas in the playground when he was seven. His eyes were slightly too far apart, his forehead wrinkled, and his eyebrows permanently conveyed a look of mild surprise. Nevertheless, despite its somewhat bizarre appearance, Dick's suntanned face somehow instantly gave the comforting impression of someone one could confide in, one could trust, one could turn to in an emergency. Julian soon learnt that they knew each other, having both been to the Sixth World Population Conference, and on hearing that Julian had also, asked his name. They both vaguely recalled seeing his name on the delegate list but neither had actually met him. The ferry docked at 17.00h hours, they were taken to their hotel by road through streets washed by heavy rain and, after signing in, agreed to meet up in an hour's time, in the bar before dinner.

In the bar Scythrop, who was the elder, and Dick vied with each other in relating tales about other delegates of the proceedings at the Sixth World Population Conference fifteen years ago.

Not of course, the formal part; this was all recorded in the Proceedings, which Julian had studied years earlier and had studied again when William told him he was to attend the Seventh WPC. Then there was the report he had written on his return, which went – together with a copy of the Proceedings – to the minister, and also his informal internal report for Departmental eyes only. He recognised that some of the yarns his fellow diners were retailing, though based on fact, were considerably elaborated for effect. Still, his new friends were interesting, obviously intelligent people with intelligent conversation, and made pleasant company.

Their talk turned to the arts, and Julian learned that whilst Scythrop was very keen on poetry, particularly that of Robert Bridges and Gerard Manley Hopkins, he was tone deaf and quite uninterested in music. Dick, on the other hand, was very fond of music and had learnt violin as a youngster, although never progressing beyond Grade 6 and had long ago given up playing. However, on discovering that his favourite composer was Gustav Mahler, Julian immediately recognised in him a fellow music lover of great discernment. They discussed listening to music, both recorded and live at concerts.

"Tell me, what do you think about when listening to music?" said Dick.

"Well, I don't often get the opportunity to really listen to music nowadays, but when I do, my mind is a complete and absolute blank."

"You're obviously very musical – the music completely fills your head if you're really listening; if I find I'm thinking about anything then I know I've lost my concentration on the music."

"Of course, it's much easier to concentrate on the music at a live performance, where you're forever looking to see where the bass clarinet is, say, hiding behind the piccolo or so on. Trouble is, live performances are so few and far between – still, interactive television's help."

'Interactive Television' was an advanced system fitted on the more expensive television sets, available only on premium channels, the ones more likely to feature broadcast orchestral concerts. A handheld controller enabled the user to home in on an enlarged section of the picture, at will – just like being there.

The conversation continued on the topic of the symphony, and Mahler and Bruckner in particular. Suddenly Julian noticed that Scythrop had quietly got up and wandered over to another table, where he was talking animatedly to two other people.

"Oh dear, I hope he doesn't think we're rude, sort of cutting him out of our conversation."

"No, no – Scythrop and I got talking to the one on the left a couple of months ago. He's an old friend of Scythrop's, from their college days. I bet they'll be talking about philately, they're all three mad on it."

It turned out later that the two people Scythrop was talking to, a stocky man in early middle age, and a youngish woman, along with Julian, Dick and Scythrop, made up the British delegation to the forthcoming WPC. The middle-aged man, he was told, was Dr Frayne Wilberton from the Department of Gerontology at Southampton University, and the woman Dr Sarah Lees from a similar department at the University of Bath. With the shrinking world population, it was of paramount importance to extend the useful working life of everyone, especially those with valuable skills in engineering, medicine, civil administration etc. Apart from his serious look, thick horn-rimmed spectacles and shiny bald head, Julian did not notice anything else about Dr Wilberton, but he could not fail to be struck by Sarah's unrestrained honey-blonde hair, tumbling down below her shoulders, framing a face which was – with its sparkling blue eyes, generous mouth and bright red lipstick – if not exactly beautiful, nonetheless distinctly pleasant to look at despite the fact that the features all seemed slightly too large.

Later, over dinner, the conversation ranged far and wide, but settled obstinately, after a while, on the start of proceedings on the morrow. The general opinion was that a further decline in the viability of the human race would be revealed, and none of them had any great faith that a promising line of action to improve things would appear. On this depressing note, the gathering broke up, and Julian went to his room wondering what the next day would bring. He washed, cleaned his teeth, carefully laid out his things for the morning and set his travelling alarm clock for 06.55 hours. In bed, he turned over and over, sleep eluding him. Infuriatingly, each time he started to drift off, he realised that he was doing just that, and was instantly wide awake again.

Later he found himself standing around with other delegates of various nationalities, African, Arab, Chinese, Malayan and many others staying in the hotel. To his surprise, he realised there were naked young women standing around also, and the man next to him took one in his arms, purely to hide her nakedness. He did the same for a young woman standing near him, hiding her front with his suit-clad body and covering as much of her back as he could with his arms. She was the same height as him, and he felt the pleasant sensation of her soft cheek against his ear, as she looked over his shoulder at he knew not what; he realised he had absolutely no idea what her face looked like. He guessed she was about his age, and he felt slightly guilty to be holding her and not Inez. But then he realised the explanation was that at that age, he had probably not met Inez yet. Now this was perplexing: If he had not met Inez yet, how could he know that he would do, sometime in the future; that such a person as Inez even existed?

But another problem came to his attention. The other delegates were each holding a fat folder of papers, doubtless the timetables and other information concerning the conference which was soon to start – the young women seemed to have disappeared. He couldn't go to the Conference without his folder; he assumed that they had collected theirs at the hotel reception desk when they booked in and that he should have done the same. He turned abruptly to go to the reception desk in the foyer, and that woke him up with a start. Eventually, he drifted off to sleep again, a sleep populated by dreams as his sleeping always was. But they were the usual sort, not involving naked women and so inconsequential that on waking he could not actually remember any of them, only the fact that he had been dreaming, as he always did. He could not remember ever having had such a vivid dream as that earlier one, which stuck in his mind in its bizarre entirety.

The alarm clock roused him, and he got up, washed, cleaned his teeth (his dental hygienist told him that once a day was not enough as plaque can form in less than 24 hours), shaved, dressed, glanced briefly at the information William had provided him with on his last visit to the Department, and prepared to go down to breakfast. Whilst many delegates were busy with continental breakfast, Dick, Scythrop and Frayne, but not Sarah, were tucking into full English breakfast. Julian asked if he could sit at the same table as her, they were all small tables laid for just two and this seemed the only place free. She nodded, finished a mouthful of cornflakes and mumbled, "Please do." He had helped himself at the buffet to his usual breakfast, consisting of three and a half dessertspoonful of Muesli with milk, and a cup of coffee, which he refilled later.

"Is that all you're having?" she asked, and without waiting for him to reply, added, "no wonder you're so slim. I wish I could keep my weight down."

"But you're –" He paused, embarrassed, and blushed.

"Not actually fat, I know. But do you know how much I weight?"

Basically, a shy man, he feared the conversation might be drifting in a personal direction, and after last night's dream that was something he felt he could not face. So, he assumed it was a rhetorical question and merely smiled politely. To fortify himself for the day's proceedings, he allowed himself, exceptionally, a third cup of coffee, which he always took white, but without sugar.

They all arrived at the Conference Centre through more heavy rain, negotiated security, registered and collected the fat folder of paperwork, the lack of which had so worried him in last night's dream. It detailed the main, subcommittee and working party timetables, and gave a list of delegates by country, with their specialisms, together with a lot of other information, some useful, some less so and some apparently totally irrelevant. On the way into the main auditorium, for the opening speech by the Belgian prime minister, there was a green baize-covered table with a carafe of water covered by a glass and half a dozen other up-turned glasses. Julian couldn't help smiling, remembering Sam Goldsmith, Nick Wagner and the 'gin' at an earlier conference.

They settled into their seats and sat through what turned out to be, for a politician, quite a surprisingly interesting and thought provoking speech, laced with a little subtle humour. But the most serious point in his address was the statement that the world population was now down to 37% of that at the start of the third millennium. This figure and the figures of 49% at the 5th and 43% at the 6th WPCs plotted on a graph, lay more or less on a straight line giving a predicted extinction date for the human race of 2374AD. This was less than a century away, or about four generations, assuming of course that the rate of decline remained constant. This emphasised how desperately urgent was the task of the many universities, research institutes and indeed the WPC's own subcommittees, in identifying the cause of reduced human fertility, and finding a remedy thereto. At the end, he received a round of appreciative applause, and Sarah, who was sitting in the next seat, leant across close to Julian and murmured, "His English is so excellent; you've got to be really good to work in a little humour and make it sound quite natural, in a language not your own." Julian noticed the delicate floral perfume she was wearing, the very same which was Inez's favourite, and suddenly felt very lonely.

At the coffee break, there was a minor mishap as Sam carried a cup of coffee away from the table at which it was available. Carelessly he brushed against one of the pillars supporting the ceiling and the cup nearly fell off the saucer. He managed to avoid complete disaster but finished up with lots of the coffee in the saucer and more down his right trouser leg. He shouted, "Triple bugger!"

Nick said, "It's usually just 'bugger' and occasionally 'bugger and bugger', but I've never heard anyone come out with 'triple bugger' before."

Scythrop commented, "If you're not going to pronounce all of the buggers individually, you could always up the ante to pentabugger, octobugger, dodecabugger, or whatever suits your frustration at the time."

After coffee break, there was an interesting presentation by a middle-aged American on studies in gerontology carried out by a team at UCLA. It described the effect of certain alkaloids extracted from various species of the order Solanaceae in not merely delaying, but positively reversing, the effect of mental decline in old age. Intrigued, Julian looked again at the timetable and saw that the paper was presented by the leader of the team, none other than Dr Nicholas Wagner. The papers in the afternoon Julian found less interesting, and those on the following morning, worse. The first paper on the afternoon of the second day was very technical in the medical sense, dealing with measures to maximise both male and female fertility. Finding some of it stretching his knowledge to the limit, Julian wondered how other delegates without any medical background were faring. During the next paper he resorted to looking through the list of names of delegates, and thought he vaguely recognised several.

After tea, came a paper that the prime minister in his introductory talk had promised would be interesting, even though it did not concern human fecundity. It was presented by the chairman of a committee dealing with simians and it dealt with their ever-increasing use in all walks of life. Some were even used as general assistants in hospitals. One of the less urgent tasks of the main sub-committee dealing with this important topic was the invention of a general term to cover all simians used by humans, for whatever purpose. After many discussions and after discarding many suggestions, the chairman said the committee had come up with 'Simian Auxiliary Population Elements'. The creatures inevitably thereafter became universally known by the acronym SAPEs. The ignorant interpreted this as meaning 'servant apes' although the creatures were not related to apes in any way. As the chairman explained, the term was very carefully tailored to underline the nature and role of simians.

"It emphasises the fact that they are not, never were and never will be people; they are just animals, as useful as horses or cows say, or more so even, but just animals, that's all."

At dinner that evening, the five British delegates were joined by Dr Wagner, by the elderly distinguished-looking Frenchman who introduced himself as Henri Duparc of the Curie Institute, and by a Pole whom Julian could see was called Jan Plessner; he had forgotten to take off his conference name badge. Julian had met the first two but was uncertain about the other until it came out in conversation that Jan was the son of a Dr Anton Plessner, the world famous rheumatologist. As the dessert came around Dr Wagner complained that Antwerp seemed a depressing sort of place, and he was looking forward to getting back to California.

"I do not agree; it is just the weather," said Henri Duparc. "I have always had a liking for Anvers, since when I was a small boy, and our family visited an uncle who lived here. I always look forward to when I will be in Anvers again." Many of the others thought they would reserve judgment until they could see the city in better weather.

The following day was cold, the light poor and the rain heavy yet again – by now most of the delegates would probably have agreed with Dr Wagner rather than Henri Duparc. Day 4 of the Conference dawned bright, but by the time they left the hotel it had clouded over and was already spitting. Julian was not sorry when the fifth and final day arrived. The morning he spent in the deliberations of the subcommittee dealing with sapes, to which he had been seconded by William, where his medical knowledge was again stretched to the limit, this time by some of the ideas floated by other members of the committee. However, when the maximum load that a sape could be expected to lift and carry was discussed, his specialised knowledge of anatomy gave him the authority to contradict the excessive estimate given by the committee's chairman. He pointed out that the skeleton of sapes was more lightly built than that of humans, and that the musculature of any vertebrate was proportional to the build of the skeleton. So, they would not be able to carry a burden that a human could manage, even if they were the same height as a human, which they were not. He was relieved when the chairman, a short stout dark featured Colombian with a perpetually worried expression, accepted eventually, with great reluctance and evident displeasure, his suggested amendment on that point.

There were no other items on the agenda and – its work done – the subcommittee meeting came to an end. The participants collected up their papers amid an animated buzz of conversation; they would not see each other again until the next WPC. Julian did likewise and they all headed out of the committee room – meeting up with those leaving the main hall – and made their way towards the large room where the usual buffet lunch was laid out. Afterwards, all the delegates left in little groups or one by one, making their way back to the main hall. But Julian, almost the last to leave, headed for the gents' toilet and afterwards hurried towards the main hall, across the large foyer. He did not pay any particular attention to the sound of hurrying footsteps behind him, evidently someone in a great hurry. Suddenly he felt a thump against his right side as a heavy body collided with him, sending him flying. He feared he would go sprawling but was fortunately fleet enough of foot to regain his balance, with difficulty. As he straightened up he was just in time to see a large swarthy heavily built man he did not recognise disappearing round a turning into a corridor, without a word of apology. He stood a moment to get his wind back and then headed toward the main hall for the afternoon session. The door was now shut but the attendant dutifully opened it for him, with an expressionless face ignoring Julian's questioning glance, as though he had seen nothing, though clearly he must have. Julian shrugged, went in and took the nearest seat, as the chairman of the session was already starting his opening remarks. As it happened, he found himself sitting next to Sarah.

"Whatever's the matter? You're white as a sheet."

"Oh, it's all right, nothing really." Sarah could see it was not all right and definitely not nothing. But people were looking at them and shushing – the chairman was not a good speaker, and his voice did not carry well – so Sarah had to be content with determining to ask again later.

The last session of the day, and of the Conference, was the usual wash-up session and produced some lively exchanges between the floor and the panel of presenters and committee chairmen on the stage. Of the few reporters accredited to the conference, one from the Telegraph asked if the panel were aware of the developments in sape breeding in South America, where research was being undertaken, on behalf of one of the larger commercial breeders, into developing a sape so intelligent that it could undertake many of the tasks currently only possible for humans. Julian thought the reply from the panel was unsatisfactory, not really addressing the issue raised in any cogent way. But he was also intrigued to know who had posed the question. Fortunately, he was much nearer the door than the questioner, a tall gaunt middle-aged man with slightly greying straight black hair swept back and plastered down. So, he quickly took up position by the door as the delegates, observers and reporters filed out. At last, he saw the man he was looking for.

"Hal, how are you then?"

Hal looked non-plussed for a moment, then said, "Well, I'd never have recognised you, Julian."

Hal and Julian had not seen each other since the wedding, although they exchanged Christmas cards each year.

"Not surprising we never met in all this throng; where're you staying?"

"At the Antwerp Inn."

"Me, I'm just down the road at the Wellington," said Hal, and he promised to come round to Julian's hotel after dinner, as he would like to see more of some of the delegates: There were none at all in the Wellington, which was a very small hotel.

Good as his word, Hal turned up at the Antwerp Inn and was soon in animated conversation with Sarah. After dinner, Julian introduced him to some of the delegates, not necessarily the ones who were concerned with improving human fecundity or with increasing useful human longevity, but those who were particularly interested in the question of sapes, although this included some of the former – among whom was Sarah. The whole group was eager to hear what was really going on in this direction, rather than the carefully tailored anodyne stories presented by the official channels in the countries where these developments were occurring. So, Hal had an attentive audience. He said, "Simians have been employed for as long as people can remember by hunter-gatherer Amazonian Indian tribes, to harvest fruit and nuts that they could not reach. Being so light, the smaller animals can venture much, further along branches and had learnt to use forked sticks to dislodge bunches of fruit etc.; in return the tribe's people tended any ill or wounded animals and assisted the females in parturition. The animals have also apparently been employed by Peruvian farmers for much longer than had at first been thought. The sapes used by the latter had, from the early days, been selectively bred for large size and muscle power and with these creatures you can get twelve, fourteen or more generations to a century. So, with human direction added to the power of natural selection, you get astounding results in no time at all."

"Yes, but what do they look like?" said Sarah, adding, "I've never seen one." A chorus of 'me too' made it clear that she was not the only one.

"Well, they're a large tailless monkey, like a gibbon only bigger. Standing about one and a half metres at a guess, though there are short ones and tall ones, just like us. Short light brown fur all over – except white on faces and backs of hands – that's about it, really. Oh, normally walk upright, no more than a hint of a stoop – fantastically agile in trees."

"Yes, but have you ever seen one?" said someone.

"Only once," said Hal without a moment's hesitation, though Julian thought he looked slightly uncomfortable.

Hal was bombarded with further questions, to some of which he gave very specific answers, others he was vaguer about and some he brushed aside entirely. Of course, Julian knew him from long ago as not only a very intelligent man and a very helpful one also but as a man with a slightly reserved, not to say devious, streak. He could not quite make out whether Hal had been to South America recently, or whether he was relying on information from his contacts there. He knew about Hal's network of contacts worldwide who were happy to help him, as he frequently was able to pass information back to them from other sources. But sorting out the solid facts from the anecdotal, it appeared that the selective breeding of sapes for specific tasks, that they had been hearing about for some years, had proceeded further than they would have believed possible. In addition to sapes bred for agricultural labouring or domestic duties, the most go-ahead consortium, based in Bolivia, some two hundred and fifty miles northeast of La Paz, was following a potentially more lucrative goal. Their aim was to produce a more intelligent breed of sape, one that could then rapidly learn any one of a whole range of tasks. Such adaptable sapes would be more profitable for the supplier since he would no longer have to stock several blood lines to cope with different applications. The implications of this were not lost on his hearers, who looked at one another and wondered where it would all end. The group of listeners dispersed, and Julian and Hal settled down in a corner of the hotel lounge with cups of coffee, discussing the events of the day, and of the conference as a whole. He related to Hal the strange incident on the way to the main conference hall and noticed that Hal gave him a pensive look. Reaching into the right-hand pocket of his jacket for a clean handkerchief, he was surprised find a folded up piece of paper there. With a look of puzzlement, he unfolded it, and after a glance, handed it to Hal.

'*Do not underestimate sapes, or people. Accidents can happen anywhere, even in T…*' Scribbled in a foreign hand, evidently.

"Sarah told me something must've upset you just before the last session but one. Guess that's when this was popped in your pocket." Julian nodded and related in more detail the affair of the collision with the swarthy man.

"What went on in that subcommittee you attended this morning?" He briefly related the proceedings, and his part in moderating the load that a sape could be expected to bear.

"You must be careful, Julian. Big money's involved in the trade in sapes. Important people are behind it." Hal's voice, always deep, was troubled and gruffer than usual. Thoughtfully, Julian hoped his return journey would prove as uneventful as the outward but feared it might not be.

Chapter 8
Snuggling Up and Old Acquaintances

When Julian arrived home, Inez found him in a thoughtful mood. This had already lasted several days when she asked him what the problem was; had something awful been revealed at the Conference? Julian was placed in a quandary. They prided themselves that they had never secrets from each other; well, not any important ones, anyway. But he felt that serious, momentous, worldwide problems could evolve in future years, future generations, if the employment of sapes continued to expand, as seemed likely. However, he did not want to alarm her, knowing her to be one of life's worriers. Instead, he confined his fears to a long report which he prepared and emailed to William's office at the Department, ready for him to read when he came out of hospital. Even more difficult for Julian was his decision to say nothing to Inez about the ominous scribbled note that had been slipped into his pocket on his way to the buffet.

In fact, so anxious was William for news of what had transpired at the Conference, that he accessed his mailbox from the bed in his room at the hospital, downloaded the document to his laptop and perused it avidly. He was particularly interested in Julian's account of what Hal had told him. It did not in any way fall within the remit of the Department of Health and Reproduction, but William Hacker was a man of considerable intellect, and would let his mind ponder on the situation and its possible ramifications, which he could see were as potentially catastrophic, as Julian had postulated in his report.

Several months had passed, and Inez was relieved to find that, now spring was here, Julian's usual cheerful manner seemed largely to have returned. Though she had been a little surprised when, before Christmas, he had had a multi-camera CCTV system with continuous recording, installed in the house – they were lucky in the quiet corner on the outskirts of Tunbridge Wells where they lived; burglaries were unheard of, situated as they were on the opposite side of Tunbridge Wells from the isolated woodside cottage where Bill lived. What Inez didn't know was that a few days earlier, Julian had received a call from Hal, with some disturbing news.

"Are you alone?"

"Yes, what is it?"

"You know the chairman of the subcommittee you sat on at the WPC?"

"That Columbian, er, Señor Valde?"

"He's dead," growled Hal. "It could've been an accident, but if so, an unusual one. The police investigated it and concluded that it was an accident."

"You suspect it wasn't?"

"I don't know – could be. But there's a rumour he was in the pay of one of the sape breeding syndicates. They'd have an interest in maximising the load a sape could be expected to carry. No doubt he was expected to deliver."

"But the police said it was an accident."

"They'd say anything a sape breeding consortium wanted them to, for a price."

"You mean I'm –"

"Oh, I don't think you need bother too much. They've probably forgotten about you by now, the chairman was their man."

"But how could they've known it was me was responsible for setting the limit a sape could carry?"

"I expect there was another member on the committee paid to report back on the chairman and things. But don't worry, if anything were going to happen, it would have been done so by now."

Now Julian was helping Inez in the garden again from time to time and, in late March, insisted on taking her out for an evening meal. They visited their favourite restaurant, only to find it had been taken over by a new restaurateur. The meal they had was very enjoyable, quite up to the standard of the previous owner, but much more expensive than before. They returned home and after Julian had had the inevitable extra cup of coffee, sat together on the settee and listened to recorded music, with Julian's arm around his wife. They played a recording of a Vaughan William's Symphony, an unusual work in that it consists of four slow movements. Afterwards, they had a light supper and Inez said she would have a bath and then go to bed.

Julian said he would follow shortly, after replying to an email from William asking for his considered opinion on a request from a research worker for funds to investigate the economic impact of accidents resulting in bone fractures at the workplace. Having completed his reply, he duly sent it and received via online an email from Hal, with a request to know how Julian and Inez were getting on. He replied that they were fine and added an invitation to Hal to visit, and perhaps stay a day or two, if he could wangle it with the powers that be. Afterwards, Julian realised he should have cleared it with Inez, who was the keeper of the household's social diary.

Julian turned in rather later than he had intended, and found Inez half lying, half sitting, her shoulders on the pillow, her head leaning against the bed head. As he got into bed he expected to be in trouble for keeping her awake and started to apologise. But he realised she was not listening – clearly that was not the problem.

"What is it, love?"

"There's this slight pain in my chest, and a bitter taste in my throat. Do you think it's something to do with what I ate at the restaurant?"

"Not really; reflux, my dear, could happen anytime."

"What's that?"

"There's a sphincter at the top of your tummy, lets the food in and supposed to stop it coming out again. Once there, it gets attacked by gastric juices, hydrochloric acid and stuff. Your tummy's designed to cope with that, but not your oesophagus – your gullet."

"Why's stuff flowing back up?"

"It's your age, my dear." Inez hit him on the arm.

"That's what you wretched doctors say, every time."

"Sorry love but it's true – and I'm not a doctor."

"Can't you do anything about it?" said Inez as Julian was getting out of bed, adding, "Where are you going to now?" But he was already out of the bedroom. He returned from the kitchen a few moments later with a glass of water.

"Take a few sips of this, and stay sort of sitting up, like you are."

Inez took a few sips and it seemed to ease things gradually. But she stayed sitting up, afraid to lie down for fear of a recurrence, and thinking that she would never get to sleep like this, with her chest and bare shoulders outside the bedclothes. She woke at two in the morning, snug and comfy. She realised that she must have drifted off after all and found that Julian had somehow managed to get hold of his jacket and drape it over her, without waking her up. She kissed his back and snuggled up, not waking again until the sound of a busy coffee percolator filled her ears. It lived on Julian's bedside table, and next to it, on the floor, was a little Peltier cooling cabinet containing a cup and saucer with a little milk and half a glass of orange juice.

As they sat up in bed, Julian finished a freshly made cup of coffee and murmured to Inez, "A'vsmorinjoose." When she had finished it Julian put his arm around behind her, his hand gently supporting her breast, as he had done in the cafe in Duncannon Street all those years ago and asked if it would be all right if he were to invite an old friend to stay for a few days.

"Yes, of course, when is he coming?" He blushed, how well she knew him; perhaps it was not surprising, after twenty-nine years of marriage.

"Well, I haven't fixed a date yet, early next month sometime, perhaps."

The visit was duly arranged, with Hal set to arrive late afternoon on the first Friday of April, leaving first thing the following Tuesday. The day arrived, and Hal turned up in a motorcar, explaining that it belonged to the paper, though how he had wangled the loan of it, Julian neither knew nor cared to enquire. A further surprise was that he was not alone but accompanied by Sarah Lees.

"I hope you don't mind me bringing Sarah."

"Oh, no, but –" And Julian stopped short, embarrassed.

"I know, she's barely half my age, you were going to say. Well, I'm not a baby snatcher. Any man who tried to snatch her would get his wrist severely slapped if she didn't approve, believe me."

"Of course, I don't mind Sarah coming, but I don't know about Inez." They went into the house and Julian carried out the introductions.

"Oh dear," said Inez, "the spare room that we use as the guest bedroom only has the one single bed in it."

"Er, Jim's away, we could always use his room as well."

"That's okay, we're both slimmish – we'll snuggle up together." And Sarah tossed her head, smiling and sending her long blonde locks swirling like a television advertisement for shampoo. Julian and Inez looked at each other; they realised that they were hopelessly old-fashioned and that what was proposed was nothing out of the ordinary.

So, Inez simply shrugged and said, "As you like."

Hal and Julian went into the garden and were soon discussing sapes, while the two women were in the kitchen, discussing men. Inez said, "I hope you know what you're doing."

And Sarah related the background to herself and Hal, saying, "At twenty-one I married a handsome sportsman – he seemed the ideal partner. But he was always sexually very demanding and a fortnight after our honeymoon he insisted we play BDSM. Only once did he agree to play the sub and then he made so much fuss over it that after that he always had to be the dom. Over the first year of marriage, he became increasingly moody and then violent as well. After two years of marriage, I left him and obtained a divorce, vowing never to have anything to do with men again. Then, last year I met Hal at the Seventh WPC. We seemed always to be bumping into each other, and he teased me gently, like an older brother might. On the last night of the Conference, we had had a drink together and I found myself somehow very comfortable in his company; so much so that when he suggested we keep in touch I agreed readily enough, not really expecting anything to come of it. We exchanged cards, and on returning to Britain I forgot all about it."

Early that February, she had received a phone call from Hal, saying that he would be in Bath the day after next, and could he take her out to dinner in the evening.

"Again, I noticed how very much at ease I felt with him, and we had gradually become more and more close." She didn't know if anything would ever come of it and didn't really mind if it didn't. After all, she was now twenty-eight and Hal fifty-two.

"I still had plenty of time to find the right man, if I wanted to, and Hal had never suggested we share a bed, let alone actually live together, though he clearly enjoyed a kiss or two."

"So, it was your idea to 'snuggle up' to him while staying here?"

"Yes; did you see how he looked? Surprised, more than anything, I think."

"But he didn't say no, did he?"

"Would any man?" asked Sarah, asking if she could help prepare the evening meal.

Not with a face, a figure and hair like that, thought Inez, as they set to work.

Julian wanted to pump Hal for all the latest information on sapes. He knew of William's interest in the subject, so the more information he could pass on, the better it would be for his standing in the Department. The situation in South

America was confused, said Hal, which may just have been his way of saying that his contacts there were not quite as extensive as he had led people to believe, the previous year, in the Antwerp Hotel. But the most momentous item he let drop was that in the most successful sape producing syndicate, in addition to its on-going project to produce a more intelligent breed of sape, capable of turning its hand to any job after just a little training, a longer term project to cross these ultra-intelligent sapes with the large powerful types bred for heavy labouring was seriously on the cards. The expectation was that in due course the progeny would show hybrid vigour, combining the best traits of both bloodlines. But another problem needed addressing before that project made sense. One of the limitations of sapes was their limited linguistic ability.

"They've proved capable of learning lots of simple commands, but that's nothing unusual; even carthorses respond to 'gee-up' and 'whoa-back' and a sheepdog understands loads of words," said Hal. "But if a sape comes across a problem that means it can't do what you've told it to, it's just stuck – it's got no way of explaining anything to you."

Hal and Sarah's visit had passed off peacefully enough, with none of the unpleasantness that Julian had feared might transpire, given the very different characters of Inez and their two guests. Hal had sent Julian an email, a few days after the visit, thanking him for the hospitality and the next day, Monday, around lunchtime, a large bunch of flowers arrived for Inez, with Sarah's thanks. Later that afternoon, the v-phone burst into life; it was William, wanting to talk to Julian. Julian was not in his little office on the first floor, and Inez popped her head out of the back door to call him in from his daily job of watering the lettuces in the cold frame. But it was just after 17.00 hours, so William had no cause for complaint.

Julian sat down in front of the image of William on the screen and after a perfunctory exchange of courtesies, which assured each that the other was in good – or at least satisfactory – health, William started.

"Julian, we have to –" He paused and started again on a new tack. "Er, the Minister wants us to –" Another pause. "It might be better if you came up to see me. I'm completely tied up tomorrow, but Wednesday would be fine."

It was agreed that Julian would take the first train of the day arriving at Waterloo just before 09.00 hours, which with a quick walk to the office, would see him in the Department in Whitehall by a quarter past or thereabouts. On the Thursday morning, William greeted him briskly and introduced him to a Sandy

McIntosh of Edinburgh University, a cheerful pleasant-looking man in a chunky bottle-green double-knit sweater, who was in his late thirties, Julian guessed even though he was already beginning to be balding. There was no doubt where the short wiry Scotsman with his big hands and tanned face got his nickname from, though the short stiff sandy hair, like a scrubbing brush, was already just beginning to grey very slightly at the edges.

"Sandy is in charge of the SHIP project." Seeing Julian's blank look.

"It stands for sape/human interface project," William added.

"Seeing he was going to be in London for a few days, I thought it would be much better to introduce the two of you; the v-phone is no substitute for direct communication." Then, turning to Sandy said, "Perhaps you'd like to say a word or two about it to Julian. I know it's really nothing to do with Health and Reproduction, but the minister for some reason's taken it into his head to get the Department involved. Following his instructions to pick the best man for the job, it has to be Julian here. He's a gifted linguist, speaks I don't know how many languages" (William turned and indicated Julian, who however said nothing).

"But as far as I know, they don't include Sapish, if that's what you call it." Sandy's face cleared.

"That explains it – I'd heard about Julian's medical qualifications but didn't know about his languages. Perhaps the Minister knew, and that's why he wanted your Department involved."

"Possibly, but he's been in charge of almost every Ministry there is, in his time, and has the reputation of wanting to be involved in everything, all the time. Well, well, I'll leave you two together – I've another meeting shortly."

Julian led Sandy to one of the few offices in the Department. With the Department's staff mostly teleworking from home, the two small offices plus one larger one for meetings generally proved more than adequate; today, most unusually, both the small offices were in use so Sandy and Julian settled in the meeting room, where Rachel – the Department's administrative assistant, a jolly broad-hipped middle-aged spinster with a deep contralto voice, neatly permed dark brown dyed hair, tweed skirt and just a suspicion of a moustache – presently brought them regulation civil service coffee and digestive biscuits.

Sandy started off by correcting William's version of the acronym, something he had been too polite to do in front of Julian's boss: SHIP stood for Sape/Human Intercommunication Project. He went on to explain in some detail the problems being encountered in communicating with sapes generally, a problem that was especially relevant to the development of a new, more intelligent bloodline. It appeared that the linguistics department of Edinburgh University had been approached by the consultants Gelbschild Parkinson and Partners, who were retained as advisers to a South American sape breeding corporation. The university's linguistics department was in the process of setting up a co-operative panel of experts to assist the South American customer via G.P.&P. Julian appointed himself secretary to the meeting and took copious meticulous notes from which later he would prepare a detailed report for William.

They discussed the problems of communicating with simians, and Sandy's clear rugged face showed surprise to find that Julian was not only linguistically very competent but seemed to know very much more than he would have expected from one in the Health and Reproduction Department, about the current sape-breeding programmes is South America.

"But for all that," said Julian, "I've never actually seen a sape. What are they like?"

"I've never seen one either."

Julian thought this a little odd in one responsible for the type of study in question, but Sandy showed not the least trace of embarrassment. He pulled a disc out of his briefcase, popped it into the player in the corner and they watched a documentary about sapes. The first part was a condensed version of a film Julian had seen on television some time before, but it soon moved onto a series of clips of sapes making the various vocal sounds of which they were capable. They all centred around three or four different sapes and Julian soon became able to recognise each of them. Some clips showed two or more sapes having a discussion, or perhaps an argument, it wasn't always clear which. In addition to various sounds, which Julian soon began to recognise, the sapes interaction was accompanied by a lot of gesticulation and body language.

"Everyone thinks all sapes look the same, just like sheep. But you can see this isn't so," said Sandy.

"I know. There's a surprisingly large area of the human brain dedicated to recognising human faces and telling them apart, and sapes must be able to recognise each other just the same. Anyone working with sapes would soon get to tell them apart, just like a shepherd with his sheep."

After watching the documentary, which Julian found fascinating, they hammered out a plan for Julian's part in the panel of experts and discussed the need for occasional meetings of the panel. He felt he now had a much clearer idea of what a sape looked like and how it behaved.

The following day Julian set about completing a report on another urgent job he was involved in, anxious to wrap it up and turn to the SHIP business as soon as possible. It turned out lengthy, so it was not until three days later that he was finally able to produce a report of his meeting with Sandy. This did not simply recount what had passed between Sandy and himself but set it in a wider context and proposed the general direction in which the Department's future involvement in the SHIP business should proceed. Lunchtime passed, and Julian resumed work in his office, finishing just after 17.00 hours and emailing the report to the Department straight away.

He had just finished, when Inez called up the stairs to say that she was serving up dinner; they habitually dined early, as there was always plenty to do afterwards, around the house and garden, and especially now in the garden in the longer evenings of April.

"What have you been doing up there all day?" asked Inez as they sat with coffee after Julian had seen to the washing up, drying and putting away.

"I've been producing a plan of work for my involvement in the SHIP project." And then of course he had to explain what that was. He added, "It was really fascinating to see the short film of sapes 'talking' that Sandy showed and hear the sounds they can make. Some of their allophones are very similar to ours."

"What are those? The same as phonemes?"

"Not really. A phoneme is a basic unit of speech: Change it and you have a different word, another meaning. But a phoneme may represent slightly different allophones."

"You've got me lost completely."

"Well, think about the letter p in pin and spin. They're not quite the same. The p in pin is aspirated, in spin it isn't – two allophones of the letter p. In fact, you could spell spin as 'sbin', but not 'zbin'," Inez said. 'Spin' and 'pin' a few times and decided that perhaps there was a difference after all, but not very much.

Having been formally seconded by William, at the Minister's behest, to the SHIP project, the following day Julian threw himself avidly into his studies. His work for the Health and Reproduction Department had, until now, drawn only on his medical expertise. Now he had an excuse to brush up not just his languages, but the wider interest in human intercommunication of which they were a part, namely Comparative Linguistics. He had often wondered idly if he should have taken up that offer of a Chair in Comparative Philology at Cambridge, and what his life might have been like if he had.

Inez asked him, when he came down for coffee midmorning, how the new project he was involved in was going. He said it would be interesting working out how exactly to communicate with sapes.

"Almost everyone in the world seems to speak English nowadays, but they don't speak any language at all, do they?" said Inez.

"But perhaps they could manage to understand English commands, and even communicate with a mixture of vocalised sounds and sign language. Of course, it may not be anything like the SVO language that we are used to." Inez raised her eyebrows questioningly and Julian added, "Most European languages are SVO – subject, verb, object; **I ate the apple, you like knitting, he will dig the garden** and so on. But there are other languages which are SOV or OVS or any of the six possible arrangements of the three terms. Which, if any, will come most naturally to sapes is anybody's guess." He paused to pick a fragment of dead leaf out of her hair – she had been busy in the garden that morning, as so many mornings.

"Maybe they will find word order unimportant, like in Latin or classical Greek, where inflections indicate what part of speech a word is. Very handy for poets. It's only in mediaeval Latin and more modern, advanced languages where word order, prepositions and other 'helping' words have taken over the job of endings."

"Word order isn't that important – you can say either 'I gave him it' or 'I gave it him'."

"But that's because we only give things to people, not the other way round. You can't say, 'I introduced him her'."

Inez had had a good education, and naturally spoke Spanish fluently – or had done, it was now a little rusty from disuse. She had often wanted to take a more active interest in languages, but Julian had always been so busy. He went on. "They've made studies, and researchers have identified a range of distinguishable sounds that sapes can make, expressing simple feelings, wants or desires."

Julian carried out various Internet searches into all aspects of sapes over the next couple of days and was contacted in the late afternoon of the second by William, who wanted him to come up to town as soon as possible. So, he set off the following morning, catching the usual train and arrived at the Department some minutes after nine o'clock. There, he was in for a shock. Things had moved apace since his meeting with Sandy a week earlier. Sandy was there this morning too, and Julian never discovered whether he had returned to Edinburgh after their meeting or had stayed on in London.

William introduced Julian to Rodney Follet and Davina Bagley, two new recruits to Sandy's Edinburgh team reporting to G, P & P, recently graduated in psychology and veterinary science, respectively.

"They'll be working here in the Department, where they'll spend most of their time with Emma," said Sandy. Seeing Julian's blank look.

"Hasn't William told you?"

"Told me what?" Sandy explained that there was to be resident female sape in the Department.

"Rodney and Davina will spend their time exploring ways of developing communication with it. See if you can find them," he said to Davina, who returned a minute later with the sape and Rachel.

"But you can't keep a sape here, in the Department," expostulated Julian. "Where would it sleep, and who would be responsible for it when the Department's deserted?"

"She's living with me, and we come in together each morning. I've bought this dress for her; it's rather fetching, don't you think?" said Rachel proudly.

"What do you feed her on?" asked Julian.

"Oh, she's no trouble at all – a vegetarian diet; bananas, mixed dried fruit and she loves roasted salted peanuts."

"All animals love salt, they know instinctively that it's good for them," said Davina.

"And she said she loves chocolate," added Rachel.

"Said? You're not saying she can talk!" exclaimed Julian.

"I was breaking off a square of chocolate from a bar and she saw me pop it into my mouth with obvious enjoyment. She pointed to the chocolate and mimed taking a square in her fingers and popping it into her mouth."

"Interesting," said Rodney. "A clear sign of some natural degree of intelligence."

"Yes but remember sapes have lived in the Amazon with indigenous humans for centuries if not millennia. The latter have used tamed versions of the former for ages, so it's not surprising if they're used to humans," said Davina.

At that moment, William appeared, and his dark brows gathered in a frown of deep displeasure.

"Oh, I see you know about the animal now, Julian. Not my idea at all. The Minister; I think he must be off his rocker. Can't have thought it through at all. Fortunately, Rachel here has agreed to be the ''esponsible'.'' He pronounced the last word in his best French accent.

Julian eventually managed to disentangle the arrangements: Rodney and Davina were to be funded by G, P & P via Edinburgh University but would be on secondment to the Department. They would have access to Emma for as long as they needed each day, though no specific room had as yet been set aside for them to work in. Rachel was to be responsible for Emma, particularly out of hours and of course at weekends, and Julian learnt that she was to receive a generous allowance in return. How that was to be organised he had no idea; presumably, it would be classed as expenses of some sort, but not of any sort that the financial department would recognise. Meanwhile, during the whole time that Julian was in the Department that day, Emma uttered not a sound.

He returned home that evening and related the events of the day to Inez.

"In the Department? Isn't it all a little unusual?" Inez asked.

Julian exploded, "Unusual? It's positively bizarre! It's all down to the Minister, apparently. I can see William's furious, but he – can't say much. He muttered to me privately he thinks the Minister's gone stark raving mad."

"But tell me more about Emma."

"Cute little thing. Snub nose, soulful eyes, would drive a young male sape wild with desire, I shouldn't wonder. Rachel had her in a brown dress, quite a good match for her arms and legs. And she'd found some small bootees – of some sort, for its – her feet."

"Just a dress? Will that be enough during the winter?"

"I've no idea. They have fur, of course, but just how thick or effective it is I just don't know. But Rachel seems…delighted with her as a companion. I'm sure she'll look after her like a daughter."

The following morning Inez walked into the centre of town to do some shopping. She came back with a bulging shopping bag and a tabloid newspaper, which like the only other tabloid still published, was printed on two folded sheets – just eight sides, twelve at weekends; most people relied mainly on their television sets for news. It was lying on Julian's placemat when he came down for lunch. As he entered the room Inez nodded towards the paper and Julian wondered why she had bought that particular paper, regarded by most as a rag aimed at the least intelligent sector of society. But when he saw the headline he realised why she looked rather thoughtful, not to say worried. **'SERVANT APES THREATEN PEOPLES JOBS'** screamed the banner headline – the paper was commonly lax about apostrophes and other grammatical niceties, knowing that the effort would be lost on the vast majority of its readers. "Just like the Daily Diary. Simian Auxiliary Population Elements is rather a mouthful, that's why the acronym SAPEs was approved, but it never did stand for Servant Apes. They'll be able to raise a furore among the workers' syndicates with that."

"Yes but is it true?" asked Inez.

"Indisputably no. Well, not the job of anyone who didn't completely waste his time at school. Sapes are widely employed in some countries to pick crops like vining peas, fruit, cotton, hops and so on. They're taught to leave unripe tomatoes and only pick the red ones, for example, so we know they have colour vision. And they're good at digging and hoeing and things like that. But with the ever-growing shortage of human workers for jobs requiring a bit more intelligence, they don't really represent a threat to the sort of jobs that any human would like." Inez qualified this reply with an 'at present', and a worried frown.

Just at that moment Jim, who was staying with them, walked in. He too had been into town but had not met Inez there; she had left home a little later than he. He went straight up to his mother and put his arms around her in a bear hug.

"Guess what?"

"Let go, so I can breathe," she gasped; he did so.

"You and Rosemary have got engaged at long last." He looked crestfallen at the complete failure of his intended surprise.

"How did you guess?"

"I haven't been your mother for twenty-six years without learning to read you like a book. Anyway, we're both delighted, aren't we?" She turned to Julian.

"Certainly. And about high time too. You could have married her years ago."

"Yes, but at the time we weren't exactly in love, just more like brother and sister. That's what made it easy for the Carpenters and you to persuade us that we ought to go on to higher education first."

Julian was quite correct; in view of the continuing decline in world population, the legal age for marriage in Britain and most other countries had been lowered a century previously to fifteen for females, and then just twenty-seven years ago to fifteen for males and fourteen for females, in view of the fact that human fecundity was at its greatest following puberty.

"But don't you go on and delay having your first for years, like so many couples do," said Inez. She was thinking of a recent report on television they had seen about couples delaying having a baby because of the costs, only to find later that then they couldn't.

Julian added, "At least, don't use oral contraceptives. That report from the Hunter Medical School's research department reckoned that using them for any period could possibly cause permanent infertility. It even recommended banning their sale and use. After all, there's always condoms." Jim blushed: Here were his parents talking about the most intimate part of his married life, and he had only just that minute got engaged.

[Every live birth was seen as an important addition to the human stock, and legislation passed seventy years ago had made abortion illegal, with but two exceptions. One was the case of an ectopic pregnancy – though these were often managed successfully to full term, and the other was in the case of rape, and even then only if tests showed that the offspring would be male, though this provision had raised furious debate when brought in, and still did so from time to time. Men who had had more than one child were encouraged to offer their services, with the agreement of all parties, to childless wives in the hope that they were not in fact barren. The problem of keeping track of the parentage of any resultant offspring, to avoid problems due to consanguinity in marriages of later generations, was deemed too difficult to administer. So known fertile men were required to offer their services to households at least 500km away from where they lived.]

Jim and Rosemary had been childhood sweethearts at school, but her parents had moved to Cumberland when she was sixteen, and it had faded out. They had intended to keep in touch, but somehow it had lapsed. The idea had been to keep in touch by post, so they could say whatever they wanted in more privacy than email, but neither had proved a good letter writer. For some years now, since obtaining a higher degree, Jim had held a good post in a firm of economic analysts and found that one of his colleagues had relatives in Cumberland. Chatting over lunch one day, the village to which Rosemary's family had moved was mentioned. Jim asked if he knew the Carpenter family, to which the answer had been, "Yes, well."

So it was that he got in touch with Rosemary again by v-phone, just three months ago. He found that she was now a beautiful slim young woman with finely chiselled features but a rather pointed nose, long hair of a warm chestnut colour and standing, at a guess, about five centimetres taller than Inez. She had left home to train and was now working as a nurse specialising in obstetrics and gynaecology in – to Jim's amazement – the Southeast Regional Hospital in Tunbridge Wells, a huge establishment serving much of southeast England. Perhaps this explained why he had arrived, at short notice the day before, for a week's holiday with his parents. From his family home, he could see Rosemary whenever they had a spare moment, rather than travelling from his bachelor flat in Bromley, which was conveniently situated within walking distance of the offices of Baker and Daley, where he hoped soon to become a partner. Jim had with him a beautifully wrapped parcel that Inez guessed was a present for Rosemary. Julian saw her nod significantly in its direction and spoke, "I suppose you want to borrow my bike again?" Jim blushed, nodded in agreement and was soon cycling swiftly away to the other side of town, where Rosemary shared a flat with another nurse. Julian and Inez wondered when the wedding would be, and if they would soon find themselves grandparents. Or not; after all, they had had only the one child, and many young couples they knew of were childless.

Chapter 9
Demijohns 2291AD

Easter was approaching, and Inez was glad to have seen the back of winter. Jim and Rosemary had married just three months after Jim's unexpected visit and had settled in Tunbridge Wells. Since the wedding – already seven years ago, Inez reflected – Jim had continued to work for Baker and Daley, but from his home. Those seven years had seen Inez's health gradually worsen. Julian was puzzled; his medical knowledge told him that there was no one specific cause of her general decline, which must therefore be due to a number of unknown factors, making it difficult to see just what to do about it. She was however delighted that she now had a bonny fair-haired grandson Harry, just coming up to five years of age. But there was no sign of another grandchild, although Rosemary had told her on more than one occasion how much she wanted another child, be it boy or girl.

At 17.15, Julian came down from his office, gave Inez his customary pre-dinner kiss, and poured them both an aperitif. Inez served him up a meal that had always been Jim's favourite as a lad – crispy cheese-balls with deliciously gooey centres, sautéed potatoes and green broccoli, a recipe passed on to Inez by Kitty soon after she had married Julian. Jim would have loved it, had he still been living at his parents' home. It was accompanied, for Inez, by a glass of white wine from one of the many vineyards dotting the southeast of the country, and by a glass of his homemade blackberry wine for Julian. He had picked the blackberries the previous autumn, with a (very) little help from Harry. They had gathered about seven or eight kilos, enough for three 'demijohns', an archaic measure, but the large glass containers had been handed down the generations in Julian's family for over two centuries. Each demijohn had cleared beautifully all by itself, the sediment dropping down completely once the fermentation had finished, making racking unnecessary. Each produced enough wine to fill four one litre wine bottles and a little over. He was already on the fifth bottle, and vowed, as he did every year, to make more next.

He wondered whether to tell Inez his news or keep it for later. In the end, he decided that they should at least enjoy the rest of that day, and they had, unusually, a glass of Cointreau each with their coffee. The liqueur had been very expensive, the restrictions and surcharges on the transport of non-essential goods between countries meant, they knew, that as far as alcohol was concerned, it was only economic to import liqueurs and the very most expensive of wines.

The following day when Julian came down midmorning for coffee, he wondered whether to tell Inez, but somehow, he didn't, nor at lunch either. When he came down from his office for more coffee at 15.00 hours, he decided that it had to be done. He explained that the continuing decline in world population was causing such alarm that the U.N. had decided that from now on, there would be a WPC every eight years, instead of every fifteen. This meant that the next Conference would be later that year, in mid-October, and it would be held in Helsinki. William Hacker had wanted to go himself, but his poor health, entailing complicated medication, rendered that inadvisable. Julian, at 61, was in much better health and had again been selected to represent the Department, as one of the British delegation.

Inez listened to the news in silence, and when Julian had finished, she looked very pale; he could see that she was on the point of tears but was bravely holding them back. With the almost universal adoption of home-working a century and more ago, wives were used to their husbands always being on hand to deal with any emergency or upset, however little. This only partially compensated, it was true, for the fact that one's husband was constantly under ones feet, leaving a wife little time to herself. Not that Inez ever did anything that she didn't want her husband to know about on the rare occasions he was absent; it was just the feeling that then she could please herself entirely as to when she did what, providing her with a precious little 'space' to herself.

True Julian had occasionally to go to London for a special meeting, but he was rarely away for more than a day, most business being conducted by email, v-phone or, occasionally, post. Secretly, Inez had come to value the odd day when Julian was away on business, provided he was home by nightfall.

Julian put his arm around her, but she moved away, evidently not in the mood to be comforted. When he had gone to the 7th WPC, Inez had been that much younger: Now, she was not only eight years older but felt even older still.

"Why couldn't someone else go, why does it always have to be you?" she asked, in a challenging, almost angry, tone. Julian didn't know what to say; a thousand thoughts flashed through his mind. 'Always' was surely a little unfair, he had only ever been to three before, the 5th, 6th and 7th WPCs. So, he had, it was true, but the 5th was before he met Inez. Should he explain that William's declining health might mean that he would have to give up work soon? That Julian was in a good position to succeed him as head of the Department? That that would bring a substantially increased salary, and a much larger pension when in his turn he eventually might have to retire? But he judged that she was not in the mood to listen to any arguments he might adduce, however relevant they might be. So, he elected to say nothing, knowing that in a few days' time, when the unpalatable fact had had time to be digested, she would listen to and accept the arguments, albeit grudgingly. Not with any equanimity, of course, but he knew she was an eminently practical woman, who managed life's ups and downs with a certain degree of fortitude.

The summer had passed, Inez had felt much better throughout, and the flowerbeds had done wonderfully well, especially the lavatera that she had raised in the spring. The seed she had saved from the previous year's flowers, leaving off deadheading several of the most vigorous plants near the end of the season, and collecting almost an egg cupful of seed from the dried seed heads. Now, autumn was unmistakably on its way; the nights were drawing in, the day had been miserably cold and wet for late September, and Inez was feeling depressed.

In only three weeks Julian will be leaving for the 8th WPC in Helsinki, well two and a bit really, and winter will be well on the way by then, she thought and sighed. As they ate their dinner that evening Julian noticed how subdued she was and knew only too well the cause. He felt so helpless; there was really very little, if anything, that he could do about it.

The following morning dawned bright and clear, if a little chilly, and he walked into the centre of town and bought a large bunch of flowers, a small phial of Inez's favourite perfume and a large box of her favourite chocolates. When he arrived back, Inez pretended to be very pleasantly surprised and kissed him on the cheek, though he could see that it had not in fact cheered her up very much. She spoke, "By the way, there's a message for you on the v-phone."

"I'll listen to it as soon as we've had a cup of coffee." Inez was already preparing it: She had found out before their marriage, in the early days before they were even engaged, that Julian was a coffee addict.

"It's not on the answerphone bit, it's from Hal and he's left you a fax message."

They sat down to their coffee. The previous year her occasional severe stomach pains had been diagnosed as ulcers, although these were now completely under control with the aid of Zenodec, the latest in a long line of steadily improved drugs developed from the original Ranitidine. But she had been advised that she should avoid coffee, or at least caffeine, so they had changed to decaffeinated beans. Julian needed a 'fix', as Inez termed it, of coffee every hour or so throughout the day and had a filter machine in his office, besides coming down for a cup with her mid-morning and mid-afternoon. He had been dismayed at the thought of having 'decapitated', as he called it. But after trying it for a week or so, they tacitly agreed that running two separate coffee pots, one 'decaf' and one not, was too much trouble. He found that it must be some of the other ingredients in coffee, or just the taste of the stuff that he craved and was now quite used to decaffeinated. However, to get a decent tasting cup, he used about 50% more beans than before. This was a not inconsiderable expense, since like all products carted halfway round the world, the artificially high transport costs made the beans costly.

After coffee, Julian went up to his office, bent over to the v-phone control box and pulled a sheet of paper with Hal's message on it out of the integral fax. It said, "Hello you old reprobate, expect to see you at the WPC. You can expect some surprises. Both on and off the agenda. See you, Hal." Julian wondered what was in store but was little the wiser when William emailed him the Conference Agenda, travel arrangements and other details a week later.

The day before his departure dawned, and Inez helped him pack, without a murmur or a reproach, for which he was thankful, though he could sense the undercurrent of disappointment, and a distinct tinge of resentment, at his leaving. She had bought him some new pullovers when he got back from the previous WPC, and he insisted that these were still entirely serviceable. Inez thought otherwise; the sleeves were not ragged or anything like that, it was true, but they had obviously been washed a good few times. However, she did not insist, though in Helsinki in mid-October it was more than just likely that he would need them.

The following morning was misty and moist, and they ate their breakfast in silence. Julian had certainly not feared that there might be a scene when the time came to leave, but quite expected a certain coldness. But on the contrary, Inez clung to him tightly and with their arms around each other, they kissed tenderly. After a few moments, she gave him a last squeeze and released him. He turned and left, glad that the parting had been so understanding, and full of quiet admiration for the woman he had married thirty-six years earlier. At the end of the road, there was the same driver who had taken him to the ferry eight years earlier. On the way to the airport, he inquired whether it was the same car as last time, to which the driver replied with a laugh that it certainly was, "This old bus will outlast me, and my successor too, probably, if there's anyone still left alive then." He was voicing a fear that was being expressed in the papers; the rumour was that the decline in world population was still continuing relentlessly, if not faster than ever.

They were heading for Heathrow. In earlier times, it might have been Gatwick, but with the greatly reduced population and the restrictions on flying, that airport had been closed half a century earlier, and other closures had followed since then. On the way to the airport, they passed through farmland – fields and orchards – and saw many sapes busily at work. They were now a common sight, with their lightweight denim trunks and jackets, and specially shaped footwear, rather like trainers. The sick in-joke had long been that when the human race had disappeared, the sapes would inherit the earth. But it had fallen out of favour as people realised that it might be uncomfortably near the truth unless the scientists could discover the cause of humanity's low fertility and find a remedy.

At the airport, he met Hal and Sarah and they went along to find some coffee while waiting for their flight. In the coffee bar, Julian recognised a number of faces he had not seen for a while. There was Scythrop Read, looking wrinkled and much older than his fifty-five years, yet somehow the overall affect was a distinct improvement; he now looked positively distinguished instead of eminently forgettable. Dick Bailey, six years younger, could have been taken for someone in his mid-thirties, lucky fellow. Also, there were Dr Frayne Wilberton from the Gerontology Department of Southampton University, now nearing his sixties; and Sandy McIntosh, with grey hair that rendered his nickname puzzling to people who met him for the first time. Seeing a strange face, Julian said, "Excuse me, I don't think we've met?"

"I'm Richard O'Shea, always called 'Dick' rather than 'Rick', for obvious reasons."

Sandy raised his eyebrows and said, "Er," adding after a moment's thought, "oh, of course; who would want to be called an errant bullet?"

Dick O'Shea was a tall heavily built thirty-year old with heavy brows and heavy 'horn-rimmed' spectacles rather like Dr Wilberton's, except that his were black rather than brown. Dick had a slight stoop and a wild mane of hair so dark brown it appeared almost black. So, the tally of the British Delegation was seven persons; Hal did not count of course, he was there on behalf of his paper.

During the flight Julian found himself sitting next to Dr O'Shea, and asked what branch of medicine he specialised in.

"Oh, no." Laughed Dick. "I took a PhD in economics, and I've worked for the same firm all my life, pretty well. I've been co-opted from my firm by the Treasury Department, to keep an eye on the economic implications of population decline for fiscal policy."

Julian said that his son was in economics and inquired which firm his new acquaintance worked for and was told 'Baker and Daley'.

"Then you might know my son Jim Brophy."

"Ah of course. But he's in a different department of the firm, still, I should have recalled his name, sorry. Yes, he arrived straight from college. Oh, it must be ten years ago at least."

"Er," Julian did some quick thinking, "thirteen, in fact."

"Do I gather that you're a doctor?"

"No. Originally I was a journalist and linguist, but after I joined the Department of Health and Reproduction, they arranged for me to study medicine part time, specialising in Anatomy."

"You must be a rare bird, then. Isn't that the least popular of all the various medical specialisations?"

"Well, yes, it is in fact. But it's a very important one, for all that."

The conversation drifted on to other matters and when it finally petered out altogether Dick pulled a book of cryptic crossword puzzles out of his pocket. He couldn't help a smile when Julian pulled out a similar book, full of other puzzles from the same newspaper.

The plane arrived on time and following the completion of the usual formalities they were ferried to their hotel. The reception area was on the first floor of a tall building, the ground floor being a shopping mall. They booked in, then took the lift to their various rooms, having arranged to meet later for dinner. The lift sped up to the fifteenth floor, where three of their number got out, then to the seventeenth where the rest got out, with the exception of Julian, who was on the twenty second. Finding he had come down to dinner a little earlier than the rest, he looked around the spacious foyer, and collected a leaflet or two about the sights of the city, although it was unlikely that he would have the opportunity to visit any of them. He noticed the key rack behind the receptionist had spaces for rows of 'keys' – the usual credit-card sized affairs with a couple of microprocessors inside – for the fifteenth to twenty fifth floors, and in reply to his query, the receptionist explained that the floors between reception and the bedrooms were occupied by commercial offices, adding that many hotels in Helsinki were combined with office accommodation like that.

The others arrived, one by one except for Hal and Sarah, who, Julian had noticed, had got out of the lift on the same floor. They all drifted into the bar, and after an aperitif went into dinner. There were four other national delegations in that particular hotel, and each had been given a separate table. The Germans, the Guatemalans and the Chinese were all conversing volubly in their own language, but the Indians, from various parts of that vast continent, were all using English as their lingua franca. Hal commented that it might have been more interesting if the delegates had all been mixed up in multinational groups.

"I suppose so," said James, "but there might have been a problem with communications – still I suppose that any delegates here will probably have pretty good command of English."

"It wouldn't worry him," grunted Hal nodding in the direction of Julian.

"Don't you believe it; my Spanish is a little rusty and my German even more, and I never did have more than a few words of Mandarin. Those four tones in Chinese can get you into real trouble, speaking it. Depending which tone you use, 'ma' can mean either mother-in-law or horse."

After a few other pleasantries, the conversation drifted on to speculation as to what surprises, if any, the opening session of the Conference would bring, and the tone became more serious, not to say sombre. Hal muttered something about surprises in store but would not be drawn to be more specific.

At the opening session in the conference hall the following morning, the Prime Minister of Finland formally opened the proceedings with quite a short speech which, however, contained one disturbing item of news. The latest survey of world population, carried out by UNACOPS, the United Nation's Advisory Committee on Population Statistics, reported that since the seventh WPC in 2284, the population of the world had fallen from thirty seven percent to thirty two point five percent of the figure at the beginning of the millennium. This was faster than a straight-line extrapolation would predict, and clearly implied the most serious consequences for mankind.

The following paper was on extensive tests which had been carried out by a subcommittee of UNACOPS, for correlation between various chemicals which were known to have a higher than average density in specific areas, and fecundity of the population in those same areas. The problem was that of finding control areas with the same level of other pollutants as the area under investigation – the perennial multi-variable problem. The paper was presented by Jan Plessner from Poland, and Julian remembered he was the son of Dr Plessner whom both he and Bill had met years ago. The rest of the day passed with more papers, each of which was of some interest to one or other of the British Delegation, and various of them were discussed by the delegates over dinner that evening.

"The baffling thing is that there was still no real progress in determining the cause of the poor fertility exhibited by all strains of the human race," said Julian.

Sarah said, "I wonder if any progress could be achieved by studying sapes, they seem to be immune to the problem which so dogs humanity."

The following day, the second paper presented dealt with exactly the type of study that Sarah had proposed the previous night, a study which had in fact been in progress for over twenty-five years. It outlined some proposed avenues for further research but reported little if any substantial progress to date. That evening, the conversation over dinner was definitely subdued, and Julian had the feeling that Hal was keeping something back. The members of the Delegation sat on at the table long after the last course, discussing the papers read earlier that day, and then moved off into the lounge, as the staff wanted to ready the tables for breakfast the next day. The discussion continued till 21.15, when the group broke up and retired to their rooms.

Julian did not feel at all tired and settled down to catch up on the happenings in the world at large with the aid of the English language teletext channel on the room's television set. He followed that with reading a few pages of a science fiction novel he had brought with him to read on the plane. The novel described a future world in which there seemed to be pressures of neither over or under-population nor yet any shortage of energy and plans for exploring other planetary systems in this and adjacent galaxies were far advanced. The whole scenario seemed too facile to convince anyone with even a modest scientific background, and Julian put the book down and wondered what to do. He wasn't in the least tired and clearly would not get to sleep, so there seemed no point in going to bed yet. He put his jacket on again and went back down to the lounge where the bar was now closed, though there was a help-yourself coffee dispensing machine.

Pushing the appropriate buttons, he called up a cappuccino and waited the fifteen or so seconds for the machine to dispense the beverage. Picking up the paper cup and turning round, he noticed Hal sitting deep in thought in a dim recess at the far end of the lounge. He walked over and as he sat down nearby, Hal said, "So, you couldn't sleep either?" Julian nodded his assent and then challenged.

"You're holding out on us about something or other aren't you; come on now, what is it?"

"Since you ask, I'll tell you. It's not the sort of thing I could have said over dinner, with ladies present." He was referring, of course, to Sarah, and took out his handkerchief, blowing his nose noisily.

"I've known for some time something like this was in the wind, but it's only recently I've had confirmation from –" He paused. "Some of your contacts." Julian filled in for him, knowing that Hal was obsessively secretive about their identities.

"Yes, well, it started with rumours about a youngish widower in Lima, who had a female sape as a domestic, one of the larger breeds originally from the agricultural bloodline. It was said he slept with her. Then there was a sapess in Chiclayo who appeared to suffer from nymphomania; always looking for a male in any shape or form to mate with, sape or human. An enterprising sape-breeding consortium bought both the animals and bred from them both, crossing the progeny. They were only interested in the females, raising just the odd one or two males for further breeding; you know, the usual electro-gradient sperm separation process. Apparently it's been going on for umpteen generations. They finished up with a line of sapesses who are extraordinarily sexually compliant."

"What was the point of all this?" asked Julian. Hal gave him an old-fashioned look, such as an adult might give an innocent child who hasn't cottoned on.

"Most of the brothels in South America are nowadays partly staffed by female sapes, some of them entirely so. At first, the Mesdames thought they would have to charge less for a sapess than a woman, but soon found that this wasn't so; some even charge a premium – apparently the creatures have proved very popular, due to their obliging ways. There are lots of brothels in South-East Asia using them too, and I recently heard of a couple in Germany and one in

Italy." Julian could quite see it was not a topic to be floated in general conversation and wondered just what Inez would say, if she ever heard of it.

Their conversation drifted onto the subject of the papers to be presented the next day. One intriguing one was entitled 'Aspects of Sub-Atlean Fecundity', to be presented by Hercules Grönemeyer of the Institute Pasteur, Paris, also Visiting Professor of Human Biology at the University of Algiers. Several other papers sounded distinctly academic, and Julian and Hal agreed in forecasting that they would prove not only boring but of little value. In the event, come the following day, they were proved right, but they were looking forward to Dr Grönemeyer's paper, which was scheduled as the last of the day's proceedings. At the end of the very boring penultimate paper, there was an audible sense of expectation, shuffling of feet, people sitting forward on the edge of their seats, rustling of programmes.

However, Jan Plessner, the chairman of the session, did not introduce the speaker, but instead announced that Dr Grönemeyer was unfortunately not present, due to a transport problem on his way to the airport. Moreover, copies of his paper had only just arrived and had still to be unpacked and collated with some inserts covering last minute additions. That day's proceedings would therefore end with an unscheduled opportunity for further questions from the floor to the presenters of the other papers. It soon became clear that the questions forthcoming, mostly barely relevant, were almost exclusively being asked by delegates from minor states, anxious to have their names appear in the Proceedings, to impress their governments. Julian was sitting at the opposite end of the same row as Hal and Sarah. Hal and Julian looked at each other, and by mutual unspoken agreement, they got up and left with Sarah, along with a number of other delegates.

Back at the hotel, they met Scythrop Read and Dick Bailey, who had evidently also opted out of the proceedings, and at dinner they were joined by Drs Haggerty and Wilberton, and Sandy McIntosh, completing the British Delegation. Their conversation ranged far and wide but returning always to the fundamental problem faced by humanity, which the Conference was supposed to be addressing. There was general curiosity about Dr Grönemeyer's paper, but they would have to wait in patience until tomorrow, which was the last day of the Conference.

Coming down again, late in the evening, as on the previous day, he found Hal, Sarah and Frayne Wilberton deep in conversation. He joined the group and listened.

"The real mystery is why anything at all should exist," said Sarah.

"Quite," said Frayne. "It is universally accepted that the known laws of physics cannot be expected to hold through a singularity, such as the big bang."

"Consequently, what existed before that, if anything at all, is inherently unknowable, at least to humans," added Sarah.

"You mean, but not to some discarnate intelligent spirit, possibly?" asked Hal, the hard-bitten reporter, sardonically.

"Well, everything that exists needs something else outside itself, to explain its existence, so I don't see why that doesn't apply to the whole universe itself," she replied.

"As neat a modern exposition of the contingency argument as you could wish," said Julian, at which Frayne raised his eyebrows questioningly.

"What's that?"

"One of Thomas Aquinas's five ways," said Julian.

"And who's he? When he's at home?"

"One of a twelfth and thirteenth century school of Dominican Philosopher Theologians, with an interest in cosmology. He tried to unravel the secrets of the universe, though rather limited by the little scientific knowledge of the day. What there was, was largely derived from Aristotle and while Aristotle's logic was impeccable his physics was more than a bit wide of the mark any way, which didn't help matters. No, I've a lot of respect for the Schoolmen, one way and another. But I say, what a contrast to our chat last night," said Julian, looking at Hal, and immediately wished he hadn't.

"What was that all about then," asked Sarah curiously.

"The history of head-hunting in Micronesia," replied Hal, without a moment's hesitation. Julian knew, from his brief years as a junior reporter, that one always had to be prepared with a ready reply at need; he wondered whether Hal had thought it up on the spur of the moment, or, since it was so prompt, whether he had a stock of such replies, long prepared. To change the subject he ventured,

"What a deep Philosophical conversation – I didn't think that women were interested in such abstract speculation." Sarah rounded on him.

"Why shouldn't we be? Just because for the last twenty thousand years or more we've been expected to spend our time cooking and mending men-folks' clothes!"

"Sorry." Julian was smiling. "It's just that Inez always says that women are more interested in people, and men are more interested in things. Of course, I quite accept that, on average, women have the same I.Q. as men. But perhaps it was unfortunate that the Good Lord, if there is one, endowed the ladies with so much more intelligence than is necessary for the role of wife and mother."

Hal said, "Hello, we're back to a discarnate intelligent spirit again." While Sarah, good-humouredly feigning anger, swung her handbag at Julian's head. Hal growled, "You really will have to be more careful what you say while Sarah's around." With all this talk of philosophy, a little knot of bystanders had gathered.

Sam said, "Talking of philosophers, did you know that the philosopher Hegel invented the Bagel?"

"Exceedingly unlikely," said Henri, followed by cries of 'Let the lad talk' and 'what's this about, Hegel' etc., from people who could sense a story.

Sam obliged by saying, "Well then, ladies and gentlemen, as I was saying, the philosopher Hegel invented the bagel, he admired its density, his writings share that propensity."

Chapter 10
Music, Art and Nightcaps

Julian got up a few minutes later than usual and took a cold shower to wake himself up. He had slept fairly well, but they had not got to bed till later than usual the previous night. Inez had been pumping him all evening as to what had gone on at the 8th WPC, from which he had arrived home late in the afternoon. After briefly describing the contents of some of the more interesting papers, he had incautiously mentioned Hal's habit of secrecy and somehow or other she had extracted the information about the employment of sapesses for immoral purposes.

"Ugh, how disgusting. Really – men!" She exclaimed in a voice which showed her contempt and loathing for that half of the human race.

"Not all men," he countered mildly.

"No, not all men," she repeated sarcastically, in a tone that suggested she exonerated Julian, her son Jim and possibly as many as half a dozen other males throughout the entire world. Julian saw that the subject was best left severely alone and went to get himself a cup of coffee.

Now, after a night's sleep, a shower and some breakfast, he was glad to forget yesterday and get on with his SHIP work. Following up something he had found during one of his Internet searches, he had contacted a worker at the Harvard Medical School, name of Terry Harbottle, who turned out to have been a student under Sam Goldsmith. Terry emailed him a long paper produced at Harvard M. S., that he had contributed to. This addressed the sape/human intercommunication problem directly and proved most interesting. It appeared that studies had shown that sapes were not only capable of but actually did produce a surprising variety of sounds. They did not vocalise a great deal, but could produce a variety of fricatives, including 's', 'f', 'sh', 'ch' as in 'loch' as well as a deeper, more guttural 'ch' as found in the speech of amerindian tribesmen in the rain forest from which they originated. They also used three vowel sounds and a few plosives and labials, so that all the essentials were there for a limited kind of speech. Interestingly, the more intelligent ones proved excellent mimics, and could often repeat a whole sentence in a rather indistinct way, though of course with no idea what it meant. Unless, that is, they had been coached. Nouns they readily learnt to understand, starting with things that had immediate significance to them, such as the fruit on which they lived in the wild – although in captivity, they readily took to foods on which it was more convenient to feed them, such as bread and potatoes.

They also fairly readily learnt the significance of verbs, starting with ones of immediate interest or relevance, such as 'eat', 'stand', 'sit' etc. Some adjectives were or could become meaningful to them, including 'red' and 'green', so it was clear that they had colour vision. Abstract adjectives such as 'wise', 'uneventful' etc. they could not comprehend, and it was surmised that they never would be able to. Still, sapes were schooled, before sale, in a vocabulary of up to a hundred or more words relating to the sort of work they were expected to perform, be it agricultural, domestic or whatever, and easily learnt extra words 'on the job'. Besides understanding simple commands, sapes were capable of communicating with their owners in a simple way, for example saying 'broom, broom', if unable to find it, when asked to sweep up.

It was late afternoon, and Julian had been studying the Harvard report all day, apart from lunch and the inevitable innumerable cups of coffee. His line of thought was interrupted when Inez marched up the stairs carrying a large brown envelope, fully two centimetres thick. It had just been delivered by their usual postman, who had apologised for the delay in delivery, due to problems with his bicycle. Julian put it on one side while he finished some notes he had been preparing on the word processor, to be incorporated later into his contribution to the SHIP report. Inez had thoughtfully brought up another cup of coffee with the brown envelope, and after taking a deep sip and sighing with satisfaction – Inez made wonderful coffee – he set about opening the envelope, wondering what it could be. It turned out to be the missing paper from the 8th WPC, 'Aspects of Sub-Atlean Fecundity' and some other papers with a compliments slip/letter regretting that due to a misunderstanding, they had not been available for delegates to collect on the last day of the Conference, as planned.

"What's all that about?" Inez had asked.

"I've no more idea than you, till I read it," Julian had replied, and set about doing just that.

He was still engrossed in it when Inez called up for the second time to tell him dinner was ready and only when she called a third time, in an exasperated tone, did he tear himself away from it.

"What was so interesting that it kept you away from your dinner? Not something else as disgusting as what you told me about yesterday?"

"No, no, of course not. Sorry, love, if I'd known what it was I'd have been down straight away." He was looking at one of Inez's specials. In principle, it was only a pizza, but the base was homemade – and he knew of no one else who did not use a ready-prepared pizza base from the freezer cabinet, or more likely still, buy a ready-made pizza. Moreover, instead of the usual miserable thin scrape of tomato sauce with an odd olive half or two or a scrap of salami, Inez's topping was two to two and a half times as thick as the base itself, and rich with scraps of bacon, salami, chipolatas, olives, onions, cardamoms and capers, in a rich creamy tomato based sauce, all glazed with a generous sprinkling of melted grated cheese. No other accompaniments to the meal were either provided or needed, apart of course for a glass of dryish white wine; the meal would leave them not only full but not wanting any supper either. Afterwards, Julian brought Inez a cup of coffee and a glass of her favourite Limoncello liqueur, which he had brought back for her from Helsinki. She had thanked him, commenting that it must have been expensive, for lemons certainly did not grow in Finland, despite the changes in the weather that had occurred in the last two hundred years.

In return for her providing one of his favourite meals, Julian insisted on doing the washing and drying up, usually he did one and she the other. He went out to the kitchen and started, but halfway through, Inez came out, picked up a teacloth and started doing the wiping up. He half protested, but Inez said not to be silly, it would be finished much more quickly like this, a piece of feminine logic with which he was unable to argue. He soon realised that what had really brought her out, was curiosity about the contents of the brown envelope. To her annoyance, he seemed deliberately evasive, and finally she said, "I suppose it really is something as disgusting as what you told me about last night, then?"

"No, I'll tell you all about it when I've finished this – he waved at the washing up, there was still a baking tray and two saucepans to do – don't want to finish up dropping something." And Inez had to be content and wait until everything had been washed up, dried, put away and the working surfaces and cooker wiped down.

They were back in the cosy lounge, and could barely hear the late October rain, driven by a bitter wind, against the windows. All new houses had long been required to be built with foam-filled cavity walls and triple glazing, though new builds were rare, given the existing housing stock and the falling population. But their house predated the legislation. However, although the legislation was not retrospective, Julian had checked that the cavity walls were in fact foam-filled and had had secondary glazing installed. This, together plus the original double-glazed windows and extra insulation in the roof, had brought the house up to the current full thermal efficiency standard. So, for most of the year, little if any extra heating was required, beyond that provided by lighting and cooking, the roof mounted solar panel, heat extracted by a heat pump from waste bath, washing and kitchen water before it went down the drain, and body heat – 60 watts per person resting, much more in any activity.

As she settled comfortably in her favourite armchair, Inez said, "Well?" And Julian related as much as he had had time to gather from the report; fortunately, it was prefaced by a synopsis which he had had time to digest before dinner.

"If it'd been presented, it'd have been the one hopeful item in a very sombre and subdued conference. Seems that gradual climate change has actually resulted in increased rainfall all along the various ranges of the Atlas Mountains of North Africa, particularly in Morocco and Algeria. Both the northern and southern flanks of the mountains are wetter, but particularly the south. There's vegetation appearing in areas that've been barren for centuries. A big area of land to the south's become habitable, and both Tuareg and Berbers have been living there for several generations. What's more, the average family raises 2.4 children – more than the minimum needed to sustain a constant population density."

"Aren't Berbers and Tuareg related?"

"Sort of; it's complicated. The Moors of Spain were mainly Berbers, Tuaregs originally lived more to the east. Anyway, mixed marriages are particularly successful, with the few Berber/Tuareg families averaging 2.6 children. Naturally, UNACOPS are particularly interested. The additional rainfall's also raised the water table under the Sahara, and oases not too far from the mountains can now draw enough underground water to irrigate a larger area. They estimate there's now about thirty thousand additional square kilometres of habitable land, and it's increasing all the time."

"Why should mixed marriages do so much better?"

"Hybrid vigour, I guess, although the gene pools of the two groups have an awful lot in common. Anyway, there's a lot of interest and speculation why fecundity's so much better in that part of the world; there are so many unanswered questions. Like, would other nationalities living there do better at raising children too, or only the indigenous races? The report actually suggests young couples of various races, wanting children, could be resettled in that area."

"I shouldn't think that many young couples would want to uproot themselves and live in a strange land thousands of miles away from their home and family," said Inez.

"Don't you be so sure! There are many countries in the world where the majority of the population are poor peasants scraping a miserable living from poor land. Considering the valuable information that might be gained, I should think any one of several UN agencies might be willing to subsidise the experiment, cover transport and re-housing costs and provide farming implements and seed. No, it might not appeal to anyone from Britain, we're all too comfortable, but I bet there'd be no shortage of takers from places like Mexico or Bangladesh."

"I'm sure you're right dear," said Inez, picking up a book she was part way through, and a sweater she was knitting for Harry at the same time.

This was her signal, instantly recognised by Julian, that she had heard all she wanted to know about the subject. He turned on the television to get the news, selecting teletext to avoid disturbing the reading. The news was not good, which was no different from usual. A large multinational company with headquarters in the USA had gone bust, amid claims of monumental fraud on the part of the directors. Researchers at a University in Bulgaria had claimed to have made a breakthrough in identifying factors affecting fertility in city dwellers, but it was now being discounted by several other universities and research centres, among claims that the results had been at least heavily massaged, if not entirely fabricated. A recently emergent country in Southeast Asia had defaulted on interest on a large UN loan and was suffering inflation running at one hundred percent per month. The United Central African Republic had suffered another coup, the president having been murdered in a most grisly fashion, in full view of the populace, via the country's one television channel.

Julian watched the weather forecast, checked the state of the stock market, and switched off. He picked up a book of cryptic crossword puzzles, but found he wasn't concentrating, so he crept upstairs to his office and came down again with the report on Aspects of Sub-Atlean Fecundity. He had hardly opened it when he sensed disapproval, and looking up, saw Inez's eye on him. He knew she did not approve of him working on his job outside office hours, particularly if it took his attention away from her.

"Sorry dear, but you were busy with your book and your knitting, so I thought you wouldn't mind. Besides, I'm curious to know more about this Saharan business."

He got up, poured her a 'sherry', locally produced, and one for himself, took it over to her and picked up the book she was reading. It was a historical novel about the adventures, loves and misfortunes of a young French woman in Paris in the mid twenty-first century.

"I suppose historical novels can be interesting if they throw light on the period they're set in and novels about the future could be useful if they set you thinking about whether things will, or could, turn out as the writer imagines."

"Future generations will always be able to see whether he's right or not, won't they?" said Inez.

"But I really don't see the point in novels about the present. Why imagine fictional characters having all the same problems and disappointments that real people have, isn't there enough trouble in the world already, without inventing more?"

"Yes, but such books become historical novels in due course, don't they? And they're more likely to be true to life than one written by a writer hundreds of years later."

There's no answer to that, thought Julian to himself.

It was spring and Inez's winter depression was lifting by the day. She was busy tidying up the house and garden in preparation for visitors. They had had a Christmas card from Hal and Sarah: Besides the usual seasonal greetings and best wishes for the New Year, there had been a scribbled P.S. to the effect that they were shortly getting engaged. Inez and Sarah had in fact got on famously during her previous visit, almost exactly six years earlier, despite having such different outlooks on life. Ever since, they had kept in touch by letter – Sarah knew that Inez did not like using email, and at the news of Sarah and Hal's engagement, Inez had insisted that they be invited to stay, once the better weather arrived. A date in early April was arranged, when Sarah could get away from her post at Bath University for a few days, and Hal was in between assignments for the Telegraph. Julian too had arranged to take a few days holiday then. Inez had seen to the house in the morning, and after lunch had turned her attention to the garden. Julian called her in for a cup of coffee and a biscuit, a little after mid-afternoon.

"You *have* been busy; don't work yourself into an early grave, love."

"It's all right for you, but someone's got to do it."

"I'm stuck for the moment, waiting for some information to arrive by email; so, can I lend a hand?"

"It's all right, I've nearly finished; just got the roses to prune."

"Well, can I do anything else to help?"

"Yes, you can peel some parsnips to go with the roast, and a few potatoes as well." She knew he just loved roast parsnips, as indeed she did herself.

After dinner, the evening passed quietly and about 21.45 Inez said she was tired and went upstairs to get ready for bed. Shortly after, Julian followed, washed, cleaned his teeth and slipped into bed. As usual, they snuggled up in position one. And as usual, Inez was asleep in seconds, Julian a few minutes later.

Sometime later, they both woke up, turned over, and snuggled up again, Inez's left arm lying across his body and her hand holding him most intimately. Up to a few years ago, this would usually have led on to lovemaking, but now, at sixty-two and feeling unusually tired that night, he quietly savoured the pleasurable sensation. Inez amused herself by occasionally giving it a brief squeeze now and then and feeling it swell up for a second or so.

"Nice, but nothing like the effect Morella had. Oh, so many years ago." Julian enjoyed the sensation awhile, and then gradually drifted off to sleep. Feeling no response to her next squeeze, suddenly Inez was concerned.

Surely he can't have had a heart attack – please not let it be that, she thought but listening and feeling she could detect his regular slow shallow breathing. Thereafter, each turned over from time to time, sometimes sleeping back-to-back, or facing each other or this way or that way. But at six o'clock, they reverted to position one, dozing together until at seven sharp, Whiskey, their black and white cat, meowed and pawed at the bedroom door, coinciding with the time-switch controlled bedside lamp coming on. Julian slipped a dressing gown over his nightshirt, closed the window (Inez always insisted on sleeping with it open, even in the depths of winter) and went downstairs to let the cats out.

Since losing a cat some years before, found run over early in the morning, their cats were kept in overnight, and they were now anxious to go out and patrol their territory – the back garden and the footpath behind it. Whiskey bounded along in front of Julian, down the stairs and along the hall, at the back of which, Shelley the tortoiseshell female appeared from the lounge. She confidently walked into the kitchen ahead of Whiskey, who deferred without a murmur. She's obviously the boss, just like Inez, reflected Julian as they all processed through the kitchen and into the laundry room, where he unlatched the cat flap. He made a cup of coffee for himself and poured out a refreshing glass of orange juice from the fridge for Inez – since the problem of ulcers she no longer fancied coffee, even decaf, first thing in the morning. Before that, the time switch controlling the bedside lamp had also turned on a filter coffee machine each morning, but the machine had worn out, and since he had to come downstairs each morning to let the cats out and fetch chilled orange juice from the fridge for Inez, there was no point in replacing it.

He took the drinks upstairs, slipped back into bed and they watched the rising sun cast a glancing beam of light on the wall next to the window. This faced somewhat east of due north, and the sun had just started to peep into the room first thing in the morning a week or two earlier, in late March, a sure sign that spring had arrived.

"Time to get up – we've visitors arriving today, and there're still some things to sort out," said Inez.

That Friday afternoon Hal and Sarah arrived, ecologically, on a tandem. They were to occupy the visitors' room again, although the single bed they had shared on their previous visit had, in the meantime, been replaced by a double bed. Inez thought it all very strange; she and Julian had first got engaged, then married and only then slept together. Sarah and Hal seemed to be doing it all back to front; she wouldn't have been surprised to hear that they were already married and were now getting engaged afterwards. She knew that in the early years of the millennium, getting wed had for a while largely dropped out of fashion, partly due to the economic advantages of two partners being unmarried. But that had led to family instability and problem children, so a hundred and fifty years ago the law had been overhauled in such a way as to make marriage, as opposed to cohabitation, financially much more attractive.

When Hal had unpacked the two bulging pannier bags from the tandem and carried them up to the visitors' room, they gathered in the sun in the back garden, on folding chairs on the small lawn, around the garden table. Inez fetched a fresh pot of coffee and a plate of small homemade coconut fairy cakes. Julian was despatched to bring some crockery, and they all settled down to a light afternoon tea and the opportunity to catch up on each other's news. Hal had been offered the prestigious post of Assistant Editor but was agonising over whether to accept. It meant he would no longer be involved in globetrotting, possibly an advantage for someone of sixty-two, but he feared it might in practice make it difficult for him to keep up with his extensive portfolio of contacts around the world.

Sarah was considering a move from Bath University to Imperial College; it would mean promotion and greater responsibility and remuneration, but she was not sure she wanted to live in London. However, they would shortly be married and if Hal opted for Assistant Editor and she for Imperial, it would make sense, as they would both need to be in the capital.

"Will you be making your minds up soon?" asked Julian.

"Watch this space," said Hal with a quizzical look.

"And when is the great day?" Inez asked Sarah, who replied, with a maddening touch of vagueness.

"Oh, soon." And that was all they could get out of them on the matter of the forthcoming marriage.

Later that evening, after dinner, they all sat talking in the garden room, only moving back into the house well after dark, as the chilly evening foreboded a cold night. The conversation ranged over a wide field of topics, from the domestic to economics and world affairs and technology. In the latter connection, Sarah asked Julian where he thought the world was going.

"Well, certainly at the turn of the millennium there was great speculation – and trepidation – on that score. I think it was that popular science writer, 'Hot Electron' in his column, 'White Noise' in Electronics World who pointed out that since the first hominids had walked on two legs, it was millions of years before they developed speech. And then hundreds of thousands before they invented writing and thousands before really large empires appeared and then centuries before the printing press – and so it went on." His point was that the increase of knowledge and technology followed an exponential law. Hal took up the tale in his basso-profundo tones.

"The steam train lasted perhaps a hundred and fifty years before being replaced by diesels, and they in their turn barely fifty before being replaced by electric locos. The valve lasted just fifty years before being replaced by transistors, and those barely twenty before being replaced by integrated circuits. And all the time, the population of the world was also increasing exponentially."

"And anyone with even a little higher mathematics knows that an exponential curve with a positive exponent can't go on forever," added Julian.

Inez looked puzzled, and Sarah said, "It's like a chain latter; you're supposed to send twenty euros to the person who sent it to you, and to write to ten other people who are all supposed to send twenty euros to you, and each write to ten other people in their turn, and so on. If it really worked, you'd soon run out of people on the planet to keep the chain going. It just can't keep on and ongoing."

Hal said, "It applies in the arts, too. Early cave paintings were crude monochrome affairs, later came coloured representations of reality, but still crudely flat-looking. Perspective appear didn't appear generally till the fourteenth or fifteenth century."

Julian added, "And music developed in the same way, mere rhythm in some cultures, or simple unaccompanied folksong. Later, you get musical instruments and part-songs and harmony. Fourteenth century music sounds odd to our ears, with a preponderance of bare fourths and sixths; more modern sounding polyphony didn't appear till the next century. Later still, bowed instruments and whole instrumental groups, and the orchestra as we know it."

Inez looked animated and burst out. "Yes, but surely in the arts, your exponential thing came to grief centuries ago." Her favourite composers were all from the eighteenth and nineteenth centuries. "In the twentieth century, music declined again into mere cacophony, although it did improve again slightly after that. And the same in painting; after the glories of the Italian renaissance school and for the next few centuries, it developed steadily, but then declined into childish scribblings, or even just silly plain areas of flat colour."

"A clear case of the Emperor's new clothes," muttered Hal who obviously agreed on this point.

"It all underlined the impossibility of indefinite exponential growth. Politicians used to talk of 'sustainable growth', but even they've long realised it's impossible in the long run," said Julian.

On that note of general agreement, Inez went into the kitchen and prepared a special nighttime drink for them all. She took a bar of chocolate peppermint cream, broke it into pieces and dropped them into the blender. Next she poured on hot milk and blended on maximum speed for twenty seconds. The frothy liquid was poured into four glasses, each containing a dessertspoonful of rum, and topped with a sprinkling of cocoa powder. After their nightcap with biscuits, they all wished each other goodnight and retired.

As she and Julian were getting ready for bed, Inez said, "How Sarah and Hal arrange things is up to them, but I'm glad Jim and Rosemary did things the right way." And Julian knew just what she meant.

"I remember your mother once telling me about a colleague of hers, when she was a young teacher. When she heard. Kitty was expecting, she'd said how much she envied her, how she desperately wanted to have children herself. But the doctor had told her tests indicated she'd got chlamydia and that it'd almost certainly made her sterile. She said she'd never slept with anyone but her husband, but that he'd been in the merchant navy before they met. Can it really do that, and can they be sure it has?"

"Chlamydia can damage the fallopian tubes and cause infertility, yes, and there've been tests for that for years. I know they reckoned once that ten percent of the males in a lot of European countries had chlamydia, but I've no idea what the percentage is now. But it certainly doesn't help with the falling population problem," replied Julian.

And on that mournful note they lay down, eventually going to sleep.

The following morning, while Sarah and Inez were deep in conversation, Julian found a pretext to take Hal out into the garden.

"Tell me, Hal, presumably in a bordello staffed by sapesses, contraception is unnecessary?"

"Yes, that is the case. Fortunately, it appears that, although by cross breeding a donkey with a mare you can get a mule, or a lion with a tigress get a liger, the cross breeds are infertile and cannot breed further. Sapes and humans can no more interbreed than a giraffe with a rhinoceros, but simply because they are not only in different genuses but they're also not even in the same family – they parted company at the next stage up, the order of primates. Though of course there is still always the possibility of a sexually transmitted disease."

Chapter 11
Red Roses and Poison Ivy

Sleep eluded Julian; after the stimulation of the evening's discussions, his mind just 'wouldn't lie down', as he explained it to himself. Besides, Inez was being very attentive, and soon they were fast in each other's arms, just like in the early days of their marriage. Afterwards, they lay together side by side, saying nothing, and eventually did drift off to sleep, tired and satisfied by their exertions.

In the morning, Julian lay with his shoulders on the pillow, his head propped against the bed-head, while Inez lay with her head on his chest, her breasts pressing into his groins, her hips between his knees and her arms around his waist. Soon, he could tell from her deep slow regular breathing that she had gently drifted into unconsciousness. Inez found herself in a part of London she could not quite place, although it was so familiar to her. The weather was bright and warm, and she was wearing a smart costume and high heels, looking with interest at the window displays of the big shops. As she walked along, the shops got smaller and were replaced by faceless offices, and she was somehow aware that there was a man following her. She knew her costume with its brief jacket with peplum and short skirt was figure-revealing and felt uncomfortably exposed. She turned a corner and thought at first that he was gone, but soon was aware – as before, without ever seeing him – that he was still following her. However, she knew exactly what she had to do; she turned another corner, past a coffee shop that seemed vaguely familiar, crossed the road and after another turning, approached the doorway of a big building. She did not quite recognise neither the building nor the doorway, but somehow knew instinctively that they were the right place. Entering, she climbed a flight of stairs round two sides of the stairwell, round the L landing and up another. Stopping outside a door that was not quite like she remembered, but which she knew was the right one, she pressed the bell-push. She heard the steps on the lower staircase slow, falter and stop, as after a few anxious minutes the door opened, and a man was standing there. After a second or so, she recognised it was Julian. She pressed up against him, he put his arms protectively around her and she hugged him fiercely round the waist. She hugged again, so hard that it woke her up, and she was left puzzled and surprised; there had been absolutely no sensation of turning through ninety degrees, from standing to lying down. It was if an earlier vertical existence had just come to an end, and she had commenced a new life lying in Julian's arms.

She described her dream to him, marvelling that unlike her usual dreams – in which she was a purely passive spectator – she had felt in control, able to direct the course of events. He spoke, "That's 'lucid dreaming'. You're fortunate, lots of people never experience lucid dreaming in a lifetime – it's a state in which the brain's not as deeply asleep and passive as in normal dreams." She kissed his chest, snuggled down and dozed until the cats demanded attention. During this interval Julian's thoughts wandered through a thousand byways. Eventually he found himself wondering, he had no idea why, if Inez really loved him, or indeed, if he loved her. Of course, they lived together as man and wife as they had done since their wedding day. Then they had been deeply in love, he with her and, he felt sure, she with him. It certainly wasn't like that now, but then one could not hope that that initial intense love would continue, completely unchanged, throughout a lifetime, he mused. But that did not mean that they did not still love each other, in a sort of way. He decided that the question of whether she loved him, or he her, just had no answer; perhaps it was an irrelevant question or even quite simply a meaningless one. As long as they continued to act as though they loved each other, that was all that mattered; indeed, perhaps acting like that was loving each other, he concluded. At this juncture, Whiskey, the more vociferous of the two cats, meowed loudly, Inez stirred, opened her eyes and murmured ruefully, "Time to get up."

Only three days later, after Hal and Sarah had left, did Julian find out that Inez had powdered a Viagra tablet and stirred it into the peppermint-flavoured milky drink that evening, taking great care to make sure he got the right glass. Later that day, a large bunch of red roses arrived for Inez, accompanied by a card signed by both Sarah and Hal, thanking them for a most enjoyable stay.

Eight weeks later, Inez received a letter from Sarah to the effect that she was pregnant, and the wedding would consequently take place in the summer, or at latest early autumn, before she got too large. When Julian got back from the shops that Friday morning, Inez recounted the news to him, adding, "A postscript said Sarah thought it must have been while they were staying with us."

So, we weren't the only couple making love that night – I wonder if Inez got the glasses mixed up and Hal got the one with Viagra in it, thought Julian. They had a glass of sherry each to celebrate the news, and then, at nine o'clock sharp, Julian went up to his office to get on with the various jobs he had in hand.

No sooner had he sat down than there was a buzz from the v-phone controller on his desk. Julian pressed a button on the controller and from the long narrow box on the ceiling the screen unrolled, in front of the bookshelves which lined the wall opposite where he sat, stretching down to about a metre above floor level. Originally, the screen deployed automatically when the buzzer signalled an incoming call, but soon after it was installed, it had done so while Julian was bending down looking for a book on one of the middle shelves. A friend of Jim's, an electronics whiz kid called Nigel, had offered to fix it, and with some misgivings, Julian had agreed.

Nigel had come along with a laptop computer which he plugged in, via a special lead, to the interface connector on the box controlling the v-phone. After a morning's intense work, he had sussed out the control routine. He added a patch which delayed the deployment of the screen until a spare button on the desk controller (presumably meant for some possible future upgrade) was pressed. The whole exercise had been just an enjoyable challenge for Nigel, with his prematurely furrowed brow and mischievous grin. He refused any payment, but gratefully accepted a bottle of Julian's homemade blackberry wine, which had something of a reputation among family and friends.

Now, the 3D image on the screen flickered into life.

"How's the report on the SHIP project going?" enquired William.

"I had hoped to have finished it by now, but there's that much more relevant information still to come in that'll need to be incorporated, I'm afraid." William said he was going to switch to conference mode, and there, beside a half-size William, appeared a similarly sized Sandy M⁰Intosh. After a brief polite exchange of greetings, Julian repeated to Sandy the gist of what he had said to William.

"By the way, I've had some information from an old colleague of mine. It seems the employment of female sapes in brothels is widespread in South America and Southeast Asia." This was news to both Sandy and William.

Sandy said, "I don't know what sapesses do about communicating with their clients." But added facetiously that he guessed they probably got on very well with body language. However, Sandy had some news of his own. It was common knowledge that when suitably trained, sapes could communicate adequately with their masters, but what had only recently been appreciated, was that they could communicate with each other with extraordinary facility. This was achieved with a mixture of 'words' – sounds based loosely on human language, usually English or Spanish – grunts and other sounds not at all meaningful to humans, and body language.

"This has disquieting implications when two or more sapes were employed in the same location. Recently, in his residence in Paris, two male sapes had attacked the wife of the Brazilian ambassador to France, tearing the bodice of her dress," said Sandy.

"As it happened, he had heard her screams, and, dashing to the scene, shot them both dead with the miniature revolver that he carried at all times."

Ready-trained sapes were expensive, and consequently he naturally had them insured. But the insurance company had refused to pay out, since he had not been deprived of their services either by their illness, death from natural causes, accident, theft or the actions of a third party.

After lunch, Julian went back upstairs and continued work on SHIP, following up a lead from William, on the internet. Suddenly Inez heard a loud thump from upstairs and getting no reply to her enquiry as to what was going on, hurried up the narrow twisting staircase. She found Julian slumped on the floor, vainly trying to get up.

"Just stay there," she said and, fetching a pillow from the bedroom next door, propped him up while she phoned for an ambulance, which arrived ten minutes later. By that time, Julian had been able to get up with her assistance and was slumped in his chair.

The paramedic and his driver came up the stairs, took one look at Julian and insisted on taking him to hospital. With some difficulty, they carried him down the narrow stairs and, despite his protests, placed him on a stretcher. They carried him out and loaded him in the back of the ambulance, and Inez insisted on getting in too, and accompanying him to hospital. There, he was attended by a Dr Jameson. After examining him, he pronounced that he had had a minor heart attack, and that from now on, Julian should be taking three medications daily for the rest of his life, one to thin the blood, another to reduce blood pressure and a third to minimise cholesterol.

"I'll arrange for a further examination when your husband is fully recovered to see if a stent might be necessary, though with the new medication we can probably avoid the need for that, after all, no surgery is without risks. I'll notify his family doctor of the additional medication required."

"I'll make sure he always takes the pills," said Inez and gave Dr Jameson details of their family doctor. After seeing her husband installed in bed in a small room – open wards had long been a thing of the past – Inez returned to the reception area, and suddenly wondered how she was going to get home again, especially as in her anxiety she had climbed into the ambulance without a thought for a coat. Heavy clouds had rolled up and there was now a cold wind blowing. She approached the receptionist on duty, a thin bony middle-aged woman with sharp features, lank hair of an indeterminate colour, a pointed nose and thin lips which turned down at the corners. Inez asked how she might get home, and the woman replied impatiently that she had no idea.

"Didn't you make suitable arrangements before you came?" That was her unhelpful parting riposte, before disappearing into the office behind.

At that moment, the ambulance driver walked through the reception area, and seeing Inez close to tears, said, "Want to go home again, love?"

"Oh, yes please!"

"We've got to pick up a disabled patient to come in for some routine treatment; it's not too much out of our way." And he shepherded her out to the vehicle.

"We've got a passenger," he said to the paramedic, who was already standing by the ambulance.

"Jump in, then." And Inez climbed into the nearside seat of the wide cab.

"I guess you didn't get much joy from Poison Ivy?" Inez understood only too well who the driver was referring to.

"You mean the receptionist?" said the paramedic, adding, "The porters call her Deadly Nightshade."

"I know her husband just died," said the driver, "but she was always like that, as long as I can remember."

Inez arrived home about 1620 hours, where Whiskey and Shelley rubbed around her legs, glad to see her back again. She put out a little more food for them, phoned Rosemary with the news of Julian's problem, made herself a cup of coffee and sat down to drink it, with a biscuit. The house seemed strangely quiet and empty without Julian, although in truth it was little different from when he was upstairs in his office, working quietly away. It was just that, normally, she had the comforting awareness that she was not alone: Now, that had suddenly been taken away from her. Finishing her coffee, she wondered what to do next. She would have to do something, anything, to keep herself occupied and take her mind off her worry about Julian. In the end, as the wind had dropped, the clouds had dissolved as if by magic and it was now a fine warm day in late June, she decided on a little gardening.

The day lilies needed seeing to: They looked lovely in July and on into August, with their showy orange-flecked-with-black flowers but were threatening to take over the south border entirely, indeed had nearly done so. Nothing for it but to dig some up by the roots, which turned out to be heavy work for someone of Inez's build. As she struggled with the fork, Jim arrived unexpectedly. He said he had been up to the offices of Baker and Daley for a meeting with clients and was returning on the train when he got a call from Rosemary with the news of his father's illness. So, he headed for his parents' house instead of home. Seeing Inez struggle, he took the fork and spoke. "Tell me all about it while I'm digging."

She related the day's events, while he uprooted great clumps of surplus Hemerocallis rhizomes, shaking the dirt off and stacking them ready for disposal. As she finished the tale, she added, "Whoa, that's enough. I don't want to lose them entirely."

"No chance of that; they'll sprout again from any tiny little piece left in the ground – adventitious roots they're called, they're the very devil."

"I know, but what's left now will make a nice show next year. Oh dear, you've got dirt all over your best clothes; Rosemary will be furious with me. Come inside and have a bit of tea." They went into the house together and while Inez busied herself in the kitchen, Jim vigorously wielded the clothes brush that lived in the drawer of the hallstand. Fortunately, the ground had been dry, and all the dirt brushed off completely, except for one stain which with a few deft movements Inez sponged off expertly, leaving not a trace behind.

After coffee and a couple of slices of Inez's lemon sponge, Jim kissed his mother goodbye, and having ascertained that Julian should be home tomorrow, although they didn't know what time, he promised he would come over on Sunday with Rosemary and young Harry, who was now a noisy six year-old.

Back home, Jim and Rosemary discussed the implications of Julian's heart attack, and whether he was likely to have another. Should he and Inez go on living in their house right out on the edge of town? What would happen to Inez if the worst came to the worst?

133

Chapter 12
Green Baize and Straight Lines AD2300

In 2293, the year after his heart attack, Julian, Inez and the rest of the family had attended the funeral of Bill, who had died after a short illness, at the age of ninety-four. It affected seven year-old Harry: He was silent throughout the funeral and for several days afterwards, most unusual for him since he was – as his mother put it – like a clockwork toy that never ran down. It was the first time he had been confronted with the reality of death – his great-grandmother Kitty had died five years before he was born, but 'gre-gaffa' Bill had always taken a great interest in the lad, and they had been firm friends. And Inez realised from his unusually silent demeanour just how keenly Julian felt the loss, yet she was, certainly, as much upset. For she and her father-in-law had been very fond of each other from their first meeting, when he had welcomed her into his family like a long-lost daughter. Of course, she knew that he had hoped for another child, but then so had Kitty. Yet while her mother-in-law had welcomed her, seemingly as warmly as Bill, Inez was keenly aware that there had not been that immediacy of rapport between them that marks out true friendship or affection, a rapport which is so intangible and illusive that it cannot be defined or analysed and of which she was so conscious in her relationship with Bill.

In the days after the funeral, Julian said, "I wonder whether we should try and arrange to move into that lovely country cottage which was my childhood home."

But it was rather isolated, and most if not all of Inez's friends were within walking distance of where they lived now, so it was never a serious possibility.

Early that same year Sarah had given birth to a daughter which she and Hal had named Bella, the Spanish for beautiful – which the infant certainly was. At Inez's suggestion, they had added Rosa and Lees as middle names. After all, as Inez pointed out, it cost nothing and it might just conceivably come in handy for their daughter to have a perfectly legal built-in alias on the birth certificate, at some indefinite point in the future.

"Any parent who fails to do such a simple thing for their child should be ashamed," she said, adding that if William's parents had given him a few middle names as well, he wouldn't have had 'W HACKER' on his briefcase.

Three years later, in 2297, Julian and Inez had visited Hal and Sarah in their flat in Kensington. On arrival, they had been proudly shown around the flat, and then, after drinks before dinner, Julian had said, "Well, here you are then, settled in Oberon's kingdom." Their host's eyebrows rose questioningly, and he explained that Oberon, king of the fairies, held his royal seat in the gardens there.

"The mortal baby Prince Albion was stolen by the fairies and brought up there. When he grew up, Kenna, Oberon's daughter, fell in love with him but he was killed by the fairy Azuriel, Lord of Holland Park. Later, when in revenge Oberon's kingdom had been destroyed, the gardens were named Kensington, after Kenna."

"Where'd you get all that from?" asked Hal.

"Lemprière, or Brewer, can't remember which." The eyebrows shot up again and Inez continued, "We've got ancient copies of Lemprière's Classical Dictionary and Brewer's Dictionary of Phrase and Fable, handed down for goodness knows how long, in Julian's family."

"Our copies were printed in the early twentieth century," said Julian. "Although I think they were both republished several times."

"I sometimes browse through them, they're just fascinating," added Inez.

"I must look out for them when I visit second-hand bookshops," said Sarah, who never could resist browsing.

"Yes, you really must – between them, they cover everything from Zoroaster to toad eaters. Hay-on-Wye's a good place to look."

Their all too brief stay had passed off enjoyably and included a visit to Kensington Gardens. There they paused among the Italian Fountains by the statue of Jenner, the discoverer of vaccination, which neither Inez nor Julian had seen before, though of course Julian had learnt all about him during his medical studies. Before leaving, they had extracted a promise that Sarah, Hal and Bella would soon return the visit.

Three years later again, in 2300, seven years had passed since Julian's heart attack, and he had had no more. A lot had happened in the meantime. He was now a sprightly sixty-nine-year-old, enjoying life and coping well with the aid of his medication. However, old age was gradually creeping up on him, he realised. The previous evening, he had tried to make love to Inez, but to his embarrassment had had eventually to give up, being unable to reach an organism. Inez squeezed his knee sympathetically; he turned over and went to sleep with Inez holding his penis. He woke up half an hour later, heard Inez's regular breathing and knew she was fast asleep. Unconsciously, as she slept, from time to time her hand gave a little momentary twitch which aroused him greatly, until he went back to sleep. When he woke up the following morning, he admitted to himself that, regretfully, lovemaking was now a thing of the past.

He still took an interest in the Department and still did some part-time work for them, although the lengthy SHIP project had long since been wrapped up. Now that he had more time for Inez, she seemed to be finding life much more tolerable, not to say stimulating. He was now the chairman of the local National Trust Centre and Inez the secretary. They attended the monthly lecture meetings in the new Community Hall, went on the outings and the annual holiday the Centre arranged, and were involved in the local branch of what they called NADFAS although its name had been changed decades ago, and various other activities. And now at last, the return visit of Hal, Sarah and Bella had finally been arranged, and long overdue too, said Inez.

Their visitors arrived, in time for lunch, after the walk of a little over a kilometre from the station. The six year-old Bella, gorgeously pretty in a pink dress of silky material with a multi-layered full skirt, was holding Hal's hand. Inez was struck by Bella's curly golden hair, pert nose and impish smile. Hal and Sarah slept in the visitors' room as before, while Inez put Bella in Jim's old room, having looked out an ancient teddy bear of Jim's and left it on the pillow. It had not, of course, been his favourite teddy; that had been passed on to Harry. During the course of the visit, Bella became so attached to 'ancient teddy', that Jim and Rosemary said he was now hers to keep.

After a cold lunch, Inez showed Sarah round the garden, while the menfolk saw to the washing up, of which there was not a lot. While they were busy, Hal asked, "You going to the Ninth World Population Conference later this year?"

"I'd have liked to; I checked with my doctor, but he only confirmed what I knew already; it's really not on. What about you?"

"Same thing – still I'd like to know what goes on and how desperate the situation really is."

"I should get some good feedback on that. Jim's going as the economics expert in the British delegation and I've told him to bring me back spare copies of all the papers actually presented, anything else he can get hold of, and to keep his ears open as well. As you and I know only too well, some of the most important bits never make it onto Proceedings."

October came, and Jim found himself in Manchester, attending the Ninth WPC, which was held in the 'new' large conference centre cum concert hall. This replaced the old Free Trade Hall, which had been blown up by anarchist terrorists in 2077. He had parted from Rosemary the previous day with an affectionate kiss and the promise that he would only be away five days if he could get a train and travel back on the last day of the Conference.

"Can I come too?" Harry had demanded.

"Not at thirteen," said his mother. Jim adding that maybe, if the next one was in 2308 as expected, he might be able to then.

At registration on the first day of the conference, Jim collected his large folder of papers and enquired if he could have a duplicate set as well. No, apparently this was not possible, there was a shortage and delegates in larger delegations were already being asked to share. Jim knew very well what to expect from one of these conferences, having heard Julian's experiences and also the latter's account of what he had been told by Jim's grandfather. There, on a green baize covered table by the door of the main hall, was the expected carafe of water surmounted by an upturned glass, accompanied by the customary half a dozen other upturned glasses. He wondered whether to try convincing one of the younger delegates that it might contain gin, but the only other member of the British delegation he had met yet, staying at the same hotel as him, was a certain Dick Bailey from Benson Pharmaceuticals, whom he guessed, correctly, to be in his late fifties.

The opening speech by the prime minister was, as usual, unremarkable, except that, as now seemed to be the custom, it upstaged the first speaker by revealing the state of the world's population. This was now down to an estimated 30.8% of the figure at the beginning of the millennium (now referred to as the 'millennium percentage'), which was both good news and bad. The good news was that the unexpectedly low figure at the Eighth WPC, possibly indicating an increased rate of decline, was not repeated. Indeed, the rate of decline had actually decreased slightly, as the current figure was back on the straight-line prediction described at the Seventh WPC. The bad news was that this same straight-line prediction still indicated an end to the human population somewhere around 2378, just seventy-eight years away. This reflected the large number of childless unions, families in many countries managing only somewhere in the region of 1.1 children each on average, if that, far below the figure needed to sustain a viable population.

The next speaker was a tall, bearded hunch-backed Professor named Bengt Jensen, who sported pince-nez and spoke excellent but stilted English, in a booming voice which overloaded the P.A. system until the sound technician hurriedly turned down the gain. He was from the University of Copenhagen, was obviously nettled at having figures revealed which he had expected to announce himself and created something of a stir with his different analysis of the trend. He explained that the straight-line decline was in fact much faster than should be expected for the given average family size. The population versus time curve should not be a straight-line diving towards the ground at a constant angle but should follow an exponential curve with a negative exponent. This meant it should flatten out, approaching zero asymptotically like the path of a plane, flaring out as it landed. That would put the final demise of the human race well into the following century or beyond; indeed, mathematically the exponential curve never actually quite reached zero at all.

On the exponential model, mankind would end not with a bang, but with a whimper. But of course, he pointed out, below a certain size, a population would just not be viable. A point would be reached where there were too few doctors and medical staff, farmers to see to food-production, engineers to maintain essential services such as water, sanitation and power, etc. and at that point a more rapid decline, not to say a dramatic collapse accompanied by epidemics and famine, would necessarily set in. He reported that at his university, work was in hand to develop a more precise estimate of this critical millennium percentage, and he hoped to be able to report progress in this respect at the next WPC.

"And a fat lot of help that'll be, if we can't fix the birth-rate in the meantime," said Dick Bailey to Jim, as the delegates politely but unenthusiastically applauded the presentation. Most of the following presentation was inaudible, as the technician had not readjusted the amplifier gain before disappearing for an unscheduled coffee break.

Jim had had a hand, with others, in the preparation of a paper on the economic implications of continued population decline, and this was presented the following day. To some extent, it tied in with Professor Jensen's paper, in that it tried to dimension the effect of shortages of skilled staff in the professions, including medicine, technology, engineering etc. But it also attempted to take into account the extent, unquestionably limited, to which sapes could replace human effort in areas beyond their current employment in agricultural and other simple tasks. It was undoubtedly an ambitious piece of work, and in the questions session at the end of the day more questions were directed at Jim's team than any of the other speakers. They fielded them as best they could, but Jim felt slightly uncomfortable that the work – especially the part dealing with sape labour – rested upon a fairly slim basis of actual statistics. That evening, Dick offered to stand Jim a drink, and assured him that his team had performed better in the questions session than most of the other speakers. Jim was grateful for the comment, but hoped Dick was not just being kind. But from their limited acquaintance, he had come to the conclusion that Dick was a fairly genuine person, who said what he really thought.

The most interesting paper on the third day – and certainly the most entertaining, Jim thought, *was one presented by Signor Arturo Arpati, of Bologna University, a swarthy comical little man with glossy black hair, standing no more than one metre fifty-seven, so that his head only just appeared above the lectern.* He sported an enormous upturned waxed moustache which waggled as he spoke and had a habit of adding 'you see' at the end of every sentence, delivered in a melodious if eccentric English accent, the while gesticulating wildly. His department at the university had, for many years, been tracking not the decline in the world's human population, but the growth in the sape population. He quoted figures from fifty years earlier to the present day and predicted that by the next WPC, assuming it was held in 2308, the number of sapes in the world would exceed the number of humans. Over lunch Jim said to Dick, "With humans in decline, sapes steadily increasing and the crossover point in sight, it looks as though the sapes really will inherit the earth!"

"Perhaps they'll make a better job of looking after the planet than we've done. Assuming that the collapse in human numbers is mainly due to the hundreds of man-made chemicals we've released into the environment, which is pretty well certain, it'll be the biggest own goal in the history of the solar system."

In addition to the bulky folder of conference papers he had collected at registration on the first day, Jim went round the conference hall at the end of each day, and thus collected together a duplicate set from those left abandoned by various delegates, who found this or that paper of little or no interest to them. Owing to the non-appearance of the last scheduled speaker, the wash-up session on the last day was held immediately after lunch. Jim was thus able to get away in time to pick up his bag from the hotel and catch a train to London, thence on to Tunbridge Wells, arriving home in the evening to a boisterous greeting from Harry and a perfunctory embrace from a tight-lipped Rosemary. Apparently, Harry had been too boisterous at school, and been sent to see the headmaster. He had arrived home that afternoon with a note addressed to his parents, which Rosemary handed to Jim without comment. That evening he had a long serious talk with his son, which he hoped would have some beneficial effect, though he was by no means certain that it would.

The following evening, they got the washing up out of the way, as usual, straight after dinner, and then settled down with their coffee. Rosemary had not asked anything about the WPC the previous evening, rather to his surprise, but perhaps her thoughts had still been embroiled with the disgrace of Harry's behaviour. But if Jim thought he was going to have a quiet evening this evening, he was mistaken: She had evidently been saving up all her curiosity till now. So, Jim related the events, more or less in chronological order, adding his own comments and interpretation as he went along. At the end of his story, Rosemary was very quiet, and Jim could see that something was troubling her. He had no difficulty in divining what it was and said quietly, "You're thinking about the sapes, aren't you?"

She nodded and asked, "What's going to happen – in the long run, I mean?"

"I really don't know; I wish I did. But with the trends as they are, either something has to change radically or the world won't be fit for our grandchildren, if we ever have any. At present, they're all safely under the control of their owners or employers and seem to do what they're told, at least in this country. But if it gets to the stage where there are so many –" His voice trailed off; he wished he hadn't started the sentence.

He wondered whether to tell her some disturbing news he had heard at the conference, from a delegate from Peru. Before he went to the conference, Hal had given him the names of two or three of his contacts, in the hope that Jim could bring him back any useful information; he would have preferred to gather it for himself of course, but that was just not possible. Jim checked with his list of delegates and found that the only one of Hal's contacts at the conference was a certain Señor Salvador Gomez, a delegate from Peru. Jim had finally located him in the morning coffee break on the third day.

On hearing that he was enquiring on Hal's behalf, he took Jim aside and told him about some unfortunate incidents in his country.

"Two years ago, a male sape had murdered its owner, and another, from the same supplier, had done the same six months later," Señor Gomez said.

This was clearly very bad publicity for that particular sape-breeding syndicate, which had done its best to hush matters up by paying huge compensation.

"Now, as a matter of course, that sape-breeding syndicate used electro-gradient technology to maximise the ratio of females to males produced, the former being generally more amenable and biddable and less prone to outbreaks of violent behaviour." He added that from then on the few male sapes they did supply were all castrated. Several other sape breeding companies had followed suit, not only for the same reasons but also to prevent owners of sapes breeding their own replacements, the useful working life of a sape being quite short compared to that of a human. Jim related these details to Julian and Hal, but decided, not without misgivings, that it was best not to mention the matter to Rosemary, at least not yet, and guessed – correctly – that Julian would not pass on the news to Inez. If in due course it became generally known, Rosemary would worry about it, he knew.

Chapter 13
Soldiers and Shop Assistants 2301AD

A year had passed since the ninth WPC, and Jim and Julian were talking in the lounge of Jim and Rosemary's house one Saturday afternoon, while Inez and Rosemary were in the garden.

"What d'you think of the news from Africa?" asked Julian.

"Terrible – Rosemary's been worried about the potential problems with sapes, ever since hearing about the forecast at the last WPC that they would soon be in the majority." Julian was referring in particular to the news from UCAR, the so called United Central African Republic, a disparate agglomeration of African tribes in a very uneasy alliance and ruled over by Nathaniel Mbalala, a member of one of the smaller tribes, who insisted on calling the United Central African Republic 'Mbalala land' and its capital 'Mbalala-ville'. He had started out as a charismatic leader, seen as capable of calming the endemic conflict in the area and, in the ensuing stability, overseeing some much-needed economic development which would raise the desperately low living standards of the people. For despite the greatly reduced head-count of the human race worldwide, here the pressure on land and resources seemed to be as great as ever it was, if not greater, largely due to the mismanagement and consequent exhaustion of the land. It was an unfathomable conundrum; parts of the globe were now but very sparsely populated while others – such as here in the UCAR – were clearly scarcely capable of sustaining their population. There were other parts of that great continent which could easily have accommodated an overspill from the UCAR, and efforts had been made to encourage such a movement. But tribal attachments to jealously guarded traditional areas had proved enduring and impervious to reasoning. So, after a honeymoon period in which real progress had been made in fields such as education, health and housing, tribal rivalries had broken out again, threatening to undo all the progress achieved thus far.

Mbalala's response had been to try to increase the number of police, and when that proved ineffective, to call on the army to maintain order. However, his problem was that, as with the police, men were too busy scraping a living from the land to support themselves and their families, to volunteer for a force which they knew seldom got paid. He had therefore applied for, and received, a loan from the World Bank, ostensibly to further economic development, but had in fact spent much of it on acquiring several hundred male sapes. They were of the largest type designed for heavy agricultural labour, and Mbalala had by devious means succeeded in obtaining sapes that had not been castrated. These he had trained and armed, providing himself with a force which was feared, loathed and hated. They had been taught how to maintain their small arms and to fire, on the word of command, at dummy targets which had been fashioned to look like ordinary citizens. They had in fact not yet actually been ordered to fire on real people, but rumours that they had killed a man and a boy from Mbalala's own tribe circulated and were widely believed, making the mere threat that they would be deployed, a very effective damper on potential unrest and conflict.

"I wonder if they really would fire on people?" mused Julian.

"Your guess is as good as mine, but don't forget the two murders committed by sapes in Peru, or the attack on the ambassador's wife in Paris. And these were all animals that been trained for domestic duties, not taught how to kill." At that moment, Harry, who had recently celebrated his fourteenth birthday, bounced into the room.

"Hello Grandad; what's that you and Dad are talking about?"

Julian looked questioningly at Jim, who said, "He's matured amazingly over the last year. I don't mind if you tell him. But mind, Harry, not a word to Mum or…Granny." And Julian proceeded to relate the disturbing news from Africa.

Harry frowned. "The man must be mad."

"Or just desperate to hold on to power, like every dictator," said Jim. The news cast a shadow over the visit, a shadow that lingered over Julian even after they returned home the next day, Sunday.

Sapes were on Julian's mind again later that year, when the news emerged that one of the large supermarket chains planned the experimental use of sapes on the tills in a few of its stores.

"Surely that's not possible," said Inez.

"I don't see why not."

"I can understand that a sape can be trained to do simple repetitive household duties. But surely a sape can't learn arithmetic – that's an abstract subject."

"Sapes are probably much more intelligent than dogs –"

"What's that got to do with it?" interrupted Inez.

"I was going to say – that in the nineteenth and early twentieth centuries there were travelling shows called circuses, with performing animals. One popular turn was the dog that could count. A child from the audience would be asked to go into the ring and choose any two numbers between nought and five, printed on stout cards. These would be laid out on the ground, like a sum, and the dog would go and get a card with the right answer and lay it where the answer should go."

"Yes, but that doesn't mean it could do sums. It was just a trick it had been taught. It just knew that if it saw two shapes, that we call three and four, it had to go and get another particular shape that we call seven."

"Basically, all a sape at a till needs to do is no more complicated than that. It waves the barcode gun at each item until it hears the beep, swipes the customer's card and hands it the slip to sign, or puts the coins or notes tendered into the right compartments, presses a button and the readout on the till tells it what coins or notes to give back to the customer."

"But what about the odd complication that's bound to arise, where the customer has a 'two for the price of one' coupon, or fifty pence off or something like that?"

"It seems there's always going to be at least one till still manned by a human."

"'Womanned' by a human, more like, you mean."

This conversation and its implications stuck in Julian's mind, keeping him awake that night. His mind wandered over the day, the previous weeks and months and he thought. *If only I didn't feel so old. Not only is making love to Inez impossible but even the thought of masturbating in the shower just hasn't occurred to me for donkey's years.*

As he got dressed in the morning he noticed that during the night his foreskin had returned to covering the glans. During the day he wore it fully retracted, his snug fitting Y-fronts keeping it that way, as he had done ever since before his marriage to Inez. That way, the organ stayed clean and odour free, with none of the white paste of dead skin cells that would otherwise collect around the glans. He had found that his testes could be pushed up into the inguinal cavity on each side and now when he put on his Y-fronts they found their own way there by themselves.

A year later Inez arrived back home from her usual supermarket on a sunny Wednesday morning and flopped down into an armchair. Now in her late sixties, the walk back home with a heavy bag full of groceries was beginning to tell on her, the knees in particular feeling the strain. Julian had taken the bag from her at the front door, stowed the various items in the fridge, freezer or vegetable rack, as appropriate, and made a cup of coffee which he presented to Inez, with a couple of her favourite bourbon biscuits. She sighed and spoke, "Thank you, love." And Julian could see that something was not quite right.

He sat on the arm of the chair with his arm round her shoulder and spoke, "What is it?"

"It's a week since I shopped at Anderson's, and now they've gone and got sapes on the tills. I didn't realise until I'd got a basket full of provisions, otherwise I think I'd have shopped elsewhere."

"Was there a problem?"

"Well, no, not really, I suppose. It just felt awkward, being served by an animal. I'd have gone to the one till with a woman on, but there was an enormous queue for it. I suppose lots of people felt uncomfortable about it, like me."

"How did the sape behave?"

"It's difficult to say, really. Nothing objectionable – I presume it was a female; anyway, it had the same Anderson's dress that all the till ladies wear. It must've been specially made, though, being that small."

"What about all the ladies who used to be on the tills?"

"I suppose some were made redundant. They were all pretty old anyway and at least one till was usually out of use, with a supervisor often holding the fort on one of the others as well."

"Will you go on shopping there?"

"I don't know. I've never liked the other supermarket, and anyway they'll probably soon have sapes on their tills."

"You feel it's something you could do without, at our time of life?"

"I guess I'll get used to it, I suppose I'll have to."

The following autumn Inez arrived back home from the shops one day with a copy of the Telegraph. They didn't usually have a paper, and seldom watched the news on television. They were far from being uninformed about what was going on in the world, however, getting their news from the text pages, which had the advantage of conciseness compared to the various news programmes. The latter had the annoying habit of devoting the greater part of the time to one single current news story, covering it in unnecessary detail, a correspondent at the scene with really nothing new to say, filling up time ad lib, or just as exasperating, spending time speculating on what might happen, instead of sticking what had happened. With the usual coffee and biscuits by her side, she pointed out to Julian an article on one of the inside pages.

"What d'you make of that?" Julian read the indicated item, a mere five centimetres or so in the left-hand column, near the bottom.

"Well!" He looked at Inez and smiled in amusement.

"So, Mr Jason Biggar, an official of the Universal Workers' Union, is attempting to obtain negotiating rights of behalf of sapes in shops, is he? It's a novel idea, as if sapes think and behave in the same way as humans, instead of living quietly in the compounds or hostels provided by their owners." The latter were not necessarily the employers; some sapes worked for organisations, such as factories, shops or farms, to whom they were hired out by sape owning companies. These animals seemed quite used to being bussed around in special coaches, packed closely in on benches in vehicles that humans would not have dreamed of travelling in. The advantage to an employer of hiring sapes was clear: The owning company was responsible for the cost of their maintenance and care, and for providing replacements when an animal fell ill or died. On the other hand, brothels invariably owned the female sapes they employed.

The organisations owning and hiring out sapes had developed ways, based on the schemes of a panel of well-known animal behaviourists, of keeping their sapes contented and obedient. This was helped by the fact that the animals were all females – sapesses – and invariably kept in order by an elderly sapess who acted as the group's matriarch. The exploitation of the animals in this way infuriated and enraged a vociferous group of animal rights activists who proposed that all sapes should be returned to the Amazon rain forest and set free. But the time for that was long gone, it would have been simply impossible on a number of counts, firstly, the sheer number of the animals. Then again, the sapes employed by humans, through their evolution in various breeding programmes, were of an entirely different mindset from the few animals still existing in the wild and would not have survived more than a few days after being separated from human owners and being dumped in the Brazilian rainforest.

Five years had passed, and Jim was away at the 10th World Population Conference. At seventy-eight, Julian seemed in better health than for many years, and had actually wondered if he would be able to attend as well; he had missed the 9th WPC on medical grounds and would dearly have liked to attend at least one more before he died. But despite his present well-being, on hearing the place where the conference was to be held, his doctor was adamant in vetoing such an idea. The venue chosen seemed extraordinary; La Paz is well over three and a half thousand metres above sea level and visitors would find themselves short of breath, even without any exertion. On the evening of the first day, Jim phoned Rosemary and spoke, "Gosh, at three thousand five hundred metres altitude here the air is really thin, how glad I am that we are still active cyclists."

She replied, "Well at fifty years of age, you be very careful of yourself." And certainly he found the thin atmosphere often left him breathless, but he seemed to be coping much better than most other delegates. In response to Rosemary's anxiety for him, he phoned again the following evening.

"I'm really very well, but the only delegate from the United Central African Republic collapsed and had to be carted off to hospital, whilst a Thai delegate had had a heart attack during the morning session and died shortly afterwards."

Jim had not been involved in the preparation of any paper presented at this WPC, but was carefully noting, on behalf of his employers Baker and Daley, any details concerning the economic implications of the current population levels worldwide, especially those mentioned by speakers in passing but not appearing in the papers. He was also busy following up such leads in the breaks between sessions, as well as taking a keen interest in the medical papers, on behalf of Julian. As at the Ninth WPC, he managed to collect a complete set of the papers presented, to bring home for Julian and Hal to share.

On his return, he related how he had met Dick Bailey of Benson Pharmaceuticals Ltd again and had had a long discussion with him on the subject of sapes. As forecast at the 9th WPC, there were now more of these creatures on the planet than there were human beings, a fact that governments would have liked to play down or even suppress entirely, but which was widely known to and admitted by those at the Conference. The reported further decline in the human population since the previous WPC had not, in the event, turned out to be as drastic as feared. Certainly the 'straight-line' model of decline was now definitely discredited, the exponential curve proving a much better fit to the data, as forecast by Professor Jensen at the 9th WPC. However, the preponderance of sapes over humans was due more to the increase in their numbers, than the fall in the human population. The sapes bred under human guidance over many generations – man-directed evolution – were much more sophisticated than their natural cousins in the Amazon rain forest. Not only were they larger and more intelligent but they also had – as Sandy McIntosh had noted some years earlier – developed the ability to communicate with each other in a mixture of near-speech and sign language. This enabled them to cooperate to achieve objectives, in a way that was simply not possible for their wild forbears. There had been numerous instances in South America of sapes escaping their employers and fleeing to the jungle, where they had set up flourishing communities or tribes. These were becoming so successful, that they were replacing the smaller wild sapes and even exerting pressure on the indigenous Amerindian people of the Amazon rain forests. Although elsewhere this process was not anywhere like as far advanced, there were nevertheless now independent communities of sapes in the forested parts of Southeast Asia and Africa, neither owned by nor under the control of humans. The implications of this were not lost on the delegates at the WPC.

Chapter 14
Clandestine Courtship 2309AD

In the year after Jim returned from the 10th WPC, Harry – now twenty-two and with an even more rugged build and physique than his father – surprised his parents by announcing that he was getting engaged at the weekend, which as it happened, was Easter. He had done fairly well at school, after settling down and starting to take life more seriously at thirteen. From school, he had progressed to university and had taken a degree in electronics, surprising everyone, and himself more than most, by getting a 'Highly Commended', the equivalent in earlier times of an upper second. He had been working for the best part of two years with Lascar Electronics, a small local company designing, building and marketing advanced electronic measuring instruments.

"Isn't it a bit early to think of taking on such a responsibility?" said Jim, at the same moment as Rosemary simply said:

"Who?"

Harry looked from one to the other and asked, maddeningly, "Which of you do you want me to answer first?"

"Your mother, of course."

"Well then, Bella and I plan to marry sometime in the late autumn."

"Bella? But she's only fifteen!" said Rosemary.

"Legally, she could have been married over a year already."

"Yes, I know, but I mean –"

"I'll have been earning my own living for over two years by then, and Bella plans to get a job as soon as she leaves school."

"You mean she won't go on to higher education? And she's so gifted, it seems such a shame."

"Of course, legally she doesn't need Hal and Sarah's permission anyway," said Jim.

"Actually, we had thought of that for ourselves," said Harry, with quite uncharacteristic sarcasm.

Rosemary said, "I know, they should never have changed the law."

"We knew that's how you would feel; that's why we got her parent's agreement first." Rosemary stood on tiptoe, put her arm round his shoulder and gave him a little squeeze. "And of course, you're so old you don't need ours anyway, do you?"

"Would you have given it, if I did?"

After a pause, Jim said, "Yes, on balance, I think we would, although I still think it is a big responsibility to take on so young."

But Harry countered. "Granddad was only three and a bit year older than me when he married."

"But where will you live?"

Harry explained that one of his colleagues at work was a New Zealander, and was returning home that autumn, after a year's work experience in England. He had a small flat, about as far the other side of Lascar as their home was on this, and Harry had arranged with the landlord to take over the tenancy when he left.

"In that case, you won't be far from your grandmother." This was indeed so: Jim's parents' house was on the far edge of Tunbridge Wells, close to the New Zealander's flat. And so, the matter was decided, though Jim and Rosemary were intrigued to learn the details of this clandestine courtship, of which they had had no inkling. The following day, Rosemary rang up Sarah, to see if she had known about the young couple, and if so, how long. But there was no reply from the Raynor household. Rosemary mused that if you lived in Kensington, there was so much to do in the capital, right on your doorstep or within easy reach, even on foot if you were reasonably fit. She rang again in the evening, and Hal answered the phone – not what she was expecting, she had hoped for a woman-to-woman exchange on the subject. But Hal said that Sarah was out and not expected back until late.

"But perhaps I can guess what you rang up about."

"Oh, er, yes, I was going to ask Sarah if she – you – have known about it for long."

"Well then, why not ask me instead?" growled Hal teasingly.

"Well, have you?"

"We've suspected there was a boyfriend for some time, but we were still quite surprised when Bella said she wanted to get engaged. We thought she was a bit young for that, but when we learnt who the suitor was, we couldn't have thought of a better choice. After that, it was only a matter of time; they both kept on worrying us for our agreement. Of course, she's had a soft spot for Harry ever since she was six, when we came and stayed with your parents. We remember how good Harry was, playing with her and keeping her amused, just like an older brother. She never forgot that – of course, they were both only children then. We think they've been writing to each other since she was about ten."

"That would've been when Harry was seventeen. We often wondered why he never seemed interested in girls; seems he was all along, just that we didn't know about it. But they can't've met very often, surely?"

"I think they managed it more often than you might suspect; have a word with Sarah about it sometime. Hang on a minute, there's the front door."

It was Sarah returning, a little earlier than expected, and she and Rosemary had a long chat.

"You were a long time on the phone," said Jim.

"I've just had a long talk with Sarah, well, with Hal first, actually; then she got back home."

"And did they know all about it?"

"Sort of, a bit longer than us, anyway."

"What I can't understand is how the affair could have blossomed if they never saw each other."

"Apparently they've been writing to each other since she was ten. And they've seen each other, too."

"Remember Harry and his best school-friend going to stay with the friend's cousin's family in Bayswater? Apparently, Harry didn't spend much time with his friend, or the cousin. And then those long bike rides in the holidays. Bella used to go and stay with a friend at her aunt's place."

"They say true love will always find a way – remember how we used to wangle time together, sometimes even just a few short precious hours." And they clung to each other for a few moments, remembering their early love. Then Rosemary disengaged herself, saying she had to go to bed as tomorrow was washing and ironing, and tweaked his cheek. In retaliation, he patted her on the bottom, just hard enough to evoke a protest, and said he would bring her up a minty milky hot nightcap when she was in bed.

The following day, all the while during the washing and ironing, Rosemary could not stop thinking about the wedding, and making plans and them changing them again. She told herself that this was silly; it was far too early for plans, but her mind kept obstinately returning to the topic. Relief only came when she found herself reminiscing about her own marriage, and all the planning involved beforehand. And then her mind – which seemed to have a mind of its own – moved off into imagining what her life might have been like if Jim hadn't happened to work with someone who had relatives in Cumberland, or indeed who she might have married, if anyone, if Inez hadn't met Julian and had stayed in Argentina. Absently minded pondering such imponderables, she ran the iron across the collar of Jim's shirt, and accidentally right up against her left hand. When Jim heard her cry, he came down from the home office and seeing the problem, searched for the Acriflavine, an ancient ointment for burns, recently rediscovered. With that, and a large sticking plaster, he soon made her comfortable, or at least allayed the worst of the discomfort.

At last, the great day was set. It was to be the second Saturday in November, a few days after Bella's sixteenth birthday. Bella insisted on a white wedding and neither her parents' nor parent-in-laws' nor future husband demurred; they all knew that with her pale complexion, high cheekbones and long lashes, she would look absolutely stunning in a traditional wedding dress. Julian said to Harry, "You're a lucky fellow, young lad, marrying a real beauty. Makes me think of my own wedding day," he sighed. Then added, "There's few enough advantages to old age, for either a man or a woman. Don't know too much about the latter, apart from the obvious one, but for a man just about the only advantage I can think of is that he can take pleasure in admiring a beautiful woman without getting his glasses steamed up."

There was some discussion as to where the wedding should be: Inez suggested a proper church wedding. Quite why, she did not know, after all she was not a churchgoer herself and had married Julian in a civil ceremony. And she accepted that churchgoers were very much in a minority in the twenty-fourth century. So, the couple settled for a civil wedding in the special nuptial chamber at the town hall. The short honeymoon consisted of a few days with Harry's maternal grandparents in Cumberland, who kindly moved in with neighbours the while, leaving their house to the young couple entirely. Both being physically fit and energetic, they wandered the area both on foot and by bicycle, the highlight of their wanderings being an unforeseen adventure. They had cycled to Helvellyn, where they left their bikes at the foot and headed for the top, along

Striding Edge, in glorious sunshine. The path to the summit is narrow and several people have met their deaths there over the years.

As they made their way along, Bella nervously holding on to Jim, part way along the sun disappeared behind thick lowering clouds which had seemingly sprung up from nowhere. At Bella's insistence, they retraced their footsteps but after a few metres were enveloped in mist or low cloud. Immediately the temperature dropped dramatically, and they were soon chilly in their light anoraks. In the dim light, they picked their way cautiously along, mindful of the fearful drop on either side. They had not too far to go before they recognised the marker post at which they had joined the edge, and descending, soon came out of the cloud. Before long, they were back at their bikes and made their way to an inn where Bella had coffee and Harry a beer. He suggested they stay there for a hot lunch, but Bella said that as she was now a married woman, she would insist on cooking for them, back at the house.

The honeymoon passed all too quickly in a haze of mutual affection, active days and loving nights, punctuated by one serious quarrel, about which they both secretly felt ashamed afterwards. Years later they still remembered vividly the mental pain and mutual disappointment occasioned by the tiff but could not actually remember what it had been about. They returned to the flat in Tunbridge Wells and Bella secured a post as a clerical assistant at the hospital. Rosemary said this was a criminal waste of her potential, but it appeared that she would spend two afternoons a week on a management-training course at the Technical College, which might open more advanced avenues later.

The following year, at the beginning of February, Bella confided to Rosemary that she was sure she was pregnant; news which filled Rosemary with mixed feelings.

Bang goes her training and future advancement, but it would be nice to have a baby granddaughter – or grandson, she thought. By March, she was quite concerned for her daughter-in-law, who was not only having morning sickness but finding it difficult to keep food down at any time of day. But by April, Bella assured her she was fine and not having trouble with eating anymore. In early May, Bella invited Rosemary over to see the flat. She and Jim had seen it once, of course, before the couple moved in, and had thought it looked definitely spartan, and not a little shabby. As she walked the two kilometres to the flat in the early morning, Rosemary wondered what she would see. She was startled at the transformation. Harry had done some quick but effective decorating in all the rooms, with self-colour walls and ceilings in tasteful shades, and Bella had carried on from there with lots of soft furnishing fabrics and other touches, transforming the place from a barn into a comfortable home.

"How's the flat?" Jim asked that evening when Rosemary returned.

"Oh, the flat's fine."

"But?" said Jim who could tell there was more to come.

"Well, it's Bella herself."

"I thought she was okay now, no trouble eating."

"No, but she's living on biscuits – biscuits and fizzy drinks: I ask you, that's no recipe for a bonny bouncing healthy baby."

"Are you sure?"

"She didn't say as much, but that's all I saw her eating all day."

"Have a word with Harry."

"I will. What've you been doing all day?"

"The usual, work for Baker and Daley. Oh, and Dad rang, just for a chat really, I should say."

"Anything interesting? And how's Inez?"

"Inez's fine. Dad said he'd had a long chat with William Hacker, his old boss, and Bill's before him, come to that. He's seventy-seven now, two years younger than Dad, and still takes an interest in the work of the Department. Apparently, he has a grandson about Harry's age, and a granddaughter a bit older. The grandson's an electronic whiz kid, so it seems. Anyway, I phoned him afterwards, William that is, not his grandson. Introduced myself; he'd heard everything about me of course, from Dad. He's quite an interesting chap and we had a long talk."

"I know your dad always thought highly of William Hacker."

"Yes, he commented on the current state of progress or lack of it. His grandson says that we only make little minor incremental improvements nowadays. He reckons the heyday of development was the twenty-first century. Then things hit all sorts of limits. On the big engineering scale, economic difficulties, the fuel crisis, minimising greenhouse gases and so on, all conspired to stifle any big developments. The only good news on that front was the development of solar, wind and wave power; he said it now provides about ninety-five percent of our electricity. And on the microelectronics scale, something called Moore's Law hit the buffers due to leaky currents and beta particles or was it alpha? Anyway, I expect that would all mean something to

Harry. Got his grandson's email address, just in case he could be of use to Harry at some time in the future; apparently he's already quite important in the Halliday Autometrix Corporation."

"It's all beyond me, but I did hear someone on television the other day saying much the same thing. Except that he reckoned real progress had already come to an end halfway through the twenty-first century. But never mind that, it's Bella I'm still worried about. Will a baby made of biscuits and fizz ever do well?"

Chapter 15
Double Celebration 2310AD

Julian was sitting at the desk in his office looking through some old papers. Now eighty, he no longer did any work at all for the Department and was wondering whether to ditch these copies of some of his old reports. By his side was the control box of the videophone, which William's successor as head of the Department said he might as well keep; it was fully functional, but no longer the current model. Thinking better of it – after all, those reports represented many hours of labour – he sighed and put them back in the drawer. Suddenly the videophone buzzed, announcing a call, and he pressed the accept call button. He was greeted by a voice he knew well, but the screen did not deploy, indicating a call originating from an ordinary 'phone', as it happened, a mobile.

"Hello Julian, how are you?" asked Hal.

Hal had gone for an early morning walk, purchasing a copy of the Telegraph on the way. Wandering at random, he ended up sitting on a bench by the Long Water in Kensington Gardens, enjoying the spring sunshine. An item about the United Central African Republic, on an inner page, caught his eye, and on the spur of the moment he tried ringing up a young colleague, thirty years his junior, who still worked on the paper as a reporter. As it happened, Hal was in luck, he was in the office. Martin Banbury was the complete antithesis of Hal, with fair flyaway hair, a snub nose, soft grey eyes, and a penchant for wearing soft grey flannels. Thanks to the considerable help Hal had afforded him in his early days on the job, Martin had a great deal of respect, not to say affection, for the older man, and would often pass on snippets of information which were not yet in the public domain. Hal learned that there were rumours, as yet unfounded and therefore unpublished, that President Mbalala's Chief of Police had directed a troop of armed sapes to fire on a crowd of demonstrators marching on the Presidential Palace. It was said that the sapes had opened fire indiscriminately, killing some of the demonstrators, several of their own number and the Chief of Police himself, with many more wounded – both sapes and humans. The Deputy Chief of Police had managed to restore some semblance of order, helped by the fact that some of the sapes had run out of ammunition. He managed to get half of the sapes back to their barracks, but the rest had absconded into the jungle, taking their weapons and ammunition with them.

Hal now passed on this disturbing information to Julian, knowing full well that his confidence would be respected. "When we first heard about Mbalala's arming of sapes, Jim and I were appalled. Young Harry summed it up at the time, saying the man must be mad," said Julian.

"You can say that again," grunted Hal. Continuing, "Oops, forgive me. I was so intent on passing on the news that I haven't enquired how you and Inez are keeping." Julian assured him they were both well, Inez in particular being eventually delighted with her new knees after a long period getting used to them and enquired in his turn how Hal and Sarah were keeping. Apparently they were both well, apart from the minor chronic nuisances that come with age.

"Anyway, keep me posted about Bella won't you, you're so much nearer her than us. In fact, you're nearer to their flat than Jim and Rosemary are, aren't you?" Julian confirmed that this was the case, and they said goodbye. Julian sat on, immobile, lost in thought, so that when he didn't come down as usual for coffee at eleven, Inez went up to see him, fearful of another heart attack.

"What's the matter?" she enquired.

"Oh, nothing; just something Hal said just now." Inez could see only too plainly that it was not 'just nothing' and was about to press him for more information, but then thought better of it.

"Did you mention Bella to him?"

"Yes, Sarah's worried too, and wants to try and get down to see her."

As it happened, they need not have worried: Bella's appetite returned in midsummer, and in mid-September she was delivered of healthy twins. The girl was born first and a brother of almost the same weight just half an hour later. Harry chose the name Anne for his daughter, while Bella chose Bill for her son, with the proviso that it should appear as William on the birth certificate. Only later did it occur to her that she had given her son the name of his great-great-grandfather. Remembering Inez's advice when Bella was born, Sarah insisted that they should both have at least two middle names, and the local paper duly announced the great occasion of the birth of Anne Marie Raynor Brophy and

William Michael Carpenter Brophy. Pictures of the happy parents and their bonny babies appeared on the front page of the local paper, together with an article celebrating the event. With the world's shrinking population very much in mind, every live birth was an event, but twins were a very rare bonus. The reporter, in rather over-flowery language, made much of the fact that if both the twins grew up and in due course had offspring of their own, Harry and Bella would have done their bit for the preservation of mankind, whilst any further children would make them absolute heroes. The story was picked up first by regional and then by national television, whilst the national papers, not to be outdone, ran the story also, each in their own way, from a discreet single column note at the bottom of the front page in the Telegraph, to the full sentimental treatment in the popular tabloid The Daily Leaf. The twins, their parents and grandparents were even invited to lunch by the Mayor of Tunbridge Wells who expounded on what an important event each birth was.

"Our population is now barely twenty thousand, about half what it was three centuries ago. So, you can see why so many properties are standing empty, with the consequent loss to the municipal treasury of Building Assessment revenue. This makes it very difficult for me to maintain the level of services our citizens have rightly come to expect," said the short stocky mayor, puffing out his pigeon chest even further.

"People settling here and others leaving more or less balance out, so to maintain our population, we need well over two hundred children, about two hundred and sixty in fact, born in the town each year."

"Your dear children are a great blessing, both to you and to the town. I do so hope you will have more soon," said the mayoress in an unctuous tone; she was a shortish plumpish woman in late middle age, with thick ankles, improbable colour hair and rather too much lipstick.

Bella insisted on breast-feeding both her babies and managed it well enough for the first three months. Then Bill, who always seemed to be hungry, was transferred to a bottle, whilst Anne continued to suckle, until they were both weaned. Once Bill was on the bottle, Harry could help with the night feeds, until mercifully both the youngsters slept right through the night. When they were a year old, Bella went back to her clerical post in the hospital, two days a week. On Tuesdays and Thursdays, Rosemary cycled over to the flat and looked after the babies while Bella was at work: So, from an early age they grew up being almost as used to their grandmother as to their mother. Jim remarked that that was how things were a thousand years earlier, in peasant societies of the Middle Ages. Children were always brought up by their grandparents, as their parents were too busy wresting a living from the soil, and then the parents brought up their own grandchildren in their turn.

But this was not to be the case with Bella. She had been very happy on the twins first birthday, but at their second birthday party she felt somehow not quite right. It was nothing she could pin down, but she felt unusually tired at the end of the day, which she put down to the noise and bustle of the lively toddlers.

"I'll be alright in the morning," she told Harry, but she woke up with a headache and feeling so exhausted she did not attempt to get up. Later that Sunday afternoon she ate a little cake which Harry brought up to the bedroom and drank a little coffee. She seemed slightly better for a while, but then as night fell, she was violently sick. Harry was all for phoning for a doctor, but Bella said that she felt a little better and just wanted to sleep.

The following morning her breathing was irregular and her pulse rapid, and Harry was really alarmed. He decided to phone the doctor as soon as surgery opened and would ring Lascar and say he couldn't come in that day. He was just about to pull the phone out of his pocket when it rang. It was Rosemary enquiring about Bella, and Harry said she was really poorly and described the symptoms. He was still trying to contact the doctor's surgery, but it was not open yet, when there was a knock at the door. There was a paramedic standing there, with an ambulance and driver outside.

"Mrs Bella Brophy?" he enquired.

"Yes, but —"

"Suspected case of meningitis, to go to hospital straight away." Harry was stunned, then pulled himself together and showed the two men up to the bedroom.

"It's all right, love, we'll soon have you comfy in hospital," said the paramedic as they helped her onto the stretcher and carried her down to the ambulance.

Just then Rosemary arrived on her bicycle and Harry said in bewilderment, "An ambulance arrived, just like that, out of the blue, and they're taking Bella to hospital. They said something about meningitis."

"I know. I phoned your grandfather. He's never actually practised as a doctor of course, as you know, but as soon as I mentioned the symptoms you told me, he said he would phone the Medical Officer of Health – he's known him a long time – and I guess that's just what he did."

Harry wanted to go with the ambulance, but they said it would be best if they contacted him later. He went back in doors and phoned Lascar to say that he wouldn't be in that day, and then made some strong coffee for himself and his mother. She was busy reassuring the children that Mummy would soon be all right, and then set about getting their breakfast and seeing to their toilet.

"You could go to work if you like; I can always cope here."

"No, I can't concentrate on anything," said Harry, who was anxiously pacing up and down. An hour later, when the phone rang, Harry whipped it out of his pocket. "Hello?" It was a doctor at the hospital.

"Mr Brophy?"

"Yes."

"I have to confirm that your wife has suspected meningitis. We've made her comfortable and she's sleeping now. We've taken samples and sent them away for analysis, to confirm the diagnosis and if it is, find out which strain."

"When can I come in and see her?"

"As I said, she's sleeping now. This evening perhaps, about seven o'clock."

Harry never knew how he got through the rest of that day, but eventually he arrived at the hospital and was shown into the room where Bella was lying, looking pale and propped up on the pillows. On hearing him enter, she opened her eyes and whispered, "Harry." He took her hand and kissed it, and sat with her an hour or more, while she drifted in and out of consciousness. In the end, a staff nurse came in and said it would be best if the patient were left to rest, and regretfully, Harry left.

The following morning Harry rang the hospital several times asking for news, but there was none; eventually he realised they must be feeling he was wasting their time. Late that afternoon the hospital doctor rang Harry and suggested he should come in and see him. Harry did so without delay and was shown into a small room. A few minutes later, the doctor came in and spoke, "We've just had the results of the analysis. I'm afraid it's not good news. They're ninety-nine percent certain your wife has the recently identified Zempel X strain of meningitis. This is a mutant that's only appeared in the last two or three years. This is the first case in the south of England."

"But how can she have caught it? Where? Who from?"

"That's the peculiar thing about meningitis; it pops up here or there for no apparent reason. The exact mode of propagation's frankly unknown."

"Can I see my wife now?"

The doctor hesitated, then said, "You can take a look, but it's best not to go in." A nurse ushered him along a corridor to a different room from the one Bella had been in the previous day. He looked through the glass panel in the door, and an icy chill clutched his heart. Bella was lying pale and motionless, her eyes shut as if in sleep. She was hooked up to various wires and tubes, while wavy green traces processed endlessly from left to right across the screen of a monitor. He stood frozen until the nurse laid a sympathetic hand on his arm and gently turned him away. He walked back home in a daze, nearly colliding on the way with a cyclist who swore at him, and slumped down in a chair, despair written on his face. Rosemary was itching to hear his news, but she could see that it was not good, and didn't like to pry into his despondency. Having seen to the children and tucked them up, she said she had rung Jim and said she would stay the night to help with the children. She had phoned on her mobile from the kitchen, with the door closed, and told Jim that she had not liked to ask Harry how things were, but it was obvious they were pretty bad.

Chapter 16
Psophometers 2311AD

Hal was ill in bed with a severe cold. He grumbled that it was ridiculous, you couldn't get a cold in such lovely autumn weather, but Sarah said, "Anything could happen at your age." She wondered what she could do to keep him amused, and eventually hit on the idea of suggesting that he should phone or email some of his contacts to see what was happening in the world, especially about population figures and sapes, after all, they were almost halfway to the next WPC in 2316. At first, Hal seemed reluctant; to his surprise, as he grew older the passion for sniffing out news, which had been the mainspring of his professional life as a reporter, was waning. But in the end, as he considered it, its appeal slowly grew in his mind, and he asked for his famous little black notebook, where he kept the details of his many worldwide contacts. She brought it, and his favourite little cordless phone which he could almost hide in the palm of his hand and propped him up in bed with notepad and pencil on a bed tray. Then she crept away, closed the door quietly and left him to it.

From downstairs, she phoned Rosemary. Jim answered and said his wife had stayed at Harry and Bella's flat overnight and was not back yet. She had rung a few minutes earlier to say that she didn't think Harry had slept at all and had just left for the hospital. There was no more news, but as soon as there was he would ring her. Sarah was deeply troubled about her daughter's illness and knew that Hal was too: That had been the reason for his grumpiness that morning. She couldn't concentrate on knitting the fancy bed-jacket which was to be a present for Bella's wedding anniversary, and was wondering what to do when, mid-afternoon, the phone rang. It was Jim: He had just had a call from a distraught Harry at the hospital to say that Bella had died at a few minutes past three. Hal was as shocked as she was, and as she sat on the side of his bed they were both dumb with grief.

"She was always so lively and healthy."

"I know." Such banal comments, but what else was there to say? They both lapsed back into silence, each with their own melancholy train of thought.

The funeral came – attended by the twins, their father, the four grandparents (Hal still with a cough), Julian and Inez, both the mayor and the mayoress; even the Carpenters had managed to get down from Cumberland, while unnoticed at the back (and strangely silent for once) was Elsie – and went. At Rosemary's suggestion, Harry had given up the flat and moved back to his parents' house. He needed little persuasion; apart from the needs of the twins while he was at work, the flat held too many memories of their all too brief marriage, there is nothing so poignant as the memory of happy times recalled in adversity. At first, he found it difficult to concentrate on his work; the bitter memory of his loss returned about every five minutes. But after a week or two, he could concentrate on his job for a couple of hours, sometimes even a whole morning, before the gloomy thoughts resurfaced. Then his boss Mr Buckingham, the proprietor of Lascar, made him responsible for the development of a miniature battery-operated Psophometer with flat, telephone and broadcast weightings, for use on subs loops, local, toll and trunk routes carrying digital voice and other traffic. For such a small firm, this was an important contract, from one of the larger telephone companies. The tight timescale stretched Harry's talents to the limit and left him little or no time to think of other things, as Mr Buckingham had deliberately intended. The weekends, at home with the children, were however a trial still, as they missed their mother and couldn't really comprehend that they would never see her again. Towards the end of the project, as the contract completion date loomed and the electrical design and testing were complete, there was the scramble to finish the mechanical design, order all the components and metal work, and get the job onto the production floor. For the last three weeks of the project, Harry was seldom at home even at weekends, though he always made a point of being there at bed time to tuck the twins up and kiss them goodnight.

So it was that Rosemary, at fifty-four, found herself effectively a mother again, something which she had never envisaged let alone wanted and which at times she found irksome. But she also found that from time to time, when the twins were good and things went well, there was a little of the quiet satisfaction that she had sometimes experienced also with Harry when he was young, and which she had quite forgotten. And the twins both looked up to Granddad, although Jim had never been quite as good with children as Julian was. Nevertheless, she was thinking to herself one day as she was putting the kettle on, that it really was a lot of extra work. *What with a couple of two-year-olds as well as everything else, no wonder I always feel tired,* when there was a knock at the front door.

"Now do be quiet for a few moments, please," she cautioned the twins; as it happened their curiosity produced just the hush Rosemary had hoped for – perhaps they thought, *against all reason, that their mother might be standing there, somehow miraculously restored to them.*

Rosemary opened the door and there was her next-door neighbour, Elsie; Rosemary's spirits sank a little. They had always got on well enough together and had occasionally helped each other out with the odd household chore that went better with four hands than two. But apart from that, they had precious little in common and to make matters worse, Elsie was one of life's non-stop talkers. At less than one metre sixty tall and definitely on the plump side but with an inexhaustible supply of energy, Elsie was like a busy little bumblebee, with a chubby bright red face, wispy grey hair and hands that were never still.

"Oh, er, do come in, Elsie; I'd just finished giving the twins their lunch and clearing up the mess afterwards, it's amazing how much extra work they seem to make – I'd quite forgotten what it was like and anyway I only ever had the one. Tea?"

"If it's not too much trouble."

"No, no, kettle's just gone on anyway." A little white lie; like her husband, son and in-laws, Rosemary always drank coffee, but knew Elsie didn't.

"Not too strong, no milk and one and a half spoonful isn't it?" Elsie nodded as she sat down in the chair in the lounge which Rosemary indicated with a wave of the hand.

"You must be finding it an awful lot of extra work my dear. But that's just what I've come about."

Oh dear, thought Rosemary as she headed for the kitchen. *I hope she's not going to offer to help, that's the last thing I want.*

A few minutes later Rosemary was back in the lounge with a pot of tea, a spoon and sugar for Elsie and milk for herself. Before she had time to say a word, Elsie started in with, "You know that Mrs Richardson, lives in Letsby Avenue?" Rosemary shook her head.

"Don't you? Oh well, never mind, 'used to live', I should've said. I was speaking to her next-door neighbour earlier, and apparently, she died the day before yesterday – Mrs Richardson that is – and her only close relative, a nephew, was there yesterday morning. Apparently, he was very fond of his aunt – or perhaps he just hoped to inherit the house and everything. Oh dear, that's unkind of me; I shouldn't have said that should I? Anyway, seems he used to ring her up every evening to make sure she was all right. Well, when she spoke to him yesterday afternoon he was at his wits' end."

"I should think so too, didn't he have any inkling something was wrong?" said Rosemary, who decided the tea had probably had time to draw and poured for them both.

"No, one day she was fine and the next she was gone, just like that."

"Best way; it's terrible when someone goes into a long decline, and they're no good to themselves, or anyone else either. That's how I should like to go when my time comes."

"Oh, don't. We've both got a good few years yet, I should say. Anyway, like I was saying, he was at his wits' end, because of Grace."

"Grace?"

"Yes, Grace. That's its – her name. A sapesse. After he retired, Mr Richardson bought it to help his wife around the house when she started to find the housework difficult. After he died, Grace did more and more, and, well, finally finished up looking after Mrs Richardson almost entirely, as well as any nurse could've, by all accounts."

"We've got used to sapesses on the tills in shops and Bella once told us that they'd even got several working as nursing assistants in the hospital. Seems amazing what they can cope with, once they're used to it."

Barely allowing Rosemary time to get this remark in, Elsie rushed on. "Well, when the nephew didn't get an answer that evening he guessed there must be something wrong. He couldn't get over straight away, and when he arrived there the following morning, yesterday, there was poor Mrs Richardson in bed, dead, and Grace in a state, trying to wake her. He called a doctor, because the death was so sudden, and an undertaker, and late that afternoon the body was taken away."

"And Grace?"

"That's what I was coming to. No one knows what to do with the animal. The nephew can't take it, but it couldn't be left in the house alone. He said he's been told that as Grace is no longer young no one is likely to buy her, so if no one can be found to take her, she'll have to be put down."

"Oh no! After all those years of faithful service! How terrible."

"Well, anyway, the neighbour took her in, for the night at least. Apparently, the animal was as upset as any human would have been in those circumstances."

"Really? Still, I suppose it's not so surprising in fact, after all – in the wild I'm sure they live in family groups and help and look after each other, especially the females."

"But the neighbour says she can't keep Grace indefinitely, just until someone makes up their mind what to do with her. That's why I thought of you and all the extra work you've got, and maybe you could do with some help?"

There was a long pause, while just what Elsie was suggesting sank into Rosemary's consciousness. No, no, that would never do surely. It would just be yet another person to look after, in addition to Jim and the twins. Quite uncharacteristically, Elsie remained silent for many seconds – a very long time for her. Then she said, "Well, I must go now. Thanks for the tea. Let me know what you think. Only don't wait too long, or you might find Grace's been put down." And with a sympathetic glance at Rosemary and a warm smile for the twins – who had been struck silent throughout a conversation they only partly understood – she let herself out, closing the door quietly behind her.

*****

With the trauma of Bella's sudden death, Hal had quite forgotten about the notes he had made on talking to various contacts on that fateful morning two weeks earlier. Now, a week after the funeral, he remembered them. President Mbalala of the United Central African Republic was lobbying the United Nations, to have the sanctions lifted. These had been imposed in 2302, when it became known that he was arming and training sapes. He had the support of some of the neighbouring countries, ruled by virtual dictators like himself, who thought that they might one day need to take similar steps themselves to retain power. However, the Republic of South Africa reluctantly supported sanctions, as did one or two other African states, while some others had no policy (deliberately) on the question.

Hal had also found in his little black notebook the names of several delegates to the various WPCs that he and they had attended together. He had read an article in the paper about the worldwide pollution, which was generally believed to be the major factor, if not the only one, in population decline. Intrigued to probe a little deeper, he contacted Dick Bailey. Dick, twelve years his junior, was semi-retired, but still retained by Benson Pharmaceuticals as a consultant. After the introductions – they had not seen or spoken to each other for years – Hal asked, "Just how much is known about environmental pollution by synthetic chemicals?"

"There's a great corpus of knowledge on the subject. There are maps of the world indicating pollution intensity iso-contours for each of the major contaminants, and some of the minor ones as well, looking rather like seasonal rainfall or temperature maps. But in many cases, what isn't known is what effect each of these contaminants has separately on human fecundity, let alone what effect the combination of any two or more have or on that of other species either, such as sapes. You can't experiment on humans to find the effect on fecundity of Lindane or whatever. That ain't ethical, besides, you'd need hundreds in each experimental and control group, because there are no such things as perfectly average normal people."

"But surely we must know something about it by now?"

"Sure, we know about many deleterious effects of man-made chemicals in the environment. For instance, tests on house dust used to turn up brominates, used at one time as flame retardants, and phthalates. Brominates are known to affect the hormonal system and phthalates damage the reproductive system. Both long since banned of course, but they're out there in the environment, in huge quantities. If you want another example, we've known for more than four hundred years that women with above average levels of pesticides in their blood are five times more likely than others to develop breast cancer. Yet synthetic chemical pesticides are still used in some countries."

"Not in Europe or North America, surely?"

"No, not legally at any rate. Though every year there're several prosecutions for illegal use. But in any case, it has been found they can spread worldwide due to weather conditions. A deep depression following a long dry spell can suck up dust particles with traces of pesticides into the clouds. The fallout can be hundreds or thousands of miles away, even on a different continent. It's not just pesticides; we've spread all sorts of chemicals all over the place, often quite needlessly."

"Well yes, but others we couldn't do without. They must present a real problem, don't they?"

"I'm sure you're right, but often we just don't know. Take titanium, for instance. Before modern man came on the scene, this was all locked up in ores like menachanite, in Cornwall and elsewhere. For years, it was used for turbine blades in jet engines, but thousands of tons of titanium dioxide are now scattered around the world."

"Isn't that the white pigment they used in the old oil-based paints up to a century ago?"

"Yes, it's always been considered entirely non-toxic. It was even added to food at one time."

"To food? Whatever for?"

"To whiten it. The horseradish sauce you buy in the supermarket today is much the same colour as it used to be when it was homemade, five hundred years ago, a rich deep creamy colour. But two hundred and fifty years ago supermarkets persuaded themselves that housewives wouldn't buy it unless it was white. And it went into lots of other foods as well."

"Crazy, just crazy."

"The point is that while titanium and its oxide are usually considered harmless, we don't know about all its possible compounds, especially organic compounds. Phosphorus the element is very poisonous, yet it's essential to life, we all have it in our bodies; it's an essential constituent of DNA. Similarly, a harmless element like titanium might be very poisonous in some organic compound."

"I suppose there's no way of taking these compounds out of the environment, once they're out there?"

"Well, no, not at present. Benson of course are in pharmaceuticals, but one of our sister companies is in microbiology and they've had an on-going UN funded programme for years. They're trying to come up with strains of bacteria, which eat various contaminants and effectively lock them up out of the way. It sounds too fraught with difficulties to me, like what happens when a bacterium dies and decomposes. And the only useful sounding strain developed so far is not specific enough; it gets rid of its target contaminant, but also attacks other compounds which are essential to modern life."

"Thank you very much; you've really cheered me up."

"Sorry, but you did ask!"

After a further exchange of courtesies, Hal extracted a promise that if Dick were ever in London, he would drop in at Kensington and see him again and meet Sarah. An offer to visit Dick and perhaps look around the Benson establishment was regretfully declined, as at eighty-one, Hal was not as mobile as he would have liked.

In a thoughtful mood after this conversation, Hal thought he would ring Julian to discuss some of the points Dick had made. He was just looking up the number when Sarah came back from shopping. She had been to her usual supermarket, which was not the cheapest one, but the quality of the food there was excellent and the customer service beyond praise. Most of the food they sold was what would once have been called organic, but with the greatly reduced population density, intensive farming methods were no longer necessary, few agrochemicals allowed and most of the labour carried out by sapes so that produce was in fact nowadays organic anyway.

Hal got up from his chair and started stiffly towards the kitchen to make coffee. But Sarah waved him back to his chair, kissed him lightly on his balding forehead and told him to behave himself like a good boy.

He had been having trouble with low back pain and the doctor had prescribed some pills to ease it and told him to rest. It had first troubled him in his late forties and on into his middle fifties, but then he had invented some daily exercises that strengthened his back muscles, and this had kept him free from pain for years. Lately however, he was becoming so stiff it was difficult to do his exercises, an eventuality that he had foreseen, but to which, at first, he had found no answer. Then, discussing the problem with one of the contacts in his black book, the contact said, "You should wear a corset like I do. Not only does this keep me free from back pain but wearing it I am able to do the exercises that I had had to give up before."

"Where do I get one of those, and how? Anyway, they wouldn't be any good to me – men measurements are completely different to women's."

"You can get a corset made exactly to your measurements from where I get mine."

"Where's that? Anyway, it wouldn't be long enough in the body; I'm one metre seventy-nine tall."

"Just go to 'Villiers Corsets'; their model 'Nerissa' is extra-long in the body, suits the tallest women and is very popular with men. I'm one metre seventy-seven and three quarters myself, so one of those would fit you just fine." Hal had made a note of all this and decided to order one.

When he retailed all this to Sarah, she said, "Fine, it's just what you need. We should have thought of its years ago. But you'll need a minimum of two, get say three while you're at it. By the way, I've brought home some 'naughties', as you call them."

Sarah bustled about in the kitchen and came in a little later carrying a tray with cups of coffee and two little plates with a cherry lattice puff on each. She personally preferred the almond doughnut twists but had settled on Hal's favourite to cheer him up. The following day Hal rang Villiers, and they sent a form which he filled in with his measurements and was about to order three, as Sarah had advised, when he thought better of it and ordered four. In just under three weeks his four corsets arrived, and he tried one on the following morning. He did up the front busk taking care that the underbody flap covered the lacing rather than staying bunched up on the left-hand side to which it was attached and was experimenting with doing up the back lacing.

"Here, let me help," said Sarah.

To which Hal replied, "All right, but only today. I've obviously got to get the knack of doing it for myself. If I were away in a hotel overnight, I couldn't ring for a chambermaid to come and lace me up."

"But you're never away overnight are you, if you need to go up to London for a meeting, you're always back the same night." Hal had future WPCs in mind, if he were well enough to attend, he would love to go.

Once in the corset he felt agreeably cosseted and supported but worried he might be conscious of it all day long. In fact, however, when he came to take it off on going to bed, he realised that he was only conscious of it occasionally, when he wasn't busy doing anything in particular. The rest of the week, he managed to lace himself up alone, but found it advisable to put on his socks before the corset to avoid having to bend double while wearing it. Similarly, he changed to wearing slip-on shoes rather than lace-ups. The following week Sarah remarked how long it took him to get dressed nowadays.

One evening a month later Hal rang Julian, and the two men had a long conversation. Hal related the points that Dick had made and found Julian basically in agreement with them. But interestingly, he had some information, which was new to Hal. He had been in touch with William Hacker, who in turn had been in touch with his successor in the Department of Health and

Reproduction. The latter had recently received a report from the Department of Population Statistics, which sent representatives to UNACOPS. The Department of Population Statistics had received the report, entitled 'Fecundity in Certain Sub-Atlean Populations' from UNACOPS, and had passed a copy to the Department of Health and Reproduction, a sign of the improved relations between the departments following the retirement of Ken Robinson. From this document, they learnt some interesting news. The earlier paper on the subject, released just after the 8th WPC, had prompted action from a specially constituted sub-committee of UNACOPS. This had encouraged small struggling family groups of landless peasants from Central and South America and Southeast Asia to settle in the improved areas south of the Atlas Mountains, providing all removal and travel expenses, and any necessary tools, materials and seeds to start a new life. There had been no shortage of volunteers; indeed, the UN offices in the countries concerned had been deluged with crowds demanding to be among the chosen families.

This human experiment had been started shortly after the 8th WPC, so that the new communities had now been in existence for nigh on twenty years. As with the Berber and Tuareg communities in the area, fertility was markedly greater than in the countries from which the new communities had originated. Although it was clearly early days to draw firm conclusions, it really seemed that the new communities would be able to sustain at least a stable population, and possibly even a growing one. The birth rate was particularly encouraging in the few instances of intermarriage between members of the Central American and Southeast Asian communities, and Berbers or Tuaregs.

"Perhaps there's hope for mankind yet," commented Hal, when Julian had finished describing the leading points of the report.

"Perhaps, but there's no room for everyone to live in such a favoured area; elsewhere, decline continues apace," murmured Julian, as it did indeed, ominously.

Chapter 17
Encounter on the Bridge 2314AD

The year was turning from an early warm wet spring into a promising summer, and Harry, still a keen rugger player when he had the opportunity – less and less often nowadays, he was twenty-eight. He still worked at Lascar, had progressed well and was now Chief Engineer. The twins, now five, accepted the fact that they had a Granny, but no Mummy, unlike their school friends. What they did have thought was an 'aunt', but unlike any of their friends' aunts. Three years or so before, in twenty three eleven, there had been a long and serious discussion between Rosemary and Jim, about Grace.

Initially they were both against the idea of giving her a home, Jim much more so than Rosemary. In fairness, Rosemary said, "At least it's not as if it were a male sape – you know how unpredictable they can be, especially if they haven't been –" She stopped short, noticing young Bill, his hair all over the place, socks round his ankles, and freckled face, grubby as usual – listening interestedly.

"What, Granny?"

"Some of them, men sapes that is, can get violent sometimes. Now you just run along and wash your face; it's filthy, as usual."

"Wouldn't it be just more work for you, not less?" asked Jim, after Bill had scampered off.

"I don't know. Elsie and I spoke to Mrs Richardson's neighbour, and she said that Grace seemed to have a very gentle nature, and after Mr Robinson died Grace finished up looking after her mistress almost entirely. And Grace was already learning to help her around her house, after just a day or two. She said she would probably have kept Grace herself, only her husband won't hear of it, for some reason."

So eventually it was agreed that, to avoid the possibility of Grace being put down – an eventuality that Rosemary could not bear even to think about – they would give it a try for a few weeks. But already, by the end of the first week, Rosemary was surprised and indeed completely delighted with just how much help Grace was, and by the end of the second even Jim was convinced. So it was that over the next month or two, Grace – dressed in an age twelve gingham dress from the supermarket – gradually became an indispensable part of the family. She would get up at 6.30am and by the time Harry and the twins came down to breakfast Grace had already done half the housework and hot coffee and buttered toast with a scrambled egg on top, were ready and waiting for them.

Jim had always assumed that all sapes looked alike, as difficult – at least for a human – to tell apart as one sheep from another and said so.

"I know, I thought so at first," said Rosemary.

"There's an enormous area of our brains dedicated to processing the details of the human face; that's why we're so good at recognising people. We can even tell one identical twin from the other. But I suppose shepherds get used to telling their sheep apart, too," said Jim.

"I'm sure they do. I've got so's I can tell all the sapesses on the tills at the supermarket apart. And Grace looks quite different from any of them; perhaps it's because she's older than they are. And have you noticed her eyes? She usually looks a bit sad, but when she's busy with the children, she actually smiles. Especially when they're being good; I'm sure they behave better for her than they do for me. But her smile is all done with her eyes, the mouth doesn't seem to come into it at all like it does with us."

"If a sape bares his teeth it a threat, not a smile."

Young Anne, with her blonde plaits tied off with red ribbons, soft wistful features and wide innocent eyes, took to Grace almost instantly, like a second mother. Initially, Bill tried to play Grace off against Rosemary, though without success. At two years of age, the lad was no match for a grown sapess, even though she was not from the largest and heaviest type of stock, nor for his grandmother either.

*****

Now, two years later, it was a relatively peaceful household, if a little unusual, with three females and three males. Nonetheless, strains did occasionally come to the surface. Harry was conscious of his duties and responsibilities as a father to Bill and Anne, yet as he was at work five days a week, it was also to their grandparents, and particularly Rosemary (and even Grace), that the twins had had to learn obedience. But one morning, Grace wasn't down with the breakfast already as usual. Ongoing up to her room Rosemary found her semiconscious and moaning from time to time. While Rosemary attempted to wake here – with little success, Anne with great common sense picked up a phone, dialled 999 and asked for an ambulance. In a few minutes, it arrived, and Bill answered the front door, invited in a paramedic and his driver and dashed up to tell Rosemary to come. She explained that the family's servant was ill and took the two men up to see the invalid.

"Where's the invalid?" said the paramedic.

"It's our sapess servant, here," replied Rosemary.

"Sorry, can't help. The hospital only takes humans."

"Let's go. None of our business," said the driver. The paramedic could see that this left Rosemary nearly in tears.

"The driver's quite right, you know."

"Can't you do anything?" said Rosemary with a pleading look. The paramedic looked at the driver and whispered something.

"Hang on a minute. It's out of our way a bit and we have to account for our mileage you know. Still, I'll tell you what; we could drop your er – servant – off at the Wrightson Veterinary Hospital and Clinic on our way back to the hospital, couldn't we Fred?"

Fred grudgingly agreed and Grace was stretchered into the ambulance and driven off. That evening Harry phoned the Wrightson Clinic and enquired after Grace. The receptionist said she would put Harry through to the duty vet, who after a few moments picked up the call. "Mr Brophy? Yes, the creature is sleeping on and off, but the omens are not good, its heart rate is erratic and it's having breathing difficulties. Enquire again tomorrow." Harry did so mid-morning and the vet said, "I'm happy to be able to tell you that the animal is progressing well." On enquiring the following day, however, Harry was told that Grace had died in the night.

Over the last two years Harry had gradually come to the conclusion that the only solution to his responsibilities would be if he remarried and he, his wife and the twins became an independent family unit again, relieving Rosemary of the job of mothering the twins, especially as there was no longer Grace to help. Of course, he would have to ask the children, but before doing so, he considered whether it was a fair question; after all, they had only a slightly hazy memory of

Bella. But he soon found that they knew exactly what a mother was, from visits to the homes of various friends. Consequently, he had asked the twins one day, "Would you like a mummy?"

And they had replied in unison, "Yes please!"

He had not asked out of the blue: He had discussed remarriage with his father, who was all in favour of the idea. He thought it would be good for the children, a view with which both Rosemary and Inez concurred, though Julian was more cautious, fearing things might not go smoothly between the twins and their new 'mother'. Harry took the majority view and said he would see what he could do. But the obvious problem was that he knew no unattached women, at least not of an age to be interested in a widower with two small children. With the active encouragement of the government, virtually all young people were married by the time they were twenty or twenty-two at the latest, most much earlier. So, he resorted to the Introduction Service. In former times, there had been lots of these, charging substantial fees, as they were run for profit. Now, each county had its own official introduction service, operating on a free-of-charge basis via the internet. They all came under an umbrella organisation, run by the Department of Population Statistics, which financed them, and ran an overlay service. This provided a between-counties service in cases where no suitable outcome arose from within-county introductions.

It was a wet Sunday afternoon when Harry sat down at the computer in Jim's office upstairs: Unlike so many people, he worked most days at his company's premises rather than from home, reflecting the practical hands-on design and development side of his work, though now this was increasingly delegated to a very promising young graduate they had taken on a year and a half ago. He logged on to the Introduction Service's site. The twins watched spellbound, hoping for the sudden miraculous appearance of a new mummy, but soon lost interest when it seemed that their father was wading through page after page of displays, finally arriving at an Enter Personal Details page. They had started to get restless, with Anne worrying to climb on his lap while Bill began to rummage in his grandfather's desk. Hearing the commotion, Rosemary came up and tactfully led the children away with a promise of a cup of real grown-up's coffee and a cake, leaving Harry to grapple with the forms. He came down a quarter of an hour later with the news that the system had not found him any match at all.

"I'm not surprised there are no available ladies here in Tun Wells, but I thought there might have been a result from a county-wide search," said Jim.

"I think the match conditions they apply must be far too restrictive. I had to fill in an incredible amount of detail about my physical appearance; height, weight, girth, colour of hair, eyes, skin, not to mention my school details from the infants stage upwards, what I read, what I listen to, what I watch, religious affiliation if any; dependants of course – the list was endless. All quite ridiculous, none of these things might turn out to be important when you meet someone for real. As long as they've got two arms, two legs and a head in the right place, one might as well meet them and see whether it gels."

Rosemary brought him a cup of coffee and a biscuit, after which, just to see whether his theory about over restrictive match conditions was right, Harry went back up to the office and logged on under various different names, and tried changing the colour of his eyes, his height, his interests and so on; all to no avail. Finally, he logged on again under his own name, accessed the inter-county site, ticked a 'relax-match-criteria' box which did not appear on the in-county page, and with a groan found he was faced with entering all his details all over again.

Whoever wrote this software must have been a dunce, it would have been so easy to save all the personal details in a cache, ready to be used again if necessary, he thought.

The adjacent and other near counties in turn each returned a blank result, and he was about to give up, when he thought that as a last desperate throw, he would try County of London. To his surprise, up came a message box saying that an exact match had not been found, but a near match had, and an email had been sent to the inbox of a lady of thirty-two, resident in Bayswater. No further details could be given at that stage, as it was up to the person in question to review his details and contact him herself if she wanted to.

He went downstairs, poured himself yet another cup of coffee and joined his parents and the twins in the garden – the rain had stopped, the sun was brilliant, and the grass was already almost dry underfoot. He dropped into a deckchair next to Jim, and Anne climbed onto his lap, curling up with her head on his chest while Bill amused himself trying to tie his father's shoelaces together until pushed away a second time, this time more forcibly.

"Any luck?" asked Rosemary and the twins chimed in with.

"We're going to have a new mummy, we're going to have a new mummy!"

"The service has left my details with someone of thirty-two who lives somewhere in Bayswater. Whether she will think I sound worth contacting or not, I don't know. Depends how desperate she is."

"Now don't be like that – I'm sure your details sound quite attractive," said Rosemary.

They had dined, as usual at weekends, at midday. That evening, after tea and playing with the children till, they were tired enough for bed, Harry logged on and accessed his in-box. There, to his surprise, was an email from a certain Jenny Hacker saying that she would be pleased if they could meet sometime, somewhere mutually convenient – the message gave her email address, but for security reasons, not her postal address. Harry ticked the reply-to-email tab and sent a message saying that he could come up to town the following Saturday; a reply in confirmation appeared the next day – Monday – and Harry viewed it on his machine at work, during the lunch hour. He had suggested that they meet on the bridge over the lake in St James's Park at noon; this would give him plenty of time to get from home to Waterloo and walk from there to the park. That week, both at work and at home, he kept worrying about whether he was doing the right thing. But he kept telling himself that there was really no point in worrying, since probably they would mutually decide that they were not suited to each other. But what if it turned out that they decided – erroneously – that they were? If they got married and it didn't work? If Julian's reservations turned out to be justified?

Saturday morning came and the twins were up early. They had somehow got wind of what was afoot and kept asking if Daddy was going to bring their new mummy home that day. Harry dressed reasonably smartly, but not more smartly than usual. He didn't want to give the impression that he had pretensions to be anything other than what he was, a very ordinary chap, really. He chose a striped shirt and light grey jacket, adding a tie as an afterthought. On the journey, he agonised over the tie, was about to take it off and stuff it in a pocket but then changed his mind. The train ran on time, and he walked from the station to their rendezvous in bright sunlight, though the breeze was decidedly fresh.

He arrived at the bridge in St James's Park at five to twelve and found to his dismay that it was crowded. How could he have been so stupid as not to foresee the problem, and arrange to be carrying some distinguishing mark? Whatever would Miss Hacker think of him? He had just started to walk slowly across the bridge when his attention was caught by a commotion to his left. An obstreperous coot was chasing away a moorhen amid loud cries and spraying water. He returned hastily to the job in hand and continued, observing all the people as he went. There were two Japanese girls, obvious from their appearance, three Americans, obvious from their loud accents, but the vast majority were ordinary looking Londoners, black, white, yellow or swarthy. With the worldwide restrictions on travel, foreigners were few and far between, and consequently stood out noticeably.

In passing, he noticed one youngish lady, standing by the handrail, exactly in the middle of the bridge. She was smartly dressed, with high-heeled shiny black court shoes and slim shapely legs clad in fine gleaming ten denier; he was glad he had not decided to remove the tie. In contrast, her face was remarkably plain; not exactly ugly, but one definitely would not describe it as attractive. As he walked back a second time, it was obvious to anyone watching that he was expecting to meet someone. As he neared the middle of the bridge, the plain face stepped forward and said, "Mister Brophy?" With a questioning intonation.

"Yes?" He smiled in reply and was disconcerted to see not the hint of a smile in return. *This,* he thought, *did not look promising.*

"I'm Jenny, Jenny Hacker. Shall we walk round the lake?"

They set off, Harry furiously trying to think of something, anything to say, but could not.

"Have you had to come far?" What an obvious opening gambit, now why hadn't he thought of that? But then he already knew she came from Bayswater, so that wouldn't have done anyway.

"From Tunbridge Wells."

"Did you have a good journey up?"

"Yes, thanks."

Come on, he said to himself, *say something else for goodness's sake, you can't leave it all up to her.*

"The trains were on time for once. It's the same old rolling stock, must be nearly a hundred years old, but it's still very comfortable." *Not brilliant,* he thought, *but at least you're trying.* But after that, inspiration seemed to desert him. *What an earth can I say now?* he thought. At that moment, there was a loud commotion from the lake, and an angry coot, he did not know whether it was the same one, was chasing off a seagull more than twice its size.

"Just look at that," he said, and they stopped and watched the pursuit, the contestants so apparently ill-matched. It seemed to break the ice and the conversation somehow flowed more easily. He had never found conversation with Bella difficult, but then they had known each other from childhood. He never found difficulty talking to the one female engineer at Lascar, but then she was a safely married girl; no, the daunting thought was that he was possibly speaking to his future wife – or was he?

He remembered the face, what he believed Americans called 'homely', was it actually gaunt? As they walked side by side he glanced sideways: Strangely, in profile her face was much less odd, quite normal in fact, really quite attractive. She noticed his glance and slipped her hand into his; it was warm and soft. Years later, she confessed to him that she had thought that glance a good omen, she had known from a child that her profile was her best side. For his part, he was beginning to feel distinctly underdressed, an uncomfortable and embarrassing feeling. He wondered if Miss Hacker always dressed that smartly, or had she taken especial care for their first meeting? He wished he had, too.

Well, I did, didn't I? But I got it wrong; a bit too much on the informal side, he thought to himself.

They continued their circumnavigation of the lake: Now that he had got used to the necessity of trying, conversation seemed to be coming more easily. They reached the Duke of York steps, and he suggested they find somewhere for lunch. She said she knew somewhere suitable and led the way up the steps and through streets in which he rapidly found himself completely lost, even though he though he prided himself on knowing Central London fairly well. They arrived at a little restaurant which called itself The Corner House – though it was situated in the middle of a row of small shops. Jenny made her way in and showed Harry a faded framed photograph on the wall; it showed the imposing frontage of a restaurant which had long disappeared, and a label on the frame said, 'The Corner House, 1955'. Jenny was clearly known there; a waiter came up, smiled and spoke, "A table for two, Miss Hacker?" Again, Harry noticed no smile in return, and wondered.

They settled into a table by the window and chose from the very reasonably priced lunch menu. Harry said, "Would like some wine?"

"I wouldn't normally at lunch time, but I'll gladly have some if you're going to."

"I wouldn't usually at lunch time either, but let's make this an occasion. You would never believe how long I spent searching for someone on the internet, first in Surrey, then in surrounding counties and nearly giving up until I thought I might try London."

Conversation was coming much more fluently now, the ball passing back and forth from one to the other, from one subject to another. Harry said, "My grandfather had worked for the government under a Mr Hacker, and my father had met him too though I myself never met him." Jenny's face broke into a smile of surprise, which she rapidly suppressed, and then remarked, straight-faced, "He's my grandfather."

Now Harry realised the reason for the absence of smiles. Jenny's face, plain enough in all conscience in repose, twisted awkwardly into a most unbecoming bizarre grimace whenever she smiled. Harry warmed towards this poor girl, stuck with an unfortunate smile, no wonder it did not appear if she could help it. It was just the way her face was made, the unfortunate way the muscles involved in smiling worked. What embarrassment she must have gone through at school, must still go through when meeting people for the first time. He remembered the lovely legs, the smart two-piece costume, the svelte figure, the warm soft hand and thought what a shame an accident of nature had denied her at least an unremarkable smile, if not a dazzling one like Bella's.

They finished their meal, had coffee and Jenny declined to let Harry pay for them both. Their bills settled, they went back down the street the way they had come, and Harry found himself unaccountably holding her hand. He couldn't remember whether he had taken hers, or she his.

Chapter 18
Zimba 2316AD

A year had passed, and a lot had happened, both on the domestic front and on the world stage. On the former, Harry and Jenny had wed just three months after their first meeting. It had been a quiet wedding, with just the bride's and groom's parents, the groom's grandparents and the mayoress, and of course the twins, who had not behaved very well. Jenny's grandmother had died three years previously, and William, at eighty-three, was too frail to travel: Both her maternal grandparents were long dead. The wedding had been overshadowed by the death of Hal a fortnight earlier; there had indeed been some discussion of postponing the wedding, but Sarah was adamant that she would hear of no such thing. So, the wedding was preceded by a funeral, a week beforehand.

"It's an excellent thing for the twins to have a mother near their father's age; however loving, a grandmother is never a substitute," said Rosemary to Jenny.

Harry wanted the weeklong honeymoon to be as different as possible from his first honeymoon, and Sarah said they could have her flat in Kensington, while she stayed with Julian and Inez. Harry said, "That would mean Jenny would be only a few streets away from her own place."

But Jenny replied, "Thanks so much, Sarah, I'll be able to show my new husband all the sights of London, not just the tourist sites, but the more out-of-the-way places that the tourists miss, like the statue of Jenner, by the pond in Kensington Gardens, and a thousand other things besides."

Later, when they showed their holiday snaps one evening to Rosemary, Jim, Inez and Julian, Inez commented that the places they had visited had included nearly all the ones she and Julian had visited fifty-nine years earlier, but they mostly looked entirely different – except for the statue of Jenner.

After the honeymoon, Harry and Jenny moved into a flat not far from his previous home with Bella. That flat had also been available, but Harry could not bear the thought of living there with his new wife and the ghost of his old. Besides, the new flat was larger, and on the ground floor, in some communal gardens where the children would be able to play in safety. Unfortunately, Julian's fears had been largely justified. Anne and Bill had not taken readily to Jenny and refused to call her mummy. In their childish imagination, they had expected a new mummy would look the same as Bella, sound the same as Bella and almost be a reincarnation of Bella. Anne had just accepted the situation sullenly, but Bill had been openly hostile: He had beaten his five-year-old's fists in Rosemary's lap and shouted, "She's not my mummy! She's ugly."

"Your mummy was ugly too," said Rosemary, an obvious lie but it had the desired effect.

"She wasn't," shouted Bill, and he flailed his little fists again and burst into tears.

Rosemary put her arm around him. "No, no, of course she wasn't, love, but there now, that's how Daddy feels if you're nasty about Jenny." She dried his tears, and it was agreed that the twins would stay on with Rosemary and Jim for a few weeks, while Harry and Jenny settled into the new flat and got it organised and home like. There was a discussion as to what the twins should call Jenny. They all agreed that it was not a good idea to try and make them call her mummy, and Nanna didn't sound very convincing either. In the end, it was agreed that they should simply call her Jenny, and within a month or two, Jenny and her two instant children were, for the most part, on passably good terms.

As twenty-two sixteen wore on, the twins were now six, and doing reasonably well at school, though the teachers complained that Bill was short on concentration and 'could do better'. Their school dinners were excellent, so on weekdays they just had tea when they got home. Jenny had always been interested in cooking and soon after marrying Harry had got tired of the blandness of ready-made meals. So, she now followed her mother-in-law's (and her grandmother-in-law's) example of using all fresh ingredients, at least for the main meal of the day and often for other meals as well. On a hot midsummer's day, she was preparing some vegetables for the evening meal while the children got on with their sandwiches and cake. The knife slipped and blood poured from the forefinger of her left hand. Anne shrieked, but Bill got up, brought Jenny the roll of kitchen paper towels and then looked out the package of plasters from the drawer of the kitchen unit next to the cooker. Jenny staunched the wound with a paper towel and waited for the flow to stop. Then she asked Bill to take a plaster, that middle-sized one, out of its wrapper. He did so, and as she held her finger out, he deftly applied the plaster. She thanked him and gave him a little hug, and he felt very grown up. When Harry came home, he saw the plaster on her finger and learnt about the accident, and Bill's part in it. He picked up the knife, which he had not seen before, and looked at the blade, gingerly feeling the edge. Stamped on the blade, nearly worn smooth over the years, but still just legible, he read out aloud.

S Tyzack
Railway Arch
Old Street

"Where did this come from?" he asked.

"It's been handed down in my mother's family for generations. Goodness knows how old it is. I tried to find the place once, but the railway arches have disappeared. The line's gone too, or been swallowed by some tall office blocks, but they look mostly abandoned now, too. I've got a couple more somewhere, Sheffield steel, I was always told. They take a really good edge."

"I see they do. You must be more careful love, you're the only wife I've got."

"I should think so too. I'm not sharing you with anyone." And she smacked him lightly on the wrist.

The outcome of the incident was that Bill now regarded Jenny as an essential part of the household; not his mother perhaps, but someone who needed a man like him to look after her.

If there had been difficulties on the domestic front, things were no calmer on the world stage. This year was of course to be the year of the 11th WPC, scheduled as usual for the late autumn. As in other years there would be delegates attending from Britain, from the Department of Population Statistics and the Department of Health and Reproduction, along with other delegates, both from government, academia and from industry. And of course, there would be delegates from other countries all round the world. An interesting Appendix to the Final Report of the last WPC, held in La Paz, listed the participating countries and the numbers of delegates each had sent. A summary listed the total numbers of delegates by regions: There had been thirty-five from North America, two hundred and ninety from South America, three hundred and two from S.E. Asia, one hundred and eighty eight from Asia (other), ninety-seven from Arabic countries and so on for other regions as diverse as Europe, Australasia, Russia, Oceania etc. For some reason, no figure was available for Africa.

But the summer brought dire news of conflict from Asia. Some of the groups of runaway sapes living in the Vietnamese forests had taken to waylaying travellers on the country's roads. At first, they only attacked people on foot, but were now using tree trunks to stop vehicles. Their motives were not clear: In some cases, items were stolen, particularly food if they found any; in other cases, the victims were terrorised or even attacked and one or two had been killed, while sometimes they showed no interest in people, seeming simply to enjoy causing havoc.

"The problem is that the Vietnamese government has no suitable defence force. To its credit, it's never employed and armed sapes as police or soldiers, unlike some countries," said Jim.

"In any case, it'd be impossible to tackle sapes in the jungle. They're superbly fitted to survive there using their natural woodcraft skills, making them more or less completely invulnerable," replied Harry.

"And all the time, they will be breeding, presumably. Some of them were supplied before the policy of neutering all males, apart from the few stud animals." It seemed to them both, a problem with no obvious solution, perhaps no solution at all, obvious or otherwise.

Autumn came, and Jim was again away at the WPC, held this year at the University of Waterloo, Ontario. As on other occasions, he amused himself in his bedroom, before going to sleep, by looking through the long list of names of the delegates. He hardly recognised any of them: *All the delegates I knew are too old to come,* he thought. There was a Martin Banbury whom he'd heard Hal talk about, and he guessed he was there on behalf of the Telegraph. Apart from that there were the common names that always cropped up; the Smiths from English speaking countries, the Schneiders from Germany, the LeBlanc's from Francophone countries and so on, but never another Brophy.

By now, Jim was completely familiar with the rhythm of the proceedings, and found one or two papers, associated with his specialism, of interest, while the many were of little or no interest. As on previous occasions, he was able to collect a spare set of papers for Julian; Hal would have been interested too, had he still been alive. Jim was of course, on behalf of Baker and Daley, particularly interested in papers dealing with the economic consequences of population decline and made notes of a number of interesting points relating to this, which were mentioned by speakers, but did not appear in the conference papers. However, undoubtedly the highlight of the Conference was the news that swept through the delegates like wildfire, on the last morning. Although, for some strange reason, not reported in the world's press, it seems that about five weeks earlier, a troop of runaway sapes had marched on the armoury in the capital of the United Central African Republic. There were guards outside, but these were themselves sapes, and were persuaded without great difficulty to throw in their lot with the renegades. All the arms and ammunition were carried away, and similar raids made shortly afterwards on the armouries in the only other three cities or towns of any size in UCAR. Delegates from UCAR were now said to be seeking help from the United Nations to disarm the sape hordes. These had been swelled over the following weeks by runaway sapes from neighbouring countries, and now by sapes from all over the continent. The sapes were said to be led by a ruthless leader called Zemba, a specimen of giant stature for a sape, nearly as tall as an average African. What was surely a fanciful embellishment to the story, dismissed by most delegates, was that Zemba had a human Father. These reports were of course entirely unofficial, and there was no place for them on the Conference agenda, or in the Report that followed in due course. The Conference therefore concluded in the usual way, and all the delegates returned to their respective countries, wondering what, if anything, could or would be done about the African sape insurgents.

Chapter 19
A Wedding and a Funeral 2316AD

Jim had returned from the 11th WPC with a cold, but was determined to shake it off as soon as possible, as he desperately wanted to discuss with Julian the momentous news circulated by mouth on the last day of the Conference. When it became evident that it would take some little while before he was free of it, he changed his plans, as there was no way he would take the risk of visiting Julian, now eighty-six, with a cold. Luckily, two days after his return, Rosemary announced that, if it was all right by him, she intended to spend the day with Jenny. She was a little secretive as to what they would be doing, but as it suited Jim's purpose, he did not enquire. When she had finally left, he went up to his office, still coughing from time to time, and rang his father. Julian answered, and Jim enquired if Inez were there.

"No, she's gone to spend the day helping a neighbour who's rather poorly and needs a hand with her housework. Ridiculous at her age, she's older than the neighbour, by a good few year. Why, did you want to speak to her?"

"No, no, I just wanted to be sure we wouldn't be interrupted; I wanted to sound you out about some incredible rumours that circulated on the last day of the Conference. I'd value your medical opinion."

"I'm afraid I'm a bit out of date now, despite trying to keep up with the latest developments; there're so many of them."

"Still, hear what I have to say, and then I'd be interested in your comments."

"Fire away then."

Jim related in detail the reports about the sape armoury raids, and the gathering of sape reinforcements from other countries in Africa to the United Central African Republic, finishing with the reports about Zemba, and in particular the rumour that he was fathered by a human.

"Tell me it's a load of nonsense," he said.

"Yes, probably."

"Probably? Surely you don't mean it could just be true?"

"I don't think it at all likely, but nonetheless cross species sports are by no means unknown. Everyone knows about the liger, and the zebroid is a cross between a horse and a zebra."

"But those species are very closely related."

"That's why I said I didn't think it likely. But I wouldn't rule it out entirely. All the primates – erect-walking mammals – share well over 99% of their genes in common."

"So, it might be possible?"

"I've said I suppose so, even if it is very unlikely. Mind you, that reminds me that I once heard a rumour that a brilliant but unscrupulous American microbiologist specialising in gene therapy had been hired by a South American sape breeding consortium. The aim was to produce a sapeman – a human/sape crossbreed."

"What would be the point of that?"

"The idea was that such a creature would easily acquire a command of language comparable to that of a seven to nine-year-old human, completely solving the problem the SHIP project was supposed to solve but never did."

"If successful, that would create all sorts of problems. Would sapemen and women be as biddable as sapes? And would they have rights such as a human has?"

"Well, I don't think you need lose any sleep over it – I've never heard any more about it, so I assume that either the rumour was false or the project was unsuccessful."

"If we share so many genes with sapes, how come they don't suffer the same fertility shortcomings as humans?"

"All mammals share 99% plus genes in common. But that still leaves a few million genes that differ between sapes and humans. So, it's not really surprising if sapes aren't affected by some substance or other that affects us."

"It's said that as well as his great stature, Zemba shares much of the intelligence and cunning of a human Father. What if he had offspring like himself if there were lots of creatures like Zemba?"

"I don't think you need worry yourself about that, even if he were fathered by a human, which isn't at all likely anyway. Cross species progeny are sterile. If you want another mule, you've got to cross an ass with a mare again." Of course, Zemba's semi-human parentage was only a rumour anyway, but Jim certainly found Julian's opinion reassuring.

Jim went on to relate to his father the news about population decline which had been released at the Conference. The decline was still in evidence, but the exponential was not as steep as had been forecast. They had had to modify the negative exponent, Professor Jensen had explained, reducing it by twenty five percent, representing a further postponement of the crunch date for humanity.

A later speaker had enlarged upon the promising developments in the Super-Saharan or Sub-Atlean area, where the population was now reckoned to be fully self-sustaining, largely due it was thought, to the providentially low levels of contamination in the area. Doubtless also in equal measure to the hybrid vigour of the population, steadily becoming a melange of Berber, Tuareg, Central American and Southeast Asian genes.

Further evidence of hybrid vigour came from New Zealand, where there had long been a history of intermarriage between the Māori's and the European-derived stock: New Zealand was another area where the fecundity was believed to be at or very close to a self-sustaining level. A speaker from Australia reported that except in the remoter areas of the interior, where population density was very low and variable anyway, the population was still well short of being self-sustaining. However, the comparatively few reported unions (at least compared to New Zealand) between the aboriginal inhabitants and the rest of the population seemed to show the expected effects of hybrid vigour. As a result, the government had recently passed legislation aimed at encouraging such unions, by economic and other incentives.

The year after the 11th WPC, at the beginning of March of twenty-three seventeen, Inez had a phone call from Sarah on a Saturday morning. The two women had been close friends, ever since she and Hal had first stayed with Julian and Inez and shared a single bed that first Friday in April thirty-two years earlier, even though they were not married. Julian and Inez had attended Hal's funeral, even though Julian had been finding walking rather difficult, and now Inez was surprised to hear, just two years later, that Sarah was engaged to be married again.

"Who's the gentleman concerned?" asked Inez and immediately bit her lip, realising that what she should of course have asked was, 'who's the lucky fellow?'

"You might possibly know him. I met him at the eighth WPC, and Jim knows him of course. He works at Baker and Daley, but in a different department from Jim."

"Yes, but who is it?"

"James; Doctor James Richard Mannering, to give him his full handle."

"Oh dear, another Jim. I'll never know whether you're talking about your husband, or my son."

"No fear of that. He's never known as James, even at school. He's always been Dick."

The conversation continued for an hour or more, with Inez asking when the great day would be, what sort of wedding it would be and a thousand other questions. She elicited the fact that Dick was fifty-five, that – she knew – would make him five years younger than Sarah. But then Hal had been twenty-six years older when they wed: Age differences obviously didn't seem to worry Sarah. At lunch, Julian asked who the phone call had been from. Inez told him and related all the details that she had been able to glean.

"They're planning a white wedding in County Hall, with a reception after in the Banqueting Hall."

"That'll cost a pretty penny," said Julian.

"Apparently Dick is quite well off. It seems he only works because otherwise he would get bored. He jokes that his salary doesn't quite cover his income tax bill, so he must have a lot of investment income."

"Can't understand it. What will he do with himself if eventually he has to retire?"

"You never found it a problem."

"No, but I worked because we needed the money. I always had stacks of things in mind that I wanted to do in retirement. There still hasn't been time for some of them, and others I haven't been well enough to get on with."

"Well, you certainly haven't been idle, all the same."

The wedding was arranged for the early autumn, and when Inez told Rosemary the full story, Rosemary told her that Jenny had just announced that she was expecting. As it happened, it would be just about that time.

"So, we might have a double celebration."

While the ladies were talking of the future at the personal level, their menfolk, while of course delighted at the prospects, were also concerned about events on the world stage. Harry had come over to see his father with a Stilson wrench, to lend a hand replacing a washered tap with a ceramic one, which Harry said was most unlikely to drip and would probably never need attention again, ever. After, they had fallen to discussing the world news and in particular reports on television, in the papers and on TV text about events in Africa.

"Trouble continues to flare sporadically in the United Central African Republic, with random attacks on lone travellers and small villages by groups of marauding sapes," said Harry.

And Jim replied, "Yes, apparently a march by several hundred sapes on the capital, long since renamed Mbalala-ville by the countries president, has been broken up by the tiny Police force, armed with machineguns and teargas grenades. But the fear was that another armoury raid might see machineguns and ammunition falling into the hands of sapes. Armouries have been reinforced with barred windows and double locks, the keys being held by two different officers."

"Random attacks on humans have also reported from half a dozen African states, some, it was rumoured, fomented by Zemba, who was believed to travel widely in the continent, receiving shelter and food from fellow sapes. He had been spotted from a light aircraft, haranguing a group of sapes, shortly before an audacious attack on a small town in the hilly north of Taboaland, just to the east of the United Central African Republic," said Harry.

The summer passed; it had been unusually hot and damp.

"It's a veritable monsoon. The weather's going mad, and we'll soon find themselves with a monsoon season every year," grumbled Julian.

"Don't be so silly. Just because you're eighty-six, you think the world is going to the dogs and disaster is just around the corner," said Inez.

"Well, isn't it?"

"Maybe, maybe not. But it doesn't do to dwell on it. Now come and sit over here, near the window, so I can trim you hair for you." Julian found it difficult to get to a hairdresser. A home-visit hairdresser had come and done his hair once but finding that Inez was not willing to let her do hers as well, never came again.

September approached; Sarah and Dick's wedding was scheduled for the second Saturday, and all the arrangements were in place. Neither Sarah nor Dick had many surviving relatives, but such as they were, they were invited. So were Julian and Inez, although they regretfully declined due to the difficulty they found in travelling. Sarah was disappointed, and asked Jim and Rosemary to represent them on the day. On the Monday before the wedding, Rosemary was concerned to learn from Harry that Jenny had been taken into hospital with abdominal pains.

"I can't possibly go if Jenny's not well," she said to Jim. But on Thursday Harry phoned again to say that Jenny was home again, the pains had subsided, and the tests indicated that all was well, at least for the present.

The wedding went off as planned, the weather was fine and sunny, and crowds watched as the bride in a gleaming white dress and the groom, smart enough, but in an expensive suit rather than white tie outfit, made their way to the Banqueting Hall, followed by all the guests. Jim and Rosemary brought up the rear of the procession, as friends rather than family. The couple took their honeymoon in Norfolk, where Dick's relatives had a sizeable estate, and thoughtfully sent an album with photos and a video recording of the proceedings to Julian and Inez.

Rosemary was more than a little concerned to hear, on Tuesday evening ten days later, that Jenny was back in hospital. She and Jim visited the hospital the following day and found Harry and the twins at Jenny's bed side. A doctor came in and asked them all to leave, even Harry, as there were some important tests that had to be carried out. They waited and waited, dividing their time between sitting in a waiting room and pacing up and down by the flowerbeds outside the hospital. At last, a nurse came out and said, "The doctor would like to speak to you."

They were quite unprepared for what he had to tell them, though one look at his grave face gave Harry a presentiment that it was not good news. The doctor told them that as the tests were about to be carried out, Jenny had gone into premature labour. The staff had managed the emergency well, but the baby, a boy, was stillborn. Rosemary, too, had seen the doctor's long face, and had motioned to Jim to take the twins out, so it was not until much later that day that he learnt any of the details. Jenny had lost a lot of blood, but that had been replaced with transfusions, and she was now sleeping peacefully, lightly sedated. Rosemary did not think that she knew yet that she had lost her baby.

Jim phoned Julian and Inez with the sad news late that evening; they were devastated to hear of the loss of a great-grandson and enquired anxiously after Jenny. Harry of course was inconsolable, and insisted on a coffin, a funeral and an interment for his son, though both Rosemary and the hospital staff had tried to dissuade him. In the event, fortunately it was all over before Jenny was really taking any cognisance of the world. A week later Jenny left hospital, and it was agreed that until she was stronger Rosemary would stay with her and the twins, so Harry could go to work.

The twins were most unhappy that they would not have a new brother after all; at seven years old it was the first time they had really had to face the reality of death – when their mother had died they had been too young to understand at first. Bill had been looking forward to having a younger brother, while Anne had expected to be allowed to help Jenny raise the new arrival. Sarah too was deeply saddened by the news, while Julian commented what a good job it was that it had not occurred earlier. Harry's wedding had been overshadowed by Hal's death; it would have been unfortunate in the extreme if Sarah had been similarly overshadowed by Harry and Jenny's loss. Meanwhile, on the international scene, things were just as turbulent, and continued to be so.

Chapter 20
Overdue Cleaning and Nuns' Sighs 2317AD

The following year, major revolts by sapes were reported in Africa. By May Day, the Security Council of the United Nations had been in session for three weeks, such was the alarm created by these events, for fear of repetitions elsewhere in the world. But reaching a decision, of any sort, was a matter of extreme difficulty as the Security Council had been expanded over the years by the addition of new members, so that it was now not that much smaller than the General Assembly itself. There was much talk of the need for action and a proposal by the Belgian Foreign Minister, that a standing U.N. force should be assembled ready for rapid deployment to any emergency created by sapes, was met with unanimous enthusiastic support and praise. But no country had so far come up with either a firm promise of troops or even the cash to finance operations carried out by someone else. The European states were slow to feel the need for action, as there had been no notable trouble from sapes within their borders. China, on the other hand, was most concerned. The results of the introduction of a strict population control regime, in the later years of the twentieth century, had not been seen until some two hundred years later, and these results were certainly not foreseen. Like other countries which had embraced the communist experiment, an emphasis on meeting over-ambitious industrial production targets at all costs had left the country badly polluted with all sorts of chemical by-products, wastes and residues. This, combined with an ageing population brought about by the population control measures, had resulted in a spectacular population crash in the twenty-second century. As a result, China was among the largest employers of agricultural sapes.

A proposal from a group of South American nations that a force of properly trained and armed sapes should be developed was discussed at great length. It was generally agreed that Mbalala's efforts in this respect had been both ill-advised and carried into practice in an unbelievably naïve and simplistic manner. However, the majority of members of the Council were against such a course of action, believing that the risks were so great as to outweigh the possible benefits, which it was admitted could be considerable. There was also the suspicion that the proposal was at least partly, perhaps mainly, inspired by the fact that that region had a near monopoly in the breeding and sale of sapes and had an eye to the business that would be generated.

Finally, to break the stalemate Norway agreed to organise a force, drawn from its own very limited regular army. This, like most European armies of the time, was largely ceremonial, as no European army had been involved in a conflict within the borders of the continent for over two hundred years. Nevertheless, the Norwegian Army did carry out training exercises on a regular basis, in polar, temperate and tropical climes. The force would deal solely with the threat in the United Central African Republic, and the Norwegian Foreign Minister said (without much conviction) that he hoped his country's example would be followed by others. A vote of thanks to his country was proposed, seconded and carried unanimously, and the marathon Security Council session was promptly adjourned sine die.

One Monday in August, Jim came down for coffee midmorning, a habit he had inherited from his father, Julian from Bill before that, and which he had duly passed on in turn to Harry. It was a welcome return to his usual routine, having had to travel up to the offices of Baker and Daley twice the previous week. As he headed towards the kitchen, the smell of newly brewed coffee was mingled with another odour he did not recognise. He found Rosemary industriously cleaning down the working surfaces and the doors of the cabinets and wall cupboards, spraying each with a cleaner and then vigorously wiping down with a cloth that she rinsed out and wrung out between attending to each surface.

"Just doing a little long overdue cleaning," she said.

"What's that stuff you're using?" Rosemary handed him the plastic spray bottle, with its deposit and return details on the bottom of the label. Jim studied it: It contained an oxidising agent, a mixture of various ionic and non-ionic surfactants, synthetic perfume, colouring matter and half a dozen other ingredients whose names meant nothing to him. He grunted, "It's all right to use it, isn't it? I mean, it wouldn't be on the market if it wasn't, would it?"

"I hope you're right. Early in the twenty-first century they drew up a list of thirty thousand different chemicals which could be found in homes and elsewhere, and laid town a timetable to test them all for effects on human health."

"And did they?"

"Most, I believe or at any rate many. But there were so many that the funds and the will – just ran out. And the findings were never published, although a good few chemicals were banned. That's the trouble – you just can't be sure. But I guess that stuff is as good as any; it's certainly been on the market for the best part of a century, or so the label claims."

They settled down to their coffee, with some delicious little confections called 'nuns' sighs', made of meringue and chipped hazelnuts, and dusted with cocoa powder, which Rosemary had made with egg whites left over from the previous night's omelette. She always used more yolks than whites in her omelettes and left the folded-in centre with its mushroom slices just slightly runny, a trick she had learnt from Inez, and which both Julian and Jim appreciated. As an excuse for yet another nun's sigh, Jim turned on the radio and tuned to the twenty-four hours news station. They were just in time to hear a report that a force of Norwegian troops had embarked on a cargo ship sailing for Africa.

Chapter 21
The Battle of Mbalala-Ville

Captain Gunnar Johansen, who was to be in charge of the force, had felt more alarmed than honoured, when told of the appointment, and the promotion that went with it. Feeling that some knowledge of dealing with members of the order primates would undoubtedly be a good thing, he had obtained all the books on the subject that he could find, particularly those in the Norwegian Natural History Museum, and studied them assiduously. These studies were supplemented by a search on the internet, which unearthed much more information than he had found in books. But more use still, he found, were several long talks he had had with an elderly friend who had in his youth been friendly with a retired keeper in what had been one of the last zoos in the world. The old gentleman had in his time looked after chimpanzees, gorillas, baboons, gibbons and various other members of the order primates. The Captain's friend had been fascinated by the keeper's reminiscences, which he remembered vividly and passed on to Gunnar.

The Major and his forty-eight-strong force landed in the port of Douala on the first of September and set out in the vehicles they had brought with them on the trek of hundreds of miles to the United Central African Republic. Ten days later they arrived at the outskirts of Mbalala-ville, where they were met and welcomed by the country's Foreign and Interior ministers. The following day they received a visit from the President himself, who made it clear that he was hoping the Norwegian army would exterminate all the rebel sapes in his country, and hopefully those in his neighbour's lands as well: He was horrified when he found that the Major and his gallant forty-eight were the whole force, and not just the advance guard.

The Major's troops soon fortified the accommodation with which the government had provided them, a long abandoned girls' school which had been run by nuns in the days of the previous government but three. They then sent out patrols, each accompanied by a speaker of the language of the land, questioning the inhabitants as to whether any rebel sapes had been seen there and if so, how many and how long ago. From the intelligence thus gained, the Major compiled a comprehensive report, which he passed back to his Foreign Ministry. He had been provided with a satellite digital data link, but being a keen amateur radio enthusiast, communicated additionally via an HF radio link using equipment he had constructed himself, with a fellow enthusiast in his hometown. Via the satellite link he received in return the pleasant surprise that he had been promoted again to Lieutenant Colonel.

Two days later, the local police chief of a small town the other side of Mbalalaville arrived on his bicycle, in a state of great agitation. He bore news that a horde of armed sapes, headed by an enormous brute whom he was sure was Zemba, was passing his town, evidently heading for the capital. Under a leaden sky, with thunder rolling threateningly in the distance, the Colonel set out at the head of his men, marching through the capital (which was only about the size of a largish English village or very small town) to meet the menace.

In an extensive area of dried grass dotted with a few small, stunted bushes, the two armies came face to face, the Norwegians outnumbered by about fifteen to one. The Colonel ordered his troops not to fire unless a shot or shots were fired by the sapes, in which case they were to fire a volley over the heads of the crowd. Handing his rifle to his right hand man, the Colonel advanced at the head of his men, beating his chest and shouting in Norwegian, "Go! Go! Away with you!" He stopped three metres from Zemba, his men behind him all holding their rifles across their chests, ready for action. Zemba beat his chest and roared his defiance, in a mixture of shrieks, howls and grunts, interspersed with what were undoubtedly meant to be English exclamations, but he did not advance. The Colonel replied in like kind, and then advanced a pace. Zemba looked surprised. The Colonel took another step forward and was within arm's length of Zemba, who took a step back.

"Go! Go! Away with you!" repeated the Colonel at the top of his voice, and Zemba looked round at his troops, as though seeking encouragement. But not one of them moved. Zemba faced the Colonel again, but a hint of doubt was in his eyes. Seeing his leader in doubt as to what to do, a sape just to Zemba's right dropped his weapon and slunk away. The Colonel advanced another pace and Zemba backed away, colliding with the sape immediately behind him. That sape took fright also and ran away, back through the ranks of sapes, triggering a panic. Firing broke out, and a bullet whizzed past the Colonel's right ear, another passed through the flesh of his left arm, while a soldier next to him fell to the ground. Zemba turned, but a bullet hit him in the chest, and with a groan he doubled up. It seemed that some of the sapes at the back of Zemba's force, not having seen the eyeball-to-eyeball confrontation, thought the fleeing sapes from the front were from President Mbalala's small loyal bodyguard of armed sape militia, and had opened fire. When they realised the true state of affairs, they too dropped their weapons and ran.

The fallen soldier was carried to the field ambulance which had accompanied the Norwegian troops, and the Colonel's wound was dressed, while his second in command oversaw the collection of abandoned weapons and counted the dead and dying sapes. Some appeared to be suffering from some kind of illness or infection, a condition unlike any the force's medical officer had ever encountered in any human patient.

The victory was reported back to the Norwegian Foreign Ministry, via the Colonel's hometown contact, the satellite link having mysteriously failed. A return message, via the HF radio link, informed Lieutenant Colonel Johansen was now promoted to full Colonel by his government, and additionally he was awarded the United Central African Republic's highest decoration. Many of the sapes which had fled joined others in neighbouring countries, so the threat was not past, despite the Colonel's heroism, but little more was heard of them for many months. By that time, a new threat faced them, one from which they might never recover. At the medical officer's recommendation, some of the less severely wounded sapes, showing the strange symptoms, were brought back to Norway for further tests. They had quickly made a complete recovery from their wounds, but the symptoms of the mysterious illness intensified, their bodies wasting away until they ultimately died of pulmonary embarrassment, with symptoms superficially not unlike those seen in humans who had accidentally ingested the long banned herbicide paraquat.

Like thinking people throughout the world, Jim and Rosemary had anxiously followed the course of events, from the force's embarkation in Norway, through the battle and their return home in triumph. The success of the mission triggered a reconvening of the Security Council, which debated long and hard as to how to follow up and capitalise on the success. They were still in session the following spring, when a sape uprising was reported in Southeast Asia, and another followed in South America, the year after that. The large powers were shamed, at last, into action, but not for them the heroics of a small force. Massive, overpowering force was used against the rebellious sapes, to the point that even the man in the street questioned the morality of the methods used against the creatures, which were after all only equipped at best with small arms, and often not as many as one weapon to each sape. The remaining sapes retreated into forested or mountainous territory, from which it would be impossible to dislodge them.

"They're safe from any harm there. There's nothing anyone could do about them, and surely they could breed in safety there until there were innumerable hordes of them," said Rosemary, adding, "though, of course, there are few uncastrated males."

"That's right," said Jim and paused abruptly; he could think of nothing else to say, it seemed there was after all simply no solution to the problem. And nor was there, that year, nor the next, nor the next.

Chapter 22
Epilogue 2323AD

Twenty three hundred and twenty-two was an eventful year in the Brophy clan. In April, Inez died unexpectedly after a short illness, at the age of eighty-eight. At least, Inez had had the satisfaction of knowing that Jenny was pregnant again and had been looking forward to another great-grandchild in November. Julian, four years older than her, was heartbroken, inconsolable. Yet he insisted on living on in his marital home, even if that meant living alone, much to the consternation of his son and daughter-in-law. He had long lost touch with everyone in the Department, but still took a keen interest in world affairs, and in developments in the medical field. He even, at this great age, revived his interest in comparative philology, finding there had been some interesting results from recent scholarship on the subject. The subject of 'Sape Language' interested him particularly.

November came, and Jenny was delivered of a healthy baby girl, for whom she chose the name Kitty. Julian was delighted and touched that his latest great-grandchild bore his adoptive mother's name, a point of which Jenny had been vaguely aware, but insisted that she chose the name simply because she had always liked it. The twins, now twelve, were delighted with their new sister, Bill accepting philosophically that even if it had been a boy, the age difference was so large that they would never really have been playmates. Anne had actually been present, with her father, at the birth and took every opportunity to help her stepmother with the new arrival.

Another year passed, and Jim was in bed with a bad cold which had turned feverish, when on the last day of March, Rosemary heard the phone ringing. Picking it up, she heard a recorded message, stating that Mister Julian Brophy had pressed the button of his emergency beacon. Jim had insisted that if he was going to live alone, he must wear the beacon, which hung from a cord round his neck. With Jim out of action, Rosemary rang Harry and explained the situation. Harry rang the hospital, who said they would despatch a vehicle as soon as possible, and then he cycled over to Julian's, having collected the front door key from Rosemary on the way. He arrived at the same time as the hospital vehicle, which was not an ambulance but a seven-seater, used for ferrying patients between home and hospital. The driver was however a paramedic, who soon confirmed what Julian himself said, that he was bruised and had badly sprained both ankles and his right knee but was otherwise none the worse for his fall.

It was therefore agreed that he should be ferried to his son and daughter-in-law's house, and Harry helped him into the vehicle and then cycled there himself. There, he helped the paramedic install Julian in an armchair, and after the seven-seater had departed he brought a single bed downstairs and re-erected it in a corner of the lounge. This would save Rosemary, now in her sixty-sixth year and awaiting a hip replacement, having to run up and downstairs to him, and fortunately a couple of days later Jim felt well enough to get up. Julian apologised profusely for the trouble he was causing everyone and reflected ruefully that he had suffered exactly the same accident that had befallen his stepfather so many years before, when he had had to hurry over to Bill's house in similar circumstances. He added that he could see now that he would be a liability living on his own, and said he was quite reconciled to the idea of going into sheltered accommodation.

He gradually recovered from his bruises and sprains, although as he said, the healing process becomes much slower with age. Rosemary was in no great hurry to see him depart for an old people home, which she felt sure he would hate.

"Now I insist that you are not allowed to go upstairs, just in case."

"And I insist on making myself useful around the house." Which he did, eventually taking an interest in cooking, even becoming quite good at it.

In the year twenty three hundred and twenty-three the Twelfth WPC, which had been brought forward a year at the insistence of the Security Council, came and went, and Jim attended the proceedings, held in Damascus. As at the previous Conference, he collected a set of copies of the papers presented, and on his return handed them over to Julian. His father read them avidly and commented afterwards, that Hal would have been fascinated to learn the news they contained. A paper by Professor Jensen's successor had reported that the exponent had reached zero; the world's population had stabilised at last. It was true that this was an average over the globe as a whole, and the more polluted parts of the world, round the Great Lakes near Chicago, parts of Europe, round various industrial cities in the former communist states and certain other areas, population was still declining. But in parts of North Africa, Australia and New Zealand, and many other places, the population was showing a small but healthy tendency to increase, while in other areas still, it was at least stable.

Of at least comparable importance, was the situation regarding sapes. Their numbers worldwide had been halved in each of the last two years, by the mystery illness that had first been noticed after the Battle of Mbalalaville. On hearing of this, Rosemary, fearful for her grandchildren, asked what would happen if the disease spread to humans. Julian replied that of course that was a worry, but the microbiological experts reckoned that it was species-specific, and unlikely to cross a species boundary. That, at least, was the prevailing view. But he had only recently discussed the question with some of his contacts at Benson Pharmaceuticals. The present state of knowledge (or lack of it) hardly seemed to justify the assertion that the 'sape fever' could never affect humans. Indeed, there were conflicting views about the basic nature of the affliction. Six months ago, the Journal of Tropical Medicine had published an article stating that the disease vector seemed to be a particle that showed certain similarities, at least in morphology, with bacteriophages. But a month later there was an article in The Microbiological Digest that discounted any similarity with bacteriophages and said that several different microorganisms appeared to be involved in advanced cases of the disease. It was stated that these were different stages of an exceedingly complicated life cycle. This, the article maintained, was a hopeful sign, since a drug which proved fatal to any one of these stages would break the cycle and eradicate the disease.

One thing was certain, however, namely that there was frantic activity in microbiological research laboratories around the world, both in pharmaceutical companies and academia, to understand the disease. Without this knowledge it would be impossible to find an effective drug or a vaccine, either for humans or for sapes, for the decline in the available pool of sape labour was far and away much faster than the increase in the human population, which was bound to lead to severe labour shortages in the near future, indeed was already doing so, reflected in higher food prices.

It was near the end of August, and it had been a glorious summer, though now the days brought a little welcome relief from the heat. It was Julian's birthday, and would have been Inez's too, for he had been exactly four years older than her, to the day. He was in bed, and had been so for a week, feeling feverish and queasy, the severe pain in his abdomen controlled by palliative care provided by a visiting specialist. If he stood up, he felt giddy, and all the time he felt light-headed, realising that he occasionally slipped in and out of consciousness, but not quite in the same way as falling asleep. Now, in the evening of the day, and he felt, perhaps the evening of his life, he was surrounded by his family; Jim and Rosemary, Harry and Jenny, Anne and Bill, and not forgetting young Kitty, now nearly two years old. Rosemary brought in a birthday cake that she had made for him: It was a sponge cake, so that he would find it easy to eat. She cut him a tiny piece and handed it to him on a tea plate, and then cut pieces for everyone else. He thanked her, and all his descendants, for being there on his birthday, which he felt sure, though he did not say so, would be his last. He ate a little cake, and then leant back against the pillows, the plate sliding gently from his grasp.

"We've been through testing times, Inez and me and all of us. And now it seems that humanity may survive, after all, saved from its own folly, but not by anything it has done to merit it. The trouble with mankind is that its knowledge far outstrips its wisdom." And he sighed and closed his eyes. They were not sure whether he had merely fallen asleep or had embarked upon that long sleep that comes to us all in the end.

Chapter 23
Postscript 2323AD

It was four months to the day since Julian's death; the cremation had followed a few days later. The family had by now adjusted to the loss, the twins were now fourteen and Anne was doing particularly well at school. Harry was still Chief Engineer at Lascar, with a twenty percent stake in the firm, and Jenny seemed contented with her role of wife and mother. Jim, at sixty-six, was still employed by Baker and Daley, working from home, as he had done, nearly all his married life, but only two days a week, now. Kitty, now eight, was a constant delight to her grandmother, in the evenings and at weekends helping Rosemary with her current hobby, 'greenhouse gardening'. This consisted in raising plants for the garden and for friends, and for sale at local fetes in aid of charities, from seed saved from the previous year, such as shoofly, winter cherry, spider plant, or from cuttings, hebe, cistus, Peruvian lantern tree and a score of others.

Unlike his father, Jim had never studied medicine, but had picked up from Julian an interest in the subject. He had recently come across the names and phone numbers of several of his father's contacts, in some old papers. Rosemary was still worried about the possibility of sape fever affecting humans, especially since the appearance of a sensational, but ill-founded, article in the Daily Leaf. So, Jim phoned Benson Pharmaceutical and asked to speak to Dick Bailey, since he had often heard Julian speak of him. The young lady on the switchboard asked how he had got hold of the name, and Jim explained. She said that Mr Bailey had retired years ago, but he could speak to a certain Godfrey Proudfoot, who had succeeded him as head of department, and put him through. Jim noticed that this was another of the names on Julian's list of contacts, but of course there was no indication of the age of each. Having introduced himself, it became clear to Jim that his father had spoken to Godfrey on so many occasions that they were like old friends, though in fact they had never actually met. Jim said that though he had no specialised medical knowledge, he had inherited his father's interest in such matters, and explained that his wife was concerned about the possibility of sape fever crossing the species boundary, and infecting humans.

"I wondered if you could be so kind as to give me your opinion on the subject."

"Ah, well; certainly, if you've got more than a few minutes – you see the situation is more than a little complicated."

"I'd very much like to hear what you can tell me on the subject."

"Not as much as I would like. Despite the fact that the United Nations has co-opted all the laboratories in the world with a capability in microbiological research into one great research team. First, all the academic laboratories were directed to concentrate on unravelling the nature of the organism responsible for sape fever. Then, seeing progress was slow and it might be a long job, all the laboratories of commercial companies were asked to join the effort. A few refused, but one of our sister companies is part of the 'sapefevernet', and such results as are achieved by any laboratory are circulated to all the others, to try and build up the picture, bit by bit," he paused. Then continued, "The problem was that different labs found different organisms, but there was no consistency between where the samples came from, and which type of organism was found in the sample. Some of the organisms appeared somewhat similar to bacteria, but unbelievably small, others to oversize viruses and yet others to bacteriophages. It's early days yet, but we're beginning to suspect that they're all different phases of the same organism. If so, it has a very complicated life cycle, and it's not clear which of the phases is – or are – most easily passed from one individual to another, and which phase or phases actually cause the disease and subsequent death. Such a complicated organism cannot have sprung from nowhere and it appears that it's always caused the death of the occasional sape, or of their wild ancestors. But there must've been a mutation to a much more virulent form in the recent past. Until we have unravelled the whole life cycle, the means of transmission and the exact cause of morbidity, it's very difficult to see how or where to start trying to develop an effective drug or vaccine."

"So, no one could guarantee that it won't at some stage infect humans?"

"Certainly, no guarantees, but we hope it's unlikely."

"Well, that's something. Thank you for being so open with me about it."

"Oh, that's all right. Due to the collaborative nature of the effort, there's no commercial-in-confidence aspect to this work. And in fact, all I have told you, and probably a great deal more, will be available on the UN Sape Fever website in a week or two's time, when it's up and running."

Jim thanked him again, and later that day, told Rosemary that he had spoken to one of Julian's old friends, Godfrey Proudfoot, who was au fait with the great UN research effort.

"And what did he say?"

"He said that it was most unlikely that the disease will appear in humans."

"I hope he's right – I'd hoped for something more definite than just 'unlikely'." Jim felt slightly uncomfortable about changing 'hope' to 'said' and inserting 'most' into Godfrey words.

The year was passing very quickly for Jim and Rosemary, as it does when one is in ones sixties or seventies. For Harry and Jenny, it passed at just the rate they expected, neither very fast nor very slowly, while for their children, it seemed to take ages to gradually wear away. For Bill, only in the last few days of the summer holiday did it seem to flit by, bringing return to school inexorably sooner than he would have liked. As for Anne, this was no problem; she liked school, liked to please her teachers and showed a real flair for languages – just like her great-grandfather Julian, Jim commented. During the autumn half-term holiday, the twins were round one day, helping Rosemary in the garden – rather noisily – so Jim retired to his office upstairs, even though it was not one of his work days. Noticing Julian's list of contacts in a drawer, it pulled it out and looked through it again. There was Hal's name, address and phone number, crossed out, of course, following his death. And immediately following it, also on the page headed 'Telegraph' was the name and number of one Martin Banbury, Hal's protégé. On an impulse, Jim rang, and the call was answered by a young woman.

"Can I speak to Mr Banbury, please?"

"He's not on this number; I don't recognise the name. Would you hold on please." There was a pause. "I'll transfer you to the switchboard." The operator consulted an internal phone directory, found the right number, and in a moment he was talking to Martin.

Jim introduced himself and Martin Banbury said he'd often heard about him from Julian.

"What can I do for you?"

"I'm sorry to bother you, but I know you were always able to pass on newsworthy items to Julian, that were not yet in the public domain. As you know,

Julian, though not a qualified doctor, had studied medicine and was worried about the possibility of what they call sape fever crossing the species boundary to man. My wife is particularly worried about this, and I must say I am too. I had a long talk with someone working in the UN co-operative research project back in late spring, and he was not able to throw much light on the question. I wondered if you had heard anything."

"You're not the only one who's asked me that! There's little if anything to report at the present. There was a claim that a peasant in Cambodia last year had died of an undiagnosed illness which someone thought might have had something to do with sapes – he worked with them, apparently – but it turned out to be a false alarm. It was hushed up at the time, on government orders, to avoid a worldwide panic, but apart from that, there's nothing to report."

"Well, I suppose no news is good news. Thank you for talking to me."

"You're welcome. I know Hal and Julian were very good friends. I don't mind passing on anything that I have to you, as I did to Julian, on the same strictly confidential basis. What's your phone number? Best if I don't email you in case anyone else should see it, as I'm always warning people who will insist on sending multi-addressed emails by COPY instead of BLIND COPY."

Rosemary's plants, with Kitty's assistance, had done particularly well that year, and as it now drew towards its close, she prepared for the traditional family Christmas. Three days before the festival, Jim was concerned to see a slight, but persistent, frown on Rosemary's forehead. It was still there the next day, and as he poured her a digestif – homemade Limoncello – to go with the coffee after dinner, he asked her what was the matter.

"It's that Mrs Jones, down the road."

"A miserable looking woman. What about her?"

"Well, she's been going around all year telling everybody that the twenty-third is going to be the Day of Doom. She's been saying it's going to happen this year. Well, this is the last month, so that means the day after tomorrow!"

"What is?"

"That's it; she doesn't know."

"Well then, she's just a silly old woman: Take no notice of her."

"I suppose so, but she's got me worried now."

The bustle and work involved for the feast seemed to take Rosemary's mind off the prophecy in the next two days. The plan was for the two of them to spend a few days over Christmas with Jenny and Harry, and the grandchildren. The twenty-third dawned, bright and cold. They set out at nine in the morning to walk to Harry's house, a nice roomy detached house, the flat having become too small a few years after he married Jenny. They were taking great care, as the pavements were slippery with a heavy rime of frost, so it took them the best part of an hour to arrive. Jenny had prepared glasses of hot punch for the grownups, in which she included, today, the twins, but not Kitty. Congratulations and general banter were exchanged, after which Jenny said she must repair to the kitchen, and Rosemary went along to help. Harry said he would set the table, see to the drinks and generally assist, leaving Jim, the twins and Kitty playing 'Sorry', an old board game not unlike Ludo, handed down through the family for generations. Kitty won and they had just started a new game when Jim's mobile phone rang.

"Martin Banbury here. Er, are you alone?"

"Can be." And Jim headed out into the back garden, without bothering to put a coat on, to where a few thin flakes of snow were beginning to fall. "Yes?"

"Suppose I ought to wish you a happy Christmas. Have some news for you."

"What is it?"

"Are you sure you want to know, today in particular? It could wait. Probably be on television in a couple of days, and in the papers the day after."

"No, no; of course, go ahead."

"I've just received news of three confirmed cases of sape fever in humans. Fatal, in all cases. One in India – in Kerala; one in Sweden and one in Canada. The Swede had been in India a week previously, though not to Kerala. No connection whatever is known between the case in Canada and the others."

"It's really certain?"

"Afraid so. It's taken months of detailed tests to make really certain it's a human form of sape fever; there's been a news blackout until there was absolutely no doubt. Today is the first day it has been officially confirmed."

"That's strange."

"What?"

"A neighbour of ours says 23 is an unlucky number. She's certain something dreadful is going to happen on the 23rd. This being the last month of the year, that must mean today."

"You mean it's because it's the 23rd day of the last month of the 23rd year of the 2300s?"

"With all those 23s – something like that, I guess."

The End